'Fal g s
with   eme   ol ti al and the
per   l . . .   al a war   ss,
motivatio..   ..nsibility.' —*The Age*

'An analysis of racism as only a no   an
from the inside su   din
p   ctives in bala   thy literary
        ..ence. This is a magic mirror.'
                    —Jenny Pausacker, *Viewpoint*

'The whole complexity of human relationships is treated
with great delicacy yet an understated force that is quite
haunting . . . both challenging and very involving. Highly
recommended.' —*Reading Time*

'. . . a complex story that never shrinks from examining the
difficult grey areas of life and politics . . . [*Falling*] assumes
a new level of sophistication and interest in ethics by young
people, which is usually ignored.' —*Magpies*

'Chillingly disturbing . . . In Australia, where racist
views . . . are given credibility, *Falling* is a must for older
readers and adults because it shows the frightening
consequences of such views.' —*The Australian Jewish News*

'So complex that terms such as convincing, sophisticated,
layered and hair-raising don't do it justice.'
—*NRC Handelsblad* (Dutch newspaper)

'From the beginning *Falling* exhibits the traits of a classic tale
of destiny; slowly but surely it moves towards a terrifying
close.' —LIBRIS Woutertje Pieterse Prize jury report

Books are to be returned on or before
the last date below.

ALLEN&UNWIN
SYDNEY · MELBOURNE · AUCKLAND · LONDON

This twentieth-anniversary edition published by Allen & Unwin in 2017

English language edition first published by Allen & Unwin in 1997
First published as *Vallen* in Belgium by Houtekiet/Fontein in 1995

Allen & Unwin – Australia
83 Alexander Street, Crows Nest NSW 2065, Australia
Phone: (61 2) 8425 0100
Email: info@allenandunwin.com
Web: www.allenandunwin.com

Allen & Unwin – UK
Ormond House, 26–27 Boswell Street, London WC1N 3JZ, UK
Phone: +44 (0) 20 8785 5995
Email: info@murdochbooks.co.uk
Web: www.murdochbooks.co.uk

A Cataloguing-in-Publication entry is available from the National Library of Australia:
www.trove.nla.gov.au. A catalogue record for this book is available from the British Library.

ISBN (AUS) 978 1 76029 392 5
ISBN (UK) 978 1 76063 398 1

Cover and text design by Ruth Grüner
Cover photography by Maikka Trupp
Set in 10.25/15.5 pt Sabon by Midland Typesetters, Australia
Printed in Australia by McPherson's Printing Group

10 9 8 7 6 5 4 3 2 1

www.anneprovoost.be/en

Translation of this book was assisted by:
the Department of Music, Literature and Performing Arts,
Administration of Culture,
Ministry of the Flemish Community, Belgium,
and by the Literature Fund of the Australia Council for the
Arts, through the translation grants program,
administered by the National Book Council, Australia.

The paper in this book is FSC® certified.
FSC® promotes environmentally responsible,
socially beneficial and economically viable
management of the world's forests.

falling

WHEN THEY BRING Caitlin home, I'm standing by the side of the road. Nobody has told me when she will be discharged from the hospital, but I have a premonition and have been standing there all morning. I wander about a bit, nip the dead heads out of the geraniums on the windowsills with my barely healed fingers, and grind blades of grass, green again after the rain, into brown shreds. Because of the dense cloud, it looks as if the house, covered in climbing roses, and the convent further down the hill are sheltered under a gigantic waterproof tent. What strikes me most is that the shutters are open: they've been closed all summer to keep out the heat. Now, moist air is blowing in through them.

When the ambulance drives past, I'm standing with my back to the house, on the inside of the bend. Because of the rustling of the wind in the trees, I haven't heard it coming. It's driving up the slope slowly from around the curve, the engine rumbling in low gear. I have plenty of time to look in through the windows. Caitlin is not on the stretcher in the back, as she was three weeks ago, when she was being carried away with sirens screaming. She sits on the driver's right, confidently looking ahead, as if she is used to travelling in ambulances. ('I can't figure you out,' I said to her once. She turned half towards me and answered: 'We were forced to move time and again. That makes you forget how to make close friends.')

The driver takes the bend cautiously. I follow their movement not just with my eyes and my head, but with my whole body, slowly turning, my arms hanging limp by my sides and my chin sticking out a little. Before I quite realise, we are looking into each other's eyes. I want to nod, blink my eyes at her, call out something, but my face turns to stone. She looks at me the way you look at a passing building, or at a pedestrian you don't know and take no notice of. She looks normal, no different from usual, except for the yellowish tinge of her face. She is sitting up straight, stretching her neck out the way some waterbirds do just before flying off. I know how she talks, and how she moves when she says something. I can see the way she will look at something, blink, turn round and say: 'What did you say?' She seems like quite an ordinary girl, the way she is sitting there, a girl who rides her bike down a slope and climbs back up on foot, a girl who, on warm days, walks up to her knees into the water of the pond and suddenly, unexpectedly, with a shout, throws herself full length into the water. A girl who yells: 'Shit, the brakes aren't working!' when she is driving through the hills without her mother knowing.

Our eye contact lasts no longer than half a second—my eyes instantly focus on a point in the distance and she looks down to the road surface—but it feels like an eternity. I become totally conscious of the way I am standing here, in jeans, bare feet in my shoes, craning my neck to see her properly. My hands are still bandaged in a few places. I rub my fingers together to feel the pain, but the wounds are dry, and nearly all have healed over. I am only aware of a kind of insensitivity round my fingernails, and a velvety hypersensitivity where new skin has grown. Suddenly I know why I am standing there so openly: I want to behave as if I am not ashamed of what has happened.

As soon as the white ambulance has disappeared behind the trees, I walk around the house. I say nothing to my mother, who is bringing the garden chairs onto the back porch and covering the cushions with plastic. I go inside and upstairs to the bedroom that was once my grandfather's. I shut the door behind me, and, when I hear my mother coming inside, turn the key. The two suitcases which I have been packing earlier this morning are standing in the middle of the room. I pick them up and put them next to the wall. Next I try to shift the writing desk under the skylight without making a noise, but I can hardly manage: the timber floor is uneven and the desk heavy. The legs make a scraping noise. I climb onto the table and, through the gap in the foliage of the treetops, I look at the courtyard in front of the convent building.

I'm in time. The ambulance is just arriving. It slows and stops. The driver gets out, jumps almost, as if to show how healthy he is. Half skipping, he walks round the car and opens Caitlin's door. First he brings out two grey crutches and leans them against the open car door. He offers his left arm. Caitlin's hand appears on his white sleeve. As I see the movement of the hand to the sleeve, the hair on the back of my neck stands on end. For a moment it is as if I feel her hand on my arm. I know her hands are never clammy, but always cool and dry, as if she regularly washes them under the cold tap. I have touched them nearly every day, every time we went down to the town along the path that shepherds once used, and took the shortcut, clambering over Challon's Bluff.

He helps her get out. While she is laboriously busy moving herself out of the car, I can see nothing unusual. For long seconds I believe that everything has actually turned out all right. But then she makes a quarter turn. She now has her face towards me, throws her head back lightly and stays motionless for a moment. Of course she knows I'm here, standing on the table watching her. I can't see the expression on her face, because the distance is too great. It starts raining gently. A flight of doves drifts in, as if lost, and lands awkwardly a few metres behind her. She takes a crutch under each arm and places her legs apart a little. Now I can see clearly that her left foot is gone.

'LUCAS!' MY MOTHER calls from downstairs.

'Yes,' I reply without moving. Caitlin keeps looking in my direction while the driver reaches inside the car to get her luggage. He brings out a blue striped sports bag, is about to put it down but hesitates and, after a few quick words from Caitlin, slings it over his shoulder by its strap. He disappears half into the car again and produces two bunches of flowers.

'I know what you're doing,' my mother calls. I hear her coming up the stairs. Like a cat, I jump from the table. Using every last ounce of strength, I lift and put it back in its place without letting it touch the floor. There are two books on it, great hefty novels which my grandfather must have been reading in the long months before his death. They have shifted, and I put them back where they were. Before my mother gets to the door I turn the key again. She comes in, her hands still wet from the rain on the garden chairs, quickly glances round the room and smiles.

'I could have sworn you were standing on the table,' she says and sits down on the edge of the unmade bed. She dries her hands on her shirt and gets a packet of cigarettes out of the breast pocket.

'I heard she'll be allowed to go home soon,' she says, flicking a metallic coloured lighter. With her head she gestures towards the skylight. 'It's as well we are leaving. There is still such a lot of gossip down there. I am so fed up with this bloody little town. Perhaps they will have forgotten about it all by next summer.'

I say nothing, can say nothing, because all this time I see the amputated leg in front of me and realise that for three weeks I have refused to think about this scene. In my head I become aware of a strange sound that wasn't there before. It's like a Chinese orchestra with lots of bells, and then it changes into a buzzing noise. I sit down so I'll hear it less.

'How is the packing going?' She points at the suitcases. 'I've looked in all the cupboards. They're clear of our things. My bathers I'll leave here, I never use them at home anyway. It's odd, but I seem to have more room in my suitcases than when we came. Yet I'm leaving hardly anything behind. On the contrary, there are a few things I am taking, things he would never let me have.' She sucks on her cigarette in a childish sort of way. 'If we can, I would like to leave tonight. The last train's at seven-twenty.' The buzzing noise in my head is now echoing around the hills. Somewhere a tree is being pulled down and cut into firewood. Because I don't answer, she leans over until her face is nearly against my ear. She is so close I can see the join in the paper of her cigarette. 'That way there might be just enough time for you to say goodbye to Caitlin. I've got a pot of begonias which will only die here. It's on the windowsill outside. Just say they're from me.'

'I went in yesterday,' I say quickly. The noise of chain-saws in the hills has a strange effect on me: I keep hearing the whine of the saws even at night, the way a young mother keeps hearing her baby crying even though it is already asleep. 'We've said goodbye.' She looks at me as if she knows full well that I am lying. Two streams of smoke come from her nostrils. She lets the ash drop into her free hand.

'And you'd better hurry,' she says as if she hasn't heard me. 'While she's still in hospital you can see her. Once she's home, Soeur won't let you in and you'll be left out in the cold. You know what she is like. Since the accident even Copernicus isn't allowed through her gate.' Copernicus is my grandfather's old tomcat who always lies by the back door, even when the house is deserted. His whiskers reach down to the ground, and he is about as easy to move as a mountain range. Fortunately, his independent and cheeky way of walking melted Soeur's heart, and until three weeks ago she'd let him share the dishes she put out in her garden for her numerous cats. The week after the accident, Copernicus became very thin. One afternoon we saw Soeur throwing stones to chase him out of the convent garden, and since then we've been buying cat food in the supermarket.

My mother stands up. The mattress is filled with old wool which has no more bounce in it, and gives off the smell of winter rooms with every movement. 'If you don't, Caitlin might think you don't *want* to see her again,' she says, nearly whispering. The whining in my head is now so loud that I don't dare let my jaws move apart. I nod, but even that hurts. When she is gone, I stare for minutes at the cigarette smoke which hangs beneath the skylight.

MY MOTHER KNOWS it as well as I do: I can't visit Caitlin. Yet, for the last couple of days, she's been sending me down to town where the hospital is, one time with nut biscuits she baked herself, the other with flowers from her garden. Each time, I've wrapped the presents. I've taken the old shepherds' path down, but at Challon's Bluff I've stopped and sat down. I've stayed there the whole afternoon, thinking, constantly running the film of that summer through my head, and always surrounded by the noise of chainsaws. Mostly it was misty, occasionally it rained. Each time, towards evening, I returned home empty-handed. The presents from my mother would be lying in the gorge next to the bluff.

This time, of course, I feel stronger. I *know* Caitlin isn't in the hospital, so I tie a ribbon round the pot of begonias and begin the descent along the old shepherds' path. Besides, I have a particular question for the doctors and nurses. It has been hounding me for the past three weeks, and I want an answer. I slither down Challon's Bluff, more slowly than usual because I can't use my hands properly, and walk on along the winding road. Since my last visit to the town—the day I went to the police station—everything seems changed. The leaves lie ankle deep and the berries on the bushes spread a sweetish smell. At the foot of the cypress near the plateau lie stones which have rolled there from higher up, and the mosquitoes that normally swarm here have been replaced by solitary wasps, attracted by the smell of rotting fruit. I walk carefully. Caitlin always got down first; she loved speed and the sound of stones rolling under her feet. ('Why do you always go so fast?' I asked her once. 'Because I'm made to win,' she replied.)

7

The road seems shorter but more dangerous than it used to be. The last stretch is the most difficult. You have to cut through Monsieur Orchamp's garden, making sure he doesn't notice. If he does, you risk having to go halfway back up the hill because he'll come after you, waving his stick, his dog at his heels. The best place to wait for the coast to be clear—Orchamp inside, the dog busy with something, no cars in the street—is right behind the compost heap. I crouch, the pot of begonias between my feet, and while I wait, I remember the many times I have sat here waiting with Caitlin. Because of the stench, we always got away as fast as possible. We walked through the strawberry patch as far as the street, jumped over the flowerbeds beside the drive and strolled inconspicuously along the footpath, like any other couple.

This time, too, the stench is unbearable. Monsieur Orchamp is nowhere to be seen and there is no traffic, yet I stay, sitting rigid, behind the compost heap. Sweat drips down my armpits. I wait and hesitate. It is a full ten minutes before I dare go onto the street.

I walk through the streets of the town, shoulders hunched. Housewives with baskets and shopping bags walk past me, men with moustaches and glasses, carrying ladders and bags, children in prams and on bicycles. I walk close to the walls of the houses. Just past the tin works I think I hear someone call 'Lucas!', but I don't look round and pretend I am deeply absorbed in my thoughts. I make a two-kilometre detour so I won't have to go through the Cercle Meunier, where the Arabs live in dilapidated flats and where I would certainly be recognised.

The entrance to the hospital is an automatic door. For other visitors, the glass panels slide apart, but before I can manage to get through, it seems for a moment that the doors are going to slide shut in my face. The electronic eye notices me just in time. I go in and walk over the white marble floor like a skater who doesn't trust the ice. I know the building. My grandfather was in here for weeks before he went home to die. It is cool and full of pot plants. But it has become a different place: it is the burrow into which Caitlin has withdrawn like a wounded rabbit. Everyone has been to see her, except me. For hours she has talked with her visitors, probably told them all the details. Everyone knows everything and I know nothing.

The lady at reception does not ask if she can help me. She looks at me and immediately looks back to her computer keyboard.

'Name?' she says impatiently because I am silent.

'Lucas Beigne,' I reply quickly, a bit startled.

She types in a few letters and frowns at the list which appears on her screen. 'No one of that name here,' she says curtly. 'Hasn't been before either. Or are we talking about maternity? Is Lucas a baby?'

'No,' I say quickly, gulping air. I look around me. Groups of people carrying flowers are waiting. There is no one there I recognise, but many of them will have read everything in the papers. Because they have nothing to do except wait for me to get out of the way, they look at me. I wriggle my hands into my pockets to hide the bandages.

'Meadows, perhaps?' I say so softly I have to repeat it. The d-sound pops against my powder-dry palate.

'Caitlin Rose?' she asks without looking up. More heads turn in my direction. I shift my weight onto my other leg and bend over as if the brochures with the various tariffs are endlessly interesting. The receptionist taps the screen with her biro. 'You're not very well informed. Miss Meadows left this morning. She'll be coming back after the weekend.'

'Oh,' I say in order to express surprise. 'Left? What ward was she in then?' I try to read the number of her room on the screen, but the letters are too small.

'Orthopaedic, on the third floor, but she isn't there now. Really.' I thank her, but she doesn't hear me. She looks over my shoulder at the people behind me.

'Name?' she says. I move aside and walk to the end of the corridor, where the lift is.

In the lift, I can smell myself. The polished metal doors show a fantastically deformed reflection of my face and my body. When the doors open, there is no one in the long corridor in front of me. But I can sense presences everywhere. The doors to the rooms are open. The sound of TVs comes from several directions. I walk ahead, every now and then catching a glimpse of a face as it is turned towards me. They're mostly old people, their skin as faded as the light that comes through the net curtains, except for a few young girls Caitlin's age. They all have long black hair and deep-set eyes.

Behind me comes the sound of a cart being pushed along the corridor. A nurse looks over its top. Her wooden sandals flipflop on the chessboard-pattern tiles with every step she takes, and the dozens of bottles on the cart clink together in the same rhythm. I walk towards her and wave when she looks as if she is about to go into one of the rooms.

'Caitlin Meadows?' I say as I reach her. Her face has a strange colour, as if all this illness around her is making her ill. Her hairline is red and so are her eyelids. She is wearing a coverall over her bare skin.

'She's out for the weekend.'

'Did you look after her?'

'Who are you? Her boyfriend or something?'

'Her cousin,' I lie smartly. 'I'm just back from holidays. I thought she'd be here.'

'Left this morning.'

'How is she?' I stand directly in front of her as I ask the question. Immediately I realise how pushy I am being, and take a step back. 'Is she in a lot of pain?'

'Well,' she says, 'she is on painkillers. But the pain is not the problem.' She sorts the bottles on the cart by the colours of the caps. I nod as if I have been through it all.

'I suppose shock is the main problem, really,' I say wisely.

'She knows she can't complain. She could have been dead.'

'She could have been dead,' I repeat. A second nurse comes out of the room. She is a bit taller and wears a pale blue coverall instead of a white one. Her hair is tied back and she is wearing the same kind of sandals. She comes and stands next to us, a small tray in her hand. At first she pretends not to notice, but then she looks at me and says: 'Aren't you that boy . . .'

The first nurse, the one in white, looks as if the wind has suddenly changed direction and she's just caught a whiff of me.

'Ye-e-e-es,' she says. 'I recognise you from the photo in the paper. You aren't her cousin at all. You are that friend of hers, Lucas Beigne, isn't that right?' She grabs my hand to shake it.

'She had a lot of phantom pain, of course,' she says, almost in a whisper, as if it was something improper. 'You know, this persistent pain in a foot that isn't there any more. That's because of the nerves that have been cut. They keep sending signals to the brain, and the brain, of course, doesn't know that that foot has been . . . sawn off.' She hesitates a fraction before the words 'sawn off'. The taller nurse lowers her eyes, and immediately looks up again, as if she suddenly remembers something important: 'You really could have come a bit sooner, I think. How long ago is it now? Three, four weeks?' The one in white nods, full of conviction. They're suddenly speaking fast, in turns, their voices becoming more and more shrill.

'She was forever asking everybody exactly how it all happened.'

'Everything she knew about you, she knew from the papers. She asked about you so often.'

'The people from the police would only tell her the minimum, the official announcement, but of course Caitlin wanted to know a lot more than that.'

'Didn't she ring you? Every morning she said she was going to ring you, but as soon as she had a line, she said she didn't need it any more.'

'She was very confused, really. When the fire brigade people came to tell her they were thinking of giving you a medal, she didn't eat for a whole day.'

I find it almost impossible to understand what they say. The echoing of their voices against the tiled walls makes their words unintelligible. On top of that the sound of chainsaws in my head has come back. When I glance into a room, I understand why: there is an action film on, a shuddering

12

shot of Schwarzenegger tearing along a road, engine screaming. The picture alternates between his clenched jaw and his foot on the accelerator. That reminds me that I've come all this way to ask one specific question.

'And the foot?' I ask when the conversation calms down. 'Her left foot. What have they done with it?' They look at me as if something nasty is hanging out of my nose. It is the taller nurse, the one in blue, who finds her voice first.

'Well, what do you think they do with something like that? To the police first for examination in the case of accidents et cetera—not in the case of an ordinary amputation, of course—and then they burn it.'

'In the furnace of the hospital. Along with other things they don't know what to do with, blood samples, bandages and so on,' the woman in white adds.

'Burn?' I scream before I even realise that this is not a place to scream. But I can't help it. I am too bewildered. They have thrown her foot in the fire. After I did everything I could to prevent that foot from burning!

We don't go on talking for long. The patients need care, and when their shift ends the nurses have to go home, to their families. Before I leave, they remind me that Caitlin has asked for me many times. They make me promise I'll visit her and tell her how everything happened.

On the way back, I talk constantly to Caitlin in my head. I try to remember the very beginning of it all and realise I'll need to go back in time for that, to last winter.

MY GRANDFATHER DIED the week before Christmas. He had been in hospital for a long time, but had been discharged because there was no change in his condition and there weren't enough nurses over the Christmas period. He took a taxi home. My mother and I were still at home then, in the capital. We were getting ready to spend Christmas with him. I had rung him just that morning. We talked about the supply of firewood in the shed which, he said, was a bit low. He thought he would probably have to ask me to cut up some pine trunks which he had left lying around. I said that would not be a problem, and hoped he would let me use his chainsaw.

That evening we rang again, but got no answer. The same thing next morning. We had asked him to put the phone next to his bed, and he had promised to do that. About eleven my mother rang the police in the town. They said they'd look in.

As fate would have it, Soeur Béate was the one who found him. The house is higher up than the convent of Sainte-Antoine, but the garden and the shed where my grandfather kept his firewood lie a couple of metres lower than the surface of the road, just past the sharp bend which leads to the convent. She noticed something lying in the snow. At first she thought it was a blanket which had somehow been left in the snow and didn't think she would bother having a look. She and my grandfather had not spoken to each other for as long as anyone could remember, and Soeur was inclined to keep to herself no matter what happened. Her Christian sense of forgiveness must have got the better of her that morning, because she retraced her steps.

The police told us later that the nun had been thoroughly upset. For many long years the two of them had lived next to each other in silence, he alone in the house on top of the hill, and she the last nun in the dilapidated convent God seemed to have abandoned. At that time I didn't know what they had quarrelled over. As a child I never asked about it. It was simply a fact I took for granted. I assumed it was a habit rather than a real feud. But this summer, Caitlin has opened my eyes. She made me feel a fool showing that I was the only one around who didn't know what had happened.

By the time we arrived, Soeur had done all that was necessary. She had laid out my grandfather on the bed in the attic room with her own hands. Candles burned, and she had put air fresheners discreetly under the cupboard and under the bed. She had called an undertaker and ordered a coffin, the simplest and cheapest one available, but she must have thought that was appropriate. We came into the room after a nerve-racking train trip full of delays and changes, still carrying our suitcases, still wearing our overcoats. She nodded to us and disappeared, a small figure dressed completely in grey. It was the first time I had seen her so close up.

That was last winter. Towards the end of May, my mother decided that, even though my grandfather wasn't there any more, we should spend the summer in the house on the hill as we always had. The thought of being in the capital during the hot summer filled her with horror, and, anyway, she felt we should at least see to it that her parental home was cared for properly. But I had quite different plans. I was looking forward to having a good time with my new friends from the youth club I'd just joined, and could do without a holiday with my mother, all by ourselves in the hills. But she didn't give me any choice. She sublet our flat to total strangers for the summer months, and so I had nowhere to live and had to go with her. My friends tried to cheer me up by promising, hand on heart, to come and visit me. They would all come in Moumouche's car—he was a couple of years older than the rest of us, and had a licence. All I had to do was make sure there was plenty to eat and drink.

I assumed that I would be bored. I didn't take any books, because I don't like reading. On the train I registered my protest by producing a deck of cards and laying out a game of patience on the seat opposite. Sometimes I think back to that train trip, and wonder if perhaps I had a premonition. Maybe I didn't want to come because I knew my whole life would be turned upside down in a few weeks. But then I must admit I was in a foul mood because I thought *nothing* at all would happen, not because I had a premonition.

My fear of boredom wasn't the only thing, though. As the train went further south, the temperature in the compartment went up. The day had only just begun and the sun was already shining fiercely. I moved the sun shades and opened the window, but at every stop more people got in and the heat in the carriage became unbearable. I had to put my cards away to make room, and was bothered by the body odour of the man next to me.

When we arrived at my grandfather's house, we put our luggage down by the back door.

'Will there be anything to drink?' I asked.

'Nothing cool,' said my mother, searching for the key through the many compartments of her handbag. I walked into the garden. After a spring without my grandfather's care, it looked neglected. The slope up to the road at the northern end was so overgrown you could barely see that the road was there. The view of the convent was blocked by a couple of fast-growing pine trees. If you walked on, into the far corner of the triangular garden where a small rocky outcrop formed a natural terrace, you could see Montourin. The town lay shimmering in the heat. The red tiles of the roofs seemed to give off steam.

Closer by, between the town and the hill where I stood, ran the small creeks which carried the water from the hills to the Sianne River. They were crossed here and there by wooden bridges which were pulled down during winter. There were signs of human presence all over the landscape below me, and yet I suddenly had the terrifying feeling that the world was deserted.

'Lucas!' my mother called. I returned to the house with its climbing roses and grey gable roof. She stood next to the woodshed, and pointed at the stack of firewood, partly covered with plastic.

'This shows how bad he must have already been feeling last autumn,' she said. 'He obviously didn't have the strength to get firewood ready. At Christmas he had already nearly gone through his stock: barely four weeks' supply left.'

We went in. We found the house plants dried out, the fridge empty, its white door propped open with a chair, the water turned off, the easy chair and couches covered with sheets, and the side door forced. Someone had been there and had taken the TV set. I was absolutely furious. I didn't say another word to my mother but went upstairs, convinced I would be playing patience for the whole summer.

Because the windows were so well screened, the house was surprisingly cool. I carried my case along the upstairs

17

passage and noticed it was a bit warmer there, but still nowhere near as hot as outside. Almost automatically, I went towards the large room at the back, called the guest room, where my mother and I usually slept, but as I passed my grandfather's room, I stopped. I put my suitcase down and opened the door.

The small space was like a cave. Everything was where we had left it after Christmas. After the funeral, my mother had stripped the bed down to the mattress, and washed every sheet and every blanket, drying them in the freezing cold. She had put the dozens of paintings, which had stood against the walls all around the room, together behind the cupboard and covered them with a sheet. She had dusted the wardrobe and the dressing table, but the dust had come back. On the desk in the corner lay the two novels he had borrowed from someone a couple of weeks before his death. Next to it, pushed out of the way, stood a duplicating machine. It seemed to belong in a different century. For as long as I could remember, it had served as a rack for magazines and newspapers. In the sloping ceiling was a skylight which let in a subdued light.

While I was standing there, my feet almost numb after dragging those suitcases, an image from the past came into my mind. I had been quite young, still a child. The door of this room had always been locked because paintings were kept there. One day I was playing in the next room. Suddenly I was startled by the sound of someone running up the stairs, unlocking the door and going into the room. I heard a piece of furniture being shifted. I walked into the passage in my socks. The door to the bedroom was ajar. I peered in and saw that my grandfather had pushed the desk under the skylight. He stood on it peering intently through the skylight. I couldn't imagine what he could see. When he noticed me looking at him, he started talking gibberish, obviously very upset.

He had never explained to me what he was doing. Nor had I ever asked him. I had completely forgotten about it. But this sudden memory, after all those years, made the room even more attractive. I put my suitcase on the narrow bed. I opened it, took out my clothes and put them in the half-empty cupboards.

'I can't help it that the TV is gone,' said my mother, hurt, when she saw that I wasn't planning to share the guest room with her.

&

BECAUSE IT WAS terribly hot again really early the next day, I decided to go into Montourin before anything else and have my hair cut. It was sticking to my neck and my forehead, and I wanted to be rid of it. That was a mistake, I now realise. Going back over it all, I can see that this was the moment everything started to go wrong—but of course that's easy to say with hindsight. At times, I lie on the bed with my face in the pillow. I scratch my head and want to reverse time, but it's impossible. I can no longer wake up innocent, as I was that morning. Only in my dreams can I believe that it was all a bad dream.

I took the shepherds' path—I used to do that when I was still a little boy. My grandfather had shown me the quickest and safest way over Challon's Bluff. He himself hadn't gone down that way the last few years. It was too tricky, and anyway, he never needed to get down so fast that he couldn't quietly walk along the main road. I had nothing with me except some money and a plastic bottle which I had filled with tap water. I paid hardly any attention to my surroundings: my thoughts were at home, with my friends, who were probably organising barbecues in each other's backyards. When I got as far as the orchards, I did notice that there seemed to be a lot of Arabs in town for the fruit picking—a lot more even than last year; and as I walked through the Cercle Meunier I was surprised to see that in every corner, in every garden, and even in parking areas, galvanised iron shacks had been put up where seasonal workers' mattresses lay in stacks.

The hairdresser I went to was called Nadine, a woman my mother's age whom I knew because we always went to her when I was a child. She was quick, and cheaper than a hairdresser in the city. Both her front door and her window were open, to try and create some draught.

'You sure you won't be sorry?' she asked before she took the scissors to my hair. She dipped the comb in a jar of lukewarm water. Her fingertips were stained brownish black by hair dyes. Her fingernails were bitten to the quick, which made her hands look like monkey's paws.

'It's too hot for long hair,' I said firmly, listening to the grinding sound of the scissors. All the same, when I watched the tiled floor being covered in locks of brown hair, darker than usual because it was wet, I felt a mixture of excitement and regret. It was strange to feel my neck gradually becoming bare.

'Do you wash your hair with baby shampoo?' she asked. I said 'yes' without moving my head.

'I can smell it. You can't mistake that scent.' Her hand moved like a scorpion from left to right and back across my skull.

'You've got lots of hair,' she said. 'Runs in your family. Your grandfather had a good head of hair, too.' She was silent for a while, and then said unexpectedly: 'It must be a strange holiday for you, without him.' She lowered her scissors for a moment, to listen to what I would say, but when I said nothing she went on.

'And now of all times this woman and her daughter are back staying with Soeur Béate. They say it's a coincidence, but I can hardly believe that.' A hot gust of wind made the coloured fly curtain in the doorway flap. What she was saying did not catch my attention. She must have felt it, for she pressed her fingertips emphatically against my neck and said: 'Come on, you know. Those people from New York. With the girl with black hair. You used to play together, even though you weren't supposed to.' She put her hand under my chin to turn my head. She left the hair on top of my head much longer than at the back, combing it straight down.

'Your mother told us sometimes how you two hid from Soeur in the cellar of the convent.' She reached across me for a pair of serrated scissors. She was hot too. Her T-shirt was damp between her shoulderblades.

'Caitlin,' I said, surprised to have remembered the name. I hadn't thought of her for years. But the mention of the convent cellar brought it back.

'Caitlin, that's right,' she said, almost relieved. As she worked on my hair, the sleek, almost girlish shape of my

21

face became more obvious. I looked at myself in the mirror the way you look at an old photo of yourself: curious, but disapproving of the way you're dressed.

'Well, they're back, she and her mother. They obviously think the coast is clear now,' she said. She was leaving my hair quite long at the front too. It fell over my forehead and I could feel the ends moving against the skin of my face. I have lots of hair, but it is very fine. She wanted it in a particular shape, but it kept jumping away from her scissors and fell in an unruly way around my head. She undid her apron, shaking it in front of her like a bullfighter. As I paid her I looked sideways at myself in the mirror.

'But watch out!' she said conspiratorially. She folded her apron with abrupt movements. 'Watch out for their stories. They'll try and tell you all sorts of things, Caitlin's mother and especially Soeur Béate if she gets half a chance. Don't listen to them. I knew your grandfather. He was a good man.' I pulled my fingers through my hair and went towards the door. I could smell the exhaust fumes of the passing traffic. Nadine took the broom and swept the hair into a pile. She flicked the strip curtain over the half-open door, swept the hair onto the footpath in one smooth movement and let the strips fall back again.

I got back to the top of the hill quickly that day—too quickly, really, for when I got to the house I had white spots before my eyes, and the soles of my feet were so damp they itched. I walked into the house to take a shower. I had expected my mother to be there, but there was a note on the table. She had gone down into the town to report the theft. I took the paper from the table and without thinking screwed it up and threw it in the bin. I left the house and did what I had so often been told not to do: I climbed over the low, ivy-covered wall of the garden of the Convent of Sainte-Antoine and walked among the trees towards the building. When I reached the low shrubs, I went down on my knees and crept along until I could see the small courtyard of the convent. There was no one about. I walked past the old cactuses in pots and was about to risk crossing the courtyard, when a sudden shadow in the doorway and the sound of a little bell surprised me. I dived behind a couple of low willow trunks. Soeur Béate came out. She held a small copper bell in her hand which she swung carefully. When she made soft sucking and clicking noises with her mouth, striped cats appeared from different parts of the garden, among them Copernicus. She bent and put a dish down on the ground. When I had seen her last, it had been winter and she had been wearing support stockings with thick nylons over them. Not now. Her legs had a bluish sheen and were hairless.

The cats approached soundlessly, tails up in the air. They stalked around the dish and nipped like spoiled women at the sauce in which pieces of meat floated. Soeur didn't stay; she disappeared almost immediately into the coolness of the convent building. I stood up and ran past the doorway like a chicken escaping from its pen. The cats barely looked up. Their bodies undulated gently as they swallowed. I walked past the herb garden and the gravestones at the side of the building.

The hardest part was getting past the four geese in their run. The moment I appeared they started gabbling and wouldn't stop till I got to the small pond in among the greenery. I pulled my T-shirt over my head and took my shoes off. The mud felt warm on my feet. I waded through a narrow strip of tall wild irises and reeds. The roots stopped me sinking too far into the mud, and the water there was lukewarm. Only where the water reached to my waist did it get cooler. Air bubbles rose along my legs, bringing black grit to the surface with them.

'This is more like it,' I thought when I felt my body cooling off and relaxing. 'This is better than a shower. Better than sitting still near that stupid house with that boring garden. This they'd envy me, those guys back home with their barbecues.' I sniffed the scent of decaying plants. If I stayed still, dragonflies skated over the water towards me. Even though there was no wind, the surface of the water rippled occasionally. The air was full of the hum of insects.

I had already dried off and put my shoes back on when I heard voices in the courtyard. I couldn't see anything, and because I didn't dare walk past the geese, I decided to wait. I lay down on my stomach in the grass and could feel bits of mud drying and shrinking on my legs.

I got a fright when a cat walked past me. I rolled sideways, as if I had been stung, right under a shrub, and that was just as well, because the cat was followed by footsteps and a girl's voice calling: 'Come here, puss!' I hadn't seen Caitlin for ages. I guessed it was eight years since we had played together. The way she walked seemed vaguely familiar, but her face, which I only saw in a flash, far too brief to look at it carefully, I couldn't remember. She was wearing a sun hat, which covered her hair completely. The shadow of the brim fell over her face. All I could see was her chin moving every time she called 'come here!'

She disappeared, carrying the cat in her arms. Shortly after that I heard her voice again, further away now, probably somewhere near the herb garden. I stayed there for minutes, as if paralysed, while flashes of memory came into my mind, disjointed images I couldn't properly fit together. The clearest were memories of roomy, cool cellars, and the songs we sang there, not for the love of singing, but in order to hear our voices echoing off the bare, whitewashed walls.

I wanted to see more. I crept to the northern end of the convent, where she had disappeared. Crouching, I walked to the windows behind which I could sense movement. The shutters were closed because of the heat, but behind them the windows stood wide open, which made it easy to look in without being seen. I knew where I was: this whole wing was taken up by the large, rectangular dining hall where, according to my mother's stories, dozens, maybe hundreds, of nuns had taken their meals, accompanied by soft whisperings. But for as long as I could remember the tables had been pushed to the side and the chairs stacked. What remained was a huge, hollow space, with the sunlight coming in harsh stripes through the gaps in the shutters. A large mirror stood against the wall, with a silent ghetto blaster in front of it. In front of that stood Caitlin, her shoulders hunched up and her arms bent in front of her, as if she had had a fit and couldn't move any more. Around her left ankle was a support bandage. The cat sniffed at it casually, then walked around her, apparently not noticing her strange pose. Now I had a chance to have a good look at her face. It was vaguely familiar: the dark eyebrows, the thin mouth and the unusually small chin. She stayed motionless for only a moment. Abruptly, she came out of her trance. She raised one arm, moved it in a circle and let her other arm follow it as if in a lower gear. I was mesmerised. It was several seconds before I realised that she was dancing.

She was dancing without music. All I could hear was the slapping sound of her bare feet on the wooden floor and her gasping breath. In all her movements she kept her back to the mirror, except the two or three times she did a quick turn. She kept her eyes shut. At times her face was contorted, at others angry. She walked into invisible walls, appeared to hurt herself, recover again. A few times she let herself fall on the floor, painlessly, but with a thud, and she seemed to press the floor against herself.

A few times she did something I recognised, like a classical pirouette, but subtly different, because of her bare feet which caused the movement to seem to falter. But then her turn would end in an unexpected swinging movement, on stiff, spread-out legs, which made her suddenly look so like a clock I could almost hear the ticking. It was strange, and there was something magical about it. The most striking thing was the beauty of her bones. She was sinewy, and as she moved, you could see her muscles and bones. As I watched, I had the impression I was witnessing something that was not meant to be public, and a feeling of embarrassment crept over me.

It made me feel I should leave. I came out of my hiding place, tried to force my way through the low shrubs so I wouldn't have to go past the geese and the courtyard again, and reached the collapsed part of the wall. I climbed over it. There was no one on the road. The tar was melting in the cracks and the sound of crickets rose from the dry grass.

I looked at my legs, and noticed several grazes. A blackberry thorn had got stuck in my left calf. I worked it out and, instantly, a disproportionate amount of blood dripped from the small blue wound.

I SPENT THE afternoon in the shed my grandfather used to call his 'smithy'. The sun shone directly onto the corrugated iron roof and it got so hot in there that I could hardly breathe. The place smelled of my grandfather, of the past, of the old cars he used to fix while I watched. On the wall hung the objects I had seen him use over the years: hand drills, rakes, spades, saws, bicycle parts, spanners and dozens of things I didn't even know the name of, let alone what they were for.

I stood looking at all this, with the key to the padlock of the door in my hand. I had never gone into this space without my grandfather. Now that he was dead, I could touch everything. Under the well-worn workbench stood a metal box, locked with another padlock. I opened it and brought out my grandfather's relatively new chainsaw.

It was solid. I picked it up, my left hand on the grip on top, and my right hand on the handle. I pointed the tip of the blade upwards and could hear the petrol sloshing in the tank. The blade was shiny. In between the teeth were hard black beads, which smelled of resin and oil. For hours at a time I had observed how my grandfather handled it, how it made a screaming noise, almost as if touching the wood excited it, and how light brown, fragrant sawdust fell onto the grass, forming pointy little turrets, until the wind blew it away. I always had to stay clear, at least three metres away, and when he stopped the machine to go inside to drink a couple of glasses of fruit drink, he kept an eye on me through the kitchen window.

I put my finger on the safety catch. My mother was away in Montourin. Even if she was already on her way back, she wouldn't be able to distinguish between the sound of this chainsaw and that of two or three others that were busy in the hills. I pulled the starting handle. At first the motor made a sputtering noise, but after a second pull on the handle, it screamed into life. It shook in my hands, as if it would jump away from me. I braced myself. For a moment, my back and stomach felt completely dry, only to be instantly dripping with sweat again. I was amazed at how light the saw was. I had always imagined that it would be unmanageably heavy, and that only strongly built, grown-up men would be able to handle it without causing accidents.

I listened to the sound. I wondered if they could hear it, in among the thick walls of the convent. I put the blade into the top of my grandfather's wooden workbench, and, with a smooth movement, cut it through the middle. While I did this, I made a low noise, high up in my throat. In my head, that drowned out the noise of the saw.

That evening, over our meal, I asked my mother bluntly: 'Why wasn't I allowed to play with Caitlin when I was small?' She was eating a jar of cherry yoghurt, and for a moment she looked as if she had swallowed a pip. But she recovered. She smiled and continued eating with relish, her elbows spread on the table, fruit peel and apple cores around her plate, the remnants of a cheerful evening meal.

'Caitlin?' she asked, raising her eyebrows.

'The girl from New York who is staying with Soeur Béate.'

'Ah, Caitlin,' she said with a smile, realising she wouldn't be able to get out of it any other way. 'Ruth's daughter?'

'Yes. Why wasn't I allowed to play with her?'

'What makes you think you weren't?'

'They're back, Caitlin and her mother. They're staying with Soeur again.' Her hand, which was carrying a spoonful of yoghurt up to her mouth, stopped at the level of her chin. The smile on her face was replaced by an open mouth— whether from amazement or because she was about to take a spoonful, wasn't clear.

'Are they *here*? I mean *now*? In the convent?'

'Yes,' I said, waiting.

'Right now, now that your grandfather has died!' she said, more to herself than to me. She coughed behind her hand, like a child pretending to be really ill.

'Weren't you allowed to play with Caitlin?' she recovered. 'I can hardly imagine that. Perhaps Grandfather was afraid you would walk onto the road.' She started clearing the table in an exaggeratedly cheerful way, obviously thinking she'd fooled me. She pointed at my head.

'Suits you!' she said. 'It reminds me of the time you went to primary school.'

I refused to let her change the subject.

'According to Nadine, all sorts of things had happened between Soeur Béate and Grandfather, and so they couldn't stand each other.' She picked up the coffee pot, took it over to the sink, but seemed to change her mind. She came back, poured herself another cup and held the pot in my direction.

'Want any more?' she asked.

I raised my fingers dismissively, more out of annoyance than because I didn't feel like more coffee. 'You're not answering my question,' I said.

'People say so many things,' she said lightly. 'They hear the bell ringing, but don't know where the steeple is. Two personalities clash, and people start imagining things. Nonsense! There was a quarrel once about a tree your grandfather cut down which wasn't supposed to be his, but that's all there ever was.'

'And that's why I wasn't allowed to play with her?' Although I hadn't finished eating, she now started to clear away my plate and cutlery too.

'Look, the Meadows are the sort of people who think they've had a terribly raw deal in life. They can't see that everyone has a cross to bear. They make a big deal out of their problems, but won't see that they're not the only ones who've ever had bad luck.' There she stopped. She refused to say anything more about it. I insisted, but she was adamant and tried to divert my attention by showing me a large carton which she'd had delivered by taxi. It contained a second-hand TV set she'd bought for a song from an Arab. I tried to get it to work, and, when it wouldn't, I fetched the smallest screwdrivers I could find from the smithy, moved the set to my grandfather's room and screwed the back off. I don't know how long I was busy doing that. I fitted cables to sockets, took them off again, tried different connections. Every now and then I put the plug into the powerpoint. Most of the time, I got a loud hissing noise, occasionally a bit of snow and, after a lot of trial and error, a flashing picture. When I wanted to replace the back cover, I couldn't find one of the screws, but made do with a similar screw from my grandfather's old duplicator. Dusk was falling, and when I switched on the light above the table, the mosquitoes came buzzing around me.

My mother must have thought I was asleep. I heard her go to the phone in the hall and dial a number. I paid no attention to her conversation. The picture on the set was now clear, but there was no sound yet. I tried new combinations, and twiddled the knobs intently. Until I heard my mother say Soeur Béate's name.

'I don't know what got into you. What good will it do the boy?' Her voice shook, because she was trying to shout softly.

'No,' she said after a short pause. 'He just came out with it. Asking why he wasn't allowed to play with Caitlin, and all that. Yes, all right, I believe you. I assume you haven't said anything. But you have made him suspicious about a lot of things. Do you think that will do him any good, Nadine? Leave the boy in peace. And leave my father in peace.' I had moved closer to the door. I had two screwdrivers in my hand, and kept rolling them tensely between my fingers. There was a silence. I assumed the conversation was finished, but then I could hear her again, softer now, and sounding calmer. 'OK, yes, yes. Good, yes, of course you weren't to know that we've never told him anything about it. Anyway, now you know. We didn't see the point. Occasionally someone would try to bother him about it, but, you know, he was still young and didn't know what it was all about. Sometimes he would ask a question and I would tell him something, and

31

that seemed to satisfy him. He is a sensitive boy, Nadine. I've told you that before, and you should have kept that in mind . . . Yes, yes . . . That's right. Strictly speaking, you haven't said anything . . . Just forget it. It's not as bad as it sounded.' The floorboard under my foot creaked. The room smelled of the mattress. I could hear her finishing the conversation off, sending regards to Nadine's mother, wishing her goodnight and replacing the receiver.

I sat down. On the TV two men in striped ties were having an intense conversation. I no longer tried to get sound. Idly, I played with the screwdrivers and sat looking at the silent conversation deep into the night.

IN THE MIDDLE of the night, I woke up. I had been dreaming that my grandfather was standing on top of the desk, and when I opened my eyes, I was lying with my face towards the window, so I had to blink a few times before I could be sure he wasn't really standing there, intently looking out at something—what, I had no idea. I got up, pushed the desk under the skylight and climbed onto it via a wobbly wooden chair. I looked outside, but all I could see were the black silhouettes of the trees in the garden.

Because I slept late next morning, I didn't have a chance to speak with my mother. She had left early for Montourin, leaving me a plate of pancakes and a note. Although she had covered the pancakes with a second plate, flies were circling around them, attracted by the heavy scent of melted butter and syrup. I put the pancakes in the fridge, drank a couple of glasses of ice-cold milk and left the house. It was nearly midday, and already very hot. I walked straight into the smithy, knowing exactly what I had in mind. It was something I had been wanting to do for a long time. The conditions were right: there was no wind, and my mother was well out of the way. I opened the door to the smithy, got the chainsaw from the box and took it outside. I surveyed my grandfather's garden. There were some twenty trees in it, most of them old and thick, except for a few pine trees, right over on the side, on the border between the garden and the road. They had planted themselves, and had only been there a few years.

'They have to go,' my grandfather had said several times the previous summer. 'They block the view into the valley, and they throw too much shadow over my fruit trees.' Every time he mentioned it, I felt a shiver down my back. I had watched him cut down dozens of trees; I watched the slow movement of their fall, how the top of the tree was bent by the resistance of the air, then hit the ground and bounced up again a few times in a wave motion, as if resisting its fall. My grandfather jumped back as soon as the trunk made the familiar cracking noise. Before the tree even hit the ground, he walked back to it, quickly touching the trunk with his hand in order to feel its vibration. Then he laughed at me, but I never felt that the laugh was really meant for me.

'And you can do it,' he had said, 'next winter, when you come back.'

'Why don't we do it now?' I had asked.

'Because it is summer. It's better to cut down trees in winter.' But that autumn, he had become ill. When I came back, he was already dead.

I went over to the pine tree farthest from the house. Its trunk was no thicker than the leg of a young elephant, and its lowest branches were smooth and resilient. I studied the tree to see which side was most heavily covered with branches, how the roots were placed and what angle the trunk made with the sloping ground. I stood with my knees bent, the way I had seen my grandfather do, dug the heels of my shoes in the thick layer of pine needles until I could feel the hard ground underneath, and braced myself.

A moment later, the scream of the machine resounded over the hills. The birds around flew up screeching. The chain turned, jumped loose and broke with a dry crack. The motor died and the silence that followed hissed in my ears. I swore with fright. Thanks to the chain guard, my hand was undamaged, but it had been close. I put the machine on the ground and sat down next to it till the beating of my heart slowed and I could breathe normally again. The pine tree stood next to me, dead straight, shaking slightly in the passing breeze as if gloating.

I took the saw back to the smithy, letting the broken chain drag along the ground. Out of sheer anger at what had happened, I refused to put it back in the box. I laid it carelessly on the floor, somewhere between a ladder and an old bike. More than ever, I cursed this place, the holidays and the heat. I was convinced that all my friends were at the swimming pool, surrounded by fresh greenery and cool ice-cream parlours. I swore to myself that I would never, but never, go away with my mother again.

Casually, almost without thinking, I walked up to the convent wall and climbed over. I didn't wait for the coast to be clear, but walked blindly past the courtyard and the geese. It was as if I was on fire and had no time to stop. I walked straight up to the pond and into the water, shoes and all, deeper and deeper, until my shorts got wet. I was lowering my arms to cool my wrists, turning around to see if I should put my watch down on a stone on dry land, when I heard the sound of breaking twigs in the shrubs. Someone was coming. I instantly forgot the incident with the chainsaw and nearly overbalanced in the sucking mud. I started to panic. There was no time to disappear. Seconds later she stood before me, in the spot where the cracked dry earth changed into half-wet mud swarming with flies.

'Lucas!' she said, the final 's' nearly inaudible, the way she always used to say it. She didn't smile, but had a serious expression on her face, which made me wonder for a moment if the exuberant voice which had said my name had actually been hers.

'Hello, Caitlin,' I said. The water was up to my middle, and so cold I needed to pee. I tried to get out. My movements made the water go a dark colour. My shorts stuck to my body and my legs were black with mud.

'I heard a noise among the trees, and I thought . . .' She was wearing the same straw hat. Its ribbon was almost transparent against the light.

'It's so hot,' I said apologetically. I was standing before her with my hands covering my crotch, like a soccer player facing a penalty kick. 'I had to find a way of cooling off.'

'Just as well she doesn't know,' she said, nodding her head in the direction of the convent. Then she was smiling, and that put me at ease.

'I do my best to be quiet,' I said. 'She never notices.'

'You've changed,' she said. She spoke with a thick American accent. 'I didn't recognise you at first.' She took a step in my direction. She was taller than me. Only then did I notice that she was being followed by one of the tomcats, a beautifully striped tiger, with a thin, smooth tail. 'I thought you were a girl. One of my girlfriends in New York wears her hair just like that.'

'Yes . . . No . . .' I said, totally disconcerted. I stood in the grass and wanted to get away, out of this forbidden territory. I squeezed some water out of the hem of my T-shirt and started backing away from her. She followed. 'Your grandfather has . . .' she said.

'Yes,' I said, before she could go on.

'Sorry,' she said emphatically, and it was a few moments before I realised she was expressing her sympathy. With a quick movement she scooped the cat up. For a few seconds, the animal hung over her arm like a fur coat, but then it curved its body, ready to jump away.

'Are you staying long?' I asked, wanting to change the subject.

'Shush,' she said to the cat, putting her elbow against its side so it couldn't get away.

'I've come to do training,' she said.

'Training?'

'Dance. I wanted to do an audition for a dance school in New York, but that didn't work out because of this injury. Now I have to wait for a year.' She pointed at the bandage round her ankle. 'My mother is here, too.'

'So I heard.'

'Are you here with your mother, too?'

'Yes.' I looked alternately at the cat she held and at her face. There was something unusual about her. She wasn't sweating and didn't seem bothered by the heat. She looked airy, as if the heat, rather than pressing down, lightened her. She seemed to be driven by a constant inner need to move. Her eyes were brown like beer, and her skin pale.

'You remember how we used to play?' she asked. 'And do you remember the hamster?' Of course I remembered. When my hamster had escaped from its cage, my grandfather had written a very polite letter to Soeur, asking her to keep the cats inside until the hamster was found. Caitlin had brought back a note saying that the cats were far too numerous and too wild to be kept inside. I never saw my hamster again. It was all a long time ago. If Caitlin hadn't mentioned it, I would never have thought of it again.

'We weren't allowed to play together,' she added, almost in a whisper. 'But because there was nobody else around, we did anyway, and hid in the cellars.' Now I remembered: the cellars were cool. They were far from Soeur, whom I had to avoid. The thought of Soeur made me nervous. I took another step in the direction of the goose-run. Caitlin's head and the cat's followed me in a single movement.

'Wait,' she said. 'I know a better way.' She walked ahead of me. She walked quickly, without any hesitation, as if she would know every stone in this garden even in the pitch dark. Pushing her way between two rhododendrons that grew close together, she brought me to a part of the garden where I had never been. To my surprise, I saw that we were close to the wall. The ground was a little higher here than in the rest of the garden, and you could see the road which separated the convent from my grandfather's house.

'Those geese drive me mad,' she said when we had reached the wall. 'Soeur insists on keeping them. There have always been geese here, and they have to stay, she says.' Behind us, somewhere in the vicinity of my grandfather's house, a car started. I briefly tried to remember if my mother had said anything about visitors.

'It has something to do with the war, of course,' she added. 'And with your grandfather, as you realise. My mother has suggested we roast them for Christmas.'

'My grandfather?' I asked. On the road, I saw a car coming through the bend. It was going fairly fast and I tried to see who was driving. There were three men in the car. I didn't know any of them, but could see by their profiles that they were Arabs.

'Yes, of course,' said Caitlin. 'They were sort of watchdogs. Effective and cheap.' She stood on tiptoe. 'Look,' she said, 'you wouldn't say so, but we are actually really close to the pond here!' With both arms she pulled a couple of thick branches out of the way, and I could indeed see the glittering surface of the water. She bent the branches till they cracked.

'I think we can even get to the water this way,' she said, pushing her way through the shrubs. Quickly I looked over my shoulder towards my grandfather's house, and as everything seemed quiet there, I followed her.

MY FEET WERE still sloshing in my shoes when I walked home more than an hour later. Just before the fence, I was stopped by a policeman.

'Young man,' he said. I recognised him from last winter when he had come around in connection with my grandfather's death. He walked in an affected way, as if he had been a dancer or an actor in a previous life. Apart from dark trousers and a cap he was out of uniform because of the heat.

'You didn't lock the door.' A drop of sweat rolled down my thigh. The ground felt hot under my feet and my footprints dried up instantly.

'Oh, eh, no,' I said. 'I was only gone for a few minutes.'

'A few minutes is too long these days,' he said quietly. He turned his back on me and started to walk around the house.

'How come you're so wet?' he asked, and I gathered this was an invitation to walk with him.

'Stood under the sprinklers,' I lied, following him.

'Ditchwater,' he said, sniffing. 'I can smell it.' Behind the house was a second policeman. He was squatting, but stood up when he saw us. He nodded at me and spoke to his colleague.

'The same all over again,' he said.

'As per usual, eh?'

'As per usual.' In the house, behind the kitchen window, I saw my mother. She stood leaning against the sink and appeared to be talking with a third person in uniform.

'Did they take a lot of things?' I asked the policemen. The darker one, the one I had met outside, cleared his throat. His shirt collar was grey with sweat.

'The electric frying pan,' he said, almost smiling. 'With the oil still in it. I hope they didn't go too fast around the bends.'

'And the toaster,' the other one added.

'The frying pan?' I repeated sheepishly. Behind the kitchen window, my mother turned around. She noticed me and came out.

'They take whatever is easy to sell,' the dark-haired policeman said. 'Then they set up shop in the Cercle Meunier. If you look long enough, you can buy back all your own things.' Over their shoulders, I could see my mother coming towards us. The sloping path was covered in stones, and she put her feet down carefully between the sharp edges. She started talking to me while she was still twenty or thirty metres away. She didn't look at me, but at the ground.

'You didn't lock the door,' she said. She had a pack of cigarettes in her hand, which she offered the policemen when she reached us.

'You won't believe this,' she said, stretching so she could get at the lighter in her jeans pocket. 'They've even taken your TV set.' I opened my mouth to say something, but in my confusion only managed 'huh!' She pointed to the smithy, her hand hanging down limp at the end of her outstretched arm, as if it was too hot to raise it.

'They've been in there, too,' she said tonelessly. In the smithy, the expensive items were stored: the bicycles, the lawn mower, the extension ladder. They were harder to take, but easier to dispose of.

'The smithy?' I said. A warm drop rolled down my back. The bicycles were always locked. The extension ladder was fixed to the wall by a system of sliding hooks, which my grandfather had devised, so it was only possible to remove the ladder quickly if you knew exactly what you were doing. The chainsaw was normally kept under lock and key.

'They've cut through the workbench,' she said. I tried to walk calmly over to the smithy, but couldn't quite manage. Halfway there, I started to run. Because the ground sloped up in that part of the garden, my movements felt like those in a slow motion film. The lemon verbena near the door irritated my nose and made my eyes water, so it took some time before I saw that the chain was still there, but not the saw.

'They tried it out on the spot,' said my mother, who had followed me. 'It hasn't been oiled for six months, so of course it had to break.' I picked up the chain. The policemen came and stood around me.

'The lock hasn't been forced,' said one of them.

'You would be able to hear this sort of thing for miles around,' said the second one.

'They're getting more arrogant all the time,' said the last one. I saw that my mother was hugging herself as if she was cold. The back of her T-shirt hung out of her jeans. She walked through the smithy, and seemed to look at every object with great care: the rusty stirrups, the hockey stick with its faded covering, the half-empty jars of turpentine, linseed oil and fixer. She wasn't listening to what was being said. Now and then she pushed something aside with her foot, or pulled open a drawer. She shone her lighter into dark corners. Finally she lifted the tarpaulin which covered part of the tool racks, and I saw how she picked up a largish implement, inspected it carefully and pushed it under a sheet of cardboard. She came and stood with us again, and went over to the house with the policemen to fill in the official report. I went into the back of the smithy and pushed the piece of cardboard aside. Underneath it was the long, heavy, very sharp pruning knife with which my grandfather used to cut the low suckers off the tree trunks with one sweep.

FROM THEN ON, we lived in fear.

'Holidays here aren't what they used to be,' my mother said constantly. The shops were too crowded; there were beggars in the streets; bags, bicycles and prams got stolen. In the drawer next to the kitchen door was my grandfather's pruning knife.

'I'll grab that if someone breaks in,' she said. Occasionally, I caught her standing by the garden wall, looking out at the convent.

'Anything interesting?' I asked innocently. She turned, flushing.

'I'm just curious,' she said, lowering her eyes. 'I'd like to know how Ruth is. She used to come here every summer, but she hasn't the last few years. She must have aged, like me.'

I met Caitlin again, quite accidentally, when I was trying to cut through the trunk of the pine tree in the garden with a handsaw and an axe. It was early in the morning. She was walking in joggers along the road that separates the convent from our garden, and she didn't see me. She walked rhythmically, her back straight. She was wearing shorts and a thin T-shirt, and I could see how bony she was, and how, as she climbed the hill, her muscles tensed right up into her neck. At the top of the hill, a few metres from where I stood, she slowed down. Eventually she stopped altogether. She bent over, resting her hands on her knees. I was now so close to her I could hear her breathing.

'You gave me a fright,' she said when I took a step sideways. I could see hardly any sweat on her. Her hair was pulled back with an elastic band in an unattractive little ponytail, and she wore a thin gold chain round her neck. She came closer. I was standing about a metre higher up the steep slope. She seemed excited. At first I thought it was because I had frightened her, but after swallowing a few times she said: 'I saw a deer!' She gestured vaguely towards the woods behind her. 'A lovely, fully grown doe. It suddenly stood in front of me, and wasn't even frightened!' I nodded and smiled. Ever since the forest had been a protected area, I had quite often seen game. But I could understand her excitement. I imagined it was something that didn't happen every day in New York. She looked at my hands.

'What are you doing?' she asked, still panting.

'Cutting down a tree.'

'What for?' Her voice changed from excitement to indignation. For someone from New York, this wasn't so surprising either.

'It's blocking the view. We didn't put it there. It's self-seeded.'

'This tree has grown here,' she said, pointing at its branches. 'It's taken years . . .' She gasped for breath, '. . . to become what it is.' I made soothing sounds, the sort I make at my mother when she gets worked up about something.

'Only a couple of years. It's a pine. They grow fast. And it soaks up all the water from the garden. That's no good for the shrubs and flowers here.' I pointed at the flowerbeds.

She clamped her lips together as if she was not prepared to discuss the subject.

'Do you remember,' she said abruptly, 'how we used to find hoof prints near the pond? They came into the garden through the hole in the wall, but were always gone by morning.' I couldn't remember, but nodded anyway, and she smiled, pleased. I turned the axe round in my hands and let it drop on the ground. I picked up the bow saw which was lying in the grass and put the blade in the notch I had just cut. Kneeling on one knee, I pulled the saw back and forth. To my surprise, Caitlin stayed to watch. I was pleased with her interest, but a bit annoyed at the same time, for of course I wasn't doing very well. It took a terrible amount of force to make the saw move back and forth smartly, and even pulling with both hands I couldn't get a smooth sawing movement going. And it was too hot for this sort of work. I kept pretending it didn't bother me.

From the way she shifted her weight from one foot to the other, I sensed that there was something else she wanted to say or ask. She didn't speak until I let go of the saw and leaned back on both knees, puffing.

'What are you going to do with it when you've cut it down?'

'Oh, you know, get rid of it.'

'I have an idea.'

'Yes?'

'Soeur's firewood is almost finished. She doesn't have enough for the winter. She says she has, but I know there isn't enough.'

'Oh.' Her breathing was just about back to normal. Her legs were grey with dust. The longer she stood still, the more drops of sweat appeared at her hairline and dribbled down her face.

'It never used to be a problem. She burned your grandfather's wood.'

'*My* grandfather's?'

She laughed when she saw my face. It was a laugh I was to hear from her many times that summer. She managed to suggest all sorts of things with it, but at the same time it seemed to slam a lot of doors shut. She invariably looked over the top of me when she laughed like that. It was the laugh of someone who has heard a cruel joke, not someone who was being cheerful.

'Yes. It was an unspoken agreement. He would put the logs by the wall there.' She pointed at the spot where I usually crossed into the convent garden. Actually, I could remember logs piled up there. As a child I'd used them as a step onto the wall.

'Can I have this pine tree?' she asked. I didn't reply immediately, because I had to think fast. Cutting this tree into blocks without a chainsaw was an impossible task. Before I could object, she said: 'And perhaps this other one, too, if you cut that down.' She pointed out the second pine tree, the taller of the two, which stood in a bad spot on the dividing line between our garden and the road, and was a danger to passing traffic. 'I absolutely hate the cold. I'd rather stay in New York over Christmas.'

I said I'd do what I could, and considered the various possibilities. But I had to reject one idea after the other, because without a chainsaw none of them were feasible.

'Yes, OK,' I said, against my better judgement. 'I'll figure something. I'll take care of it.' She threw her head back and laughed.

'*Goo-ood!*' she called. She jumped up and down a few times. Her jumps turned into steps. She waved and continued her run. I looked after her, not quite knowing what I had promised, and why. The axe was heavy in my hand. My fingers were covered in blisters.

Twice more that morning I saw her come past. She was wearing different clothes now, and she walked downhill with long strides. With her skirt swinging up and her hair loose, she looked like a landing heron, moving its body weight backwards in order to slow its speed. I suspect she saw me both times, but she didn't wave. She swept the hair from her face and didn't look my way for a moment. I stood staring after her for minutes, even when she'd disappeared from view, and imagined seeing her here again at Christmas, and how she would carefully move down the hill over the first snow, her collar up and wearing a thick cap. I could almost feel the chill air on my skin. She would be wearing boots trimmed with artificial fur, her skin even paler than usual, her lips gleaming from the balm that protected them from the cold.

'Why the smile?' asked my mother who had come to tell me she was about to go into Montourin. I hadn't heard her coming. On the luggage rack of my grandfather's bicycle she had tied three of his paintings, carefully wrapped in plastic bubble wrap and newspaper.

'I'm going to sell them,' she said. 'To the tourists. We might get something for them.' She was wearing large sunglasses I hadn't seen before. Her shoulders were bare and a bit red after two days' sun.

'I'll bring a deadlock for the kitchen door,' she said, taking her wallet out of her handbag and putting it straight back again.

'Mum,' I said.

She looked up. I was dripping with sweat, carrying the first couple of logs I'd got ready for Caitlin in my arms. My shoes were covered in sawdust.

'What are you doing?' she said. She held her handbag so low it practically dragged on the ground.

'Mum, why did Grandfather cut wood for Soeur Béate?'

'Wood for Soeur Béate?' she repeated. 'Who told you such nonsense?'

'Caitlin. He stacked it by the garden wall. Soeur took what she needed.'

She slung the strap of her bag over her head and crossed it in front of her body. 'I would have known about it, wouldn't I?' She got ready to move off, but stopped.

'Caitlin?' she asked hesitantly. 'Ruth's daughter? Did you see her?' I nodded. 'Where did she say he put it?'

'There, where the wall is lower. All she had to do was reach over.'

She looked at the spot. Shaking her head, she laughed. 'Yes, now you mention it. He did put wood there sometimes. Always said it was just for the time being. Would he really have . . . ?' She clasped the handlebars in both hands. Her mouth was half open, as if she was about to cry out in astonishment. She took her sunglasses off and looked at me, her eyes half closed against the fierce sunlight. She put them back on, still shaking her head. 'The idiot!' she said, stressing each syllable. She stood, as if unable to recover from her bewilderment. From the branches above us, two or three crows flew up, screeching. We stood so still we could hear the flapping of their wings. Eventually she threw her left leg over the crossbar and pushed the bicycle up the bumpy garden path. The way she rode off, wobbling and with both knees sticking out, made her look like a very young girl.

'Unbelievable!' she called out again and disappeared behind the house. A few seconds later I saw her ride down the slope, pulling on the brakes. They made a high squeaking sound. I saw how she slowed down when she came to the low part of the wall, and then picked up speed again.

I managed to cut down the second, thicker pine tree. It was a fantastic experience to feel how the trunk, after resisting for minutes, finally gave out, and how the plume-shaped crown slowly came down. But it took just about all my energy, so I wasn't game to start cutting it up. When I went inside to get a glass of soft drink I passed my grandfather's woodpile, and seeing his small supply gave me an idea. I loaded up the flat wooden wheelbarrow which stood beside it, and, carefully avoiding potholes, pushed it to the road and on to the paved main entrance to the convent.

Soeur must have seen me coming from a distance. I was only halfway up the drive when she came storming into the courtyard, mousy grey, wearing orthopaedic shoes, much faster than you would expect from a woman her age, her face twitching with curiosity like a small rat. She seemed so amazed that she couldn't speak at first, which gave me time to say quietly: 'I'm bringing you some firewood from my grandfather.' I hadn't seen her so close up since Christmas. A lock of grey hair was visible on her forehead, the only proof that there actually was hair under that coif. The end of her veil flapped in the warm breeze.

Her reaction was not at all what I had expected.

'That tree didn't belong to you!' she said, her chin shaking. She stood with her arms held stiffly away from her body, as if her armpits were inflamed. 'You didn't have the right! It stood on the public road. And as for your wood, you can keep it!'

'It would have been better if you hadn't,' said Caitlin when I found her by the pond half an hour later. She stood with her feet in the water, wading further in as she talked. 'Of course she doesn't want it. She wouldn't have accepted it from your grandfather either. He never *gave* her wood. The wood she burned she'd *found*, if you see the difference.'

'I only wanted to help,' I said, feeling wronged.

'Yes, I know.'

'And it wasn't even the wood that made her angry. She was angry because I cut that tree. She's too dumb to see that the firewood didn't even come from that pine.' Caitlin slowly turned towards me. She held her arms spread out to keep her balance. Dozens of insects danced around her face.

'She's just angry,' she said. 'That pine tree represented a sort of security for her. It stood between her and your grandfather's house. Now it's gone, she can see all of you too well.'

'The woman is crazy.' I was annoyed. Then I realised I'd been speaking rather loudly and cast a quick glance in the direction of the convent. Nothing stirred. Caitlin was now standing up to her knees in the water, bending over. She moved her fingers through the surface of the water as if she was scratching it.

'Soeur is like a grandmother to me,' she said reprovingly. 'We owe her an incredible lot. So we put up with things from her.'

The way she spoke made it clear that this was the last thing she was going to say about it. She waded further in as if I wasn't there and suddenly let herself fall forward with a shout. The water sprayed up, and with a strong butterfly stroke she quickly reached the other shore where she got out, sniffling and snorting, leaving a trail of small black clouds behind in the shallows. I thought she'd forgotten I was there, but I was wrong. Without turning round, she called out: 'Just cut that wood. I'll tell her I'm getting it somewhere else.'

IN THE EARLY evening, my mother returned, her breast pocket full of dollar bills. Instead of the paintings, she carried a basket with a bottle of champagne, a vacuum-packed cooked hare, and cake. I saw her coming, pushing her bike up the steep slope, the way she walked showing her good humour.

'An American,' she said. 'He thought they were wonderful. He wanted all three of them, and he said he'd buy them before I even mentioned a price. I thought: well, it's worth a try! Lucas, he didn't even try to bargain! And now I feel like buying all sorts of things!' She was wearing a different dress from when she'd left, even shorter and brighter. She showed me the banknotes. We counted them aloud, out on the table on the terrace. We listed the things we wanted to buy. She stayed cheerful until a car slowly drove by on the road.

'Damn!'

I couldn't quite work out why she was swearing. I didn't recognise the car. I didn't think we were expecting anyone and the car seemed to just be on its way to Saint Laurent-en-Gatinne, like several other cars every day.

'What?'

'What if they see this money! The minute it's dark they'll be at the door. Where can we hide it?'

'What do you mean?'

'The Arabs. They break in all over the place. It's driving people crazy in the town. They even steal the washing from the line!' She was nearly whispering now. She covered the money with both her hands and looked at the road over my shoulder.

'Mum!' I was irritated.

'And what if they come while we're not here? They probably carry knives.' She gathered up the banknotes and ran inside, her shoulders hunched as if she was expecting it to start raining. Before she disappeared she giggled and waved her arm and sang: 'Hoo, hoo, hoo, here comes the bugaboo!'

That evening I played a joke on her. I went down in my pyjamas, pulled my grandfather's balaclava over my head and took the torch which hung above the kitchen door. It was pretty late, near eleven, but the kitchen was quite light because of the moonlight. I opened the door wide, pushed the chairs about a bit, and waited.

Seconds later, she stood in the light of my torch, in a T-shirt that reached halfway down her thighs, carrying the pruning knife. I laughed loudly, to make sure she realised it was only a joke. The thought of her taking the pruning knife into her bedroom was rather funny. But it made me uncomfortable, too, because now that she stood in front of me like that, with her hair down and in her bare feet, I could see how vulnerable she was.

'Yoo-hoo, here is the bugaboo,' I said to reassure her. But she didn't relax, not then, and not for hours after. She looked deathly pale and walked around shaking for minutes. She was so upset that I stayed talking to her till after midnight. At first about nothing in particular, but after a while about my grandfather.

'It's this house,' she said, gesturing at the walls of the living room. Because of the mosquitoes, the only lights I'd put on were a standing lamp and a table lamp on the sideboard, which spread a diffuse glow. A dry wind blew outside, and the wooden shutters banged open and shut as if they couldn't make up their mind. The hinges sounded like birds in the night.

'It has changed.'

'What do you mean, changed?'

'It doesn't give protection any more.'

'We could have an alarm put in.'

'No,' she said, stroking her upper arm. 'That wouldn't help.' I couldn't see her eyes, because the light was behind her. I only saw two black hollows turned towards me. She held her head at a slight angle while we were talking, as if she was listening intently for noises from the kitchen and the rooms upstairs.

'I grew up here, Lucas. Everything here is full of memories.'

'But it's always been like that,' I said lightly. For the third time I poured her a small glass from Grandfather's bright yellow liqueur bottle and slid it between her fingers. I'd have done anything to make up for my stupid joke.

'It's different this year,' she said. 'Totally different.'

'Because Grandfather isn't here?'

'Because of the stories. The things people say. The gossip. A lot has happened here, Lucas. More than you suspect. But the things that happened don't matter any more now. The people who are raking it all up are idiots. Now that he's dead, all that trouble seems to be coming to life again.'

'Why aren't I allowed to know?'

'Allowed to know what?'

'Everything. What happened. Nobody tells me anything.'

'I would tell you, everything, from beginning to end, if I knew what to say. But the stories contradict each other. I've always believed your grandfather's version. Everything else is just rumour mongering.'

'Tell me that version.'

She shut her eyes and held them closed tight for seconds as if she was fighting off a migraine.

'Come on,' I said emphatically.

'I can't.'

'Why not?'

'I'm confused.'

'Because I frightened you?'

'Because of the firewood.'

'The firewood?'

'Which he stacked by the wall. For Soeur. That's strange. It makes everything all confused.' She filled her glass. Her movements were so slow and concentrated that she spilled it. The piss-yellow fluid ran down her fingers and I could hear it drip onto the floorboards.

'She had to get through the winter.'

'I know,' she said, throwing her head back. She stretched her legs to restore the circulation, and crossed them again.

Her movements were uncertain. I pushed the bottle away from her, but she noticed and snatched it back.

'Or did he have to make up for something?' she asked, her eyebrows raised high. There was something theatrical about the way she looked. She drank. She cleared her throat as if she was about to start telling a story, and she did, only she didn't say the words I was waiting for. She merely repeated a few things I'd known a long time, about how she'd grown up in this house alone with her father, and how the people in the town all knew her and felt obliged to take her aside from time to time and tell her things that didn't make sense to her. I know it was wrong, but I couldn't help interrupting.

'Things about him and Soeur?' I don't know if it was my words, or if she actually just choked on her drink. Whichever, her eyes filled with tears. I did nothing to comfort her, but looked in amazement at this woman whom I had never seen shedding a tear. I knew her as cheerful and optimistic, sometimes almost superficial, because she didn't seem to really understand other people's problems and sadness. If she sensed tension, she invariably handed out flowers, or plants which she had grown herself in small earthenware pots on the terrace. She never talked about things, let alone had a good cry.

I tried to think of something to say, but all I managed was to point out the full moon and how it seemed to look much bigger here than at home in the city. Too late I realised I still had the balaclava in my waving hand. But she seemed to ignore this. Out of the corner of my eye I saw she was trying to hide the fact that she was crying. I suppose she thought I wouldn't notice because of the dark, but the opposite was true: the glittering of her eyes was particularly noticeable because of the dark with just a glimmer of light from the standing lamps.

'I talked to her today,' I said, hoping to steer the conversation in a different direction, away from the past and back to now, to this room, this summer and the American dollars in her handbag.

'Well, she talked, I listened. She carried on about that pine tree I cut down.'

'That was predictable,' she replied cryptically. 'I was going to warn you about it this afternoon, but after the business about the firewood I thought I was getting paranoid.' She got up, walked into the kitchen, blew her nose, opened and shut cupboards and soon came back with a bowl of peanuts.

'Where was I? I've lost the thread.'

'We were talking about Soeur and Grandfather.'

'Ah, yes, that's right. About Soeur and Grandfather.' But that was all she said. She ate the nuts in silence and, when they were finished, said she was tired. I suggested we share the guest room the way we used to, but to my surprise she said there was no need. She shook her hair, pulled her T-shirt back at the shoulders, and walked up the stairs faster than I expected. I followed, but when I went to walk with her to her door she stopped dead in front of me and pointedly wished me goodnight. Her breath smelled of cigarettes and alcohol, and her eyes were excited and tired at the same time, as if she had just come home from a wild party. She cut me off and practically forced me into my grandfather's room. I couldn't understand her behaviour, but was too tired to think about it.

I shut the door behind me, stretched out on the bed and snapped off the light. Because of the full moon, it was less dark than usual. I played with the twisted cord of the light switch for a while, waiting for silence to settle behind the thin wall which separated the guest room from my own. But the silence wouldn't come. I could hear bumping and shoving sounds, and the floorboards creaking as she kept walking about the room.

Besides, I was stiff with sleeplessness. Too much had happened that day to allow me to relax and doze off quietly. I tried shutting my eyes, but could feel my eyelids quivering like when I was a child and wanted my mother to think I was asleep. For some reason, my legs were pulled up in an awkward position, but when I shifted them, I couldn't keep them still. Downstairs I kept hearing the irritating squeaking of the shutters. There was too much light in the room and there was no curtain. When I opened my eyes I saw the moonlight, and when I shut them, I still saw it. I remembered stories of people who were bewitched by moonlight and must have allowed myself to be bewitched, for I slid out of bed, pushed the desk under the skylight, opened it and hoisted myself up by the window frame.

I'd never been on the roof of my grandfather's house. I put my feet on the black slates without feeling any vertigo. It seemed as if I could easily grab hold of the moon for support if I slipped. The drop next to me seemed totally harmless in the soft glow, and the warmth coming from the tiles made me feel as if I was clambering about on the back of a huge, friendly mammal. I moved on hands and feet towards the skylight of the guest room as if I had been doing this all my life. I was moving with the wind, and my T-shirt billowed out, making me feel even lighter. My hair blew over my face, and I stopped for a moment to brush it out of my eyes.

My mother's room looked like an over-exposed slide. The bright colours of her bedspread, her T-shirt and the stripes of the wallpaper stood out garishly. She was walking about the room. She had her back to the window, so I could only see her shoulders and the back of her head, but she was obviously sorting something. Small piles of documents, newspaper clippings, photos and letters lay on the floor. She took them out of cardboard boxes which stood next to the bed, examined them attentively and then put them on various piles. She held a burning cigarette between her fingers, and took an occasional puff. She shook the ash onto a piece of glossy paper with bent-up edges. I had no idea where those boxes had come from. I'd never seen them before. I tried hard to read what was written on the papers, but couldn't make out even the largest headlines on the newspaper cuttings.

After some hesitation, I risked moving my head further past the edge of the window. I was over-confident and only realised how risky this was when the support under my left foot gave way. Fortunately, my other foot stood firmly in the gutter and it was just a matter of shifting my weight onto my other hip to regain my balance. Although I had reacted fast, my mother heard the noise. I saw her jump up in fright, and she stood listening intently, her arms pressed against her body. I stayed dead quiet. I was gripping the ridge around the window so hard that my fingertips became numb. Meanwhile, the wind was blowing ever more aggressively into my T-shirt. All that time I could see my mother looking around uncertainly, listening, jumping at every sound from the shutters downstairs.

I waited until she was concentrating on her papers again, then clambered back to my room. I lowered my legs through the skylight, and when my feet touched the wooden top of the desk I caught sight of the view into the convent garden. ('Isn't our garden beautiful?' Caitlin had said when we were sitting by the pond. 'Look at those three silver birches. They're enormous now. Soeur remembers how she planted them, holding the saplings in one hand.') Since I'd cut down the pine tree, the courtyard was clearly visible through the gap in the foliage. There, in the soft light of the lamp above the patio, sat Caitlin and her mother.

Caitlin was sitting sideways on the stone seat among the trailing branches of the climbing plants which had grown beyond the support of the convent walls and fell back in long curves. Like my mother just before, she seemed to be sorting something. She was putting things down and shifting them, and at intervals she leaned back to look at the result. One arm supported the weight of her body like some fragile bird's leg. She kept repeating this sequence, arranging and inspecting, and I kept watching it without being able to see what she was actually doing.

Ruth stood next to her, looking at the circular object on the seat. I recognised her slightly bent posture, the 'hunched back' my mother used to threaten me with if I didn't sit up straight. This gave her a slightly masculine appearance, in contrast to the small, light shoes she wore under her jeans. She nodded at Caitlin. She pointed something out, and they appeared to discuss it. All around them, cats lay sleeping. On the sill of the kitchen window burned three small candles, flickering like stars.

Now and again, Ruth left the glow of the light. She walked in the direction of the pond which I could see clearly by the moonlight reflected on its smooth surface.

She would come back carrying what looked like trailing, leafless branches which were almost certainly reeds. The cats lifted their heads, watching her progress, then slept on. I tried to see exactly where she went, and what she did there, but the light was too weak.

I got into bed feeling profoundly lonely. I had no idea what my mother's boxes might contain or what kept Caitlin and Ruth busy in the garden at this hour. They obviously all sought darkness, waited for night to fall, determined to exclude me.

When I finally fell asleep, I dreamed that I had come here by train after my Christmas exams and found Caitlin and my mother, white with cold, on the half-perished couch in the smithy. Crying, they threw their arms around me, unable to speak, clearly too afraid to go into the house. It was during that dream I made two important decisions: firstly, that my mother needed some sort of protection, and secondly that I had to find a new chainsaw.

NEXT MORNING, QUITE early, I walked into my mother's room without knocking, trying to appear casual. She was in bed, reading a newspaper.

'I'm going into Montourin.'

'Can you bring something to eat for tonight?' she said. There was no sign of the boxes or the cuttings. I went down, filled a plastic bottle with water for on the way, and headed for town down the shepherds' path.

I'd never been inside a gun shop before. I tried very hard not to show my uncertainty: I walked straight up to the glass display cases, greeting the proprietor with a slight nod, almost as if I knew him. Under my left arm I was carrying one of my grandfather's paintings which I planned to sell in the market. To free my hands, I put it down on the floor against one of the cases. To the left side of the shop, by the counter, stood two young men who seemed like regular customers; they were discussing cartridges, and how their prices had gone up in the last few months. I tried not to look at them, but I couldn't help noticing that they both turned their head towards me at exactly the same time, becoming silent for a moment. Without exchanging a word or a glance, they both smiled at me. As I bent closely over the objects in the display case, I could see their reflection in the glass. They continued their discussion, but kept looking in my direction. It made me nervous. I felt even more confused when I realised from the way the weapons were grouped that there was a difference between a revolver and a pistol, while I'd always thought they were the same thing.

'. . . better off with a water pistol,' I heard the smaller of the two say. A grating noise came from his nose. I slid the glass of the case open and picked up a revolver at random. I shifted it from my left hand to my right and spun the cylinder, the way I had seen it done in films. The thing was as heavy as I'd thought. I must have looked very awkward, standing there in my basketball boots, holding the revolver, obviously having no idea what to do with it or how to load it.

The shopkeeper, with a fatherly look, came to my rescue.

'A pistol,' I said hoarsely. None of the three showed any reaction to the word. Only when I added apologetically, 'for my mother,' did they smile again. The shopkeeper showed with a wave of his arm that I should be on the other side of the shop, near the locked cases. He went to open one. He showed me things I hadn't even suspected existed. He talked about blank rounds and self-loading actions. While he explained the differences, the advantages and the possibilities of the five or six different types he had in stock, I peered at the price tags. Every single one was more expensive than I had expected, and I sidled away from the man, telling him I had to think about it. As soon as I said anything, the men in the corner became silent again. They looked at me, obviously interrupted in their discussion, but also interested.

'My mother is just like that,' the taller one said. He was obviously the elder, too; I guessed he was maybe ten years older than me. Because he'd spoken to me, I couldn't avoid looking at him. The shop was dimly lit. The only daylight came through the glass door at the front, but because it was an elongated space, artificial light was needed in the middle and the back. A few fluorescent tubes hanging from the ceiling gave a weak, flickering light. It was difficult to discern the man's face. He was wearing a bright blue Armani jacket with a lighter coloured, well-ironed shirt. He was fair, and had smooth features.

'She doesn't dare go out by herself any more. Sixty-three, she is. Fit and healthy. But what can she do when four or five of them crowd around her like a wolf pack? You hand over. There is no other choice.' The shopkeeper and the other man nodded, although it was clear he had been mainly speaking to me.

'It only has to happen to you once. Once, and you live in fear. She's not so much worried about what actually happened—what does she care about that bit of money? She's worried about what could happen. The worst things happen in her dreams.'

As he spoke, he had come closer. I could now see his intensely blue eyes, looking at me fixedly. He smelled of musk and mild soap. His friend nodded as if his head was coming loose. For a moment I thought it was my turn to say something, but the man continued: 'She never feels safe now. She would only feel safe if she had some weapon herself, like a small pistol in her handbag. Just in case. Not a real one, of course, just something to scare those men. Sons have to see to it that their mothers get something like that. I like sons who protect their mothers.' Both hands loosely on the counter, the shopkeeper stood listening to the man. A fan was revolving slowly above his head, making his thin hair stand upright at intervals.

'How old are you?' asked the blond man.

'Seventeen,' I lied. He threw a quick glance at his friend. The latter's face brightened. He seemed to be the more restless of the two, smaller and darker, and his clothes didn't look as new.

'Do you hear that?' said the blond man. 'Seventeen! Really young, a minor still, but already with such a sense of responsibility.' The shopkeeper scraped his gold ring along the glass of the counter. Immediately, the blond man turned to him.

'Come on, René, we're not going to be difficult, are we?' he said. The shopkeeper looked away quickly and shook his head. He smoothed his hair, but as soon as he removed his hand, the hair sprang up again.

'I can't do it, Benoît,' he said. 'If I sell to a minor, I've had it!'

'But, René, this isn't a weapon! It's safety equipment! And it's for his mother, anyway.'

'Can't she come and get it then?'

'René, I thought we'd agreed we weren't going to be difficult!' The exclamation hung in the air for a while, as if it had been a question.

'Yes, well,' the shopkeeper said eventually. 'I just hope I won't get caught. He looks so young, nothing like seventeen.'

'The boy *does* look seventeen,' said Benoît quietly. 'He appears young because of his haircut. But have a good look at him.' The three heads turned towards me. 'Imagine him with an ordinary short haircut. Then what do you see?' The shopkeeper kept looking at me intently. 'Yes, exactly,' Benoît said emphatically. 'A boy of seventeen.' He came and stood next to me. With a movement of his head he indicated the starting pistols the shopkeeper had been showing me and said: 'Expensive, eh?'

'Too expensive,' I agreed quickly.

'How much have you got?' asked his dark-haired friend, who had been listening all this time.

'Not enough.'

'Not enough, Alex,' said Benoît over his shoulder.

'Too bad,' said Alex. Again he made that grating noise in his nose. The fan above the counter squeaked and didn't help a bit against the heat which hung in the air like fog. The carpet felt spongy and the air smelled of melting fat. The only thing I wanted was to get outside.

'Terrible,' said Benoît while I was getting ready to leave the shop. I slowed my step, out of politeness, because he spoke to me again. 'For your mother, I mean. Did they threaten her?'

'No,' I said hurriedly. I thought of the night before, and felt engulfed by remorse. 'They only come inside when we're not there. In the shed, too. They went off with my chainsaw.'

He clenched his fist, and the muscles in his jaw tightened. 'They're . . .' said Alex, backing him.

'So which one do you think you'll get?'

'I'll have to discuss it with my mother,' I said.

'Shouldn't you have a look at the other ones?' he asked. 'The real ones?' The shopkeeper started getting agitated.

'Just have a look,' Benoît said to him emphatically.

I shook my head and repeated that there was no need. I picked up the painting, muttered a greeting and moved towards the door.

'Hang on,' said Benoît, 'Alex will hold the door for you.'

As he heard his name, Alex stretched his back. He moved past Benoît who whispered a few words to him, and walked ahead of me to the glass door.

'Is that a painting?' he asked once I was on the footpath.

'Yes.'

'Do you paint?' He peered through the gaps in the wrapping. The glass door closed soundlessly behind us.

'No, I don't. My grandfather did.'

'Really? Was he famous?'

'Felix Stockx,' I said.

His mouth fell open when he heard the name. 'Felix? You're Felix's grandson?' His reaction surprised me. My grandfather painted landscapes which weren't up to much. And Alex didn't seem the sort of person who would spend money on paintings. He pushed the door open, stuck his head in and called out: 'He's Felix Stockx's grandson!'

'I didn't know he was a painter,' said Benoît a few moments later, after he had come outside and I had unwrapped the painting to show them. Out here in the sun, his hair had a reddish sheen which I hadn't noticed inside. It was quite short, but longer than Alex's. His was so short I could see the skin of his head through it. 'A man of many talents, obviously,' he said. 'Your grandfather was a great man. They've dragged his name through the mud, but for us he remains a shining example.' They both stood facing me, slightly bent towards me as if they were about to shake my hand. They must have expected me to square my shoulders and say something memorable about my grandfather. But I did the opposite. I didn't know what they were talking about, got all confused, looked away from them and started stuttering. They must have assumed it was because I felt ashamed, because Alex nudged me and said: 'Hey, you're not one of those, are you?' He made a gesture I could not read.

'One of which?' I said squawking like a turkey.

'Someone who pretends the past does not exist? Who shrouds everything in a cloak of silence?' Fortunately, Benoît, who was obviously more sensitive and noticed my confusion, intervened and said: 'Of course not, Alex. This boy is simply careful. He doesn't know who we are, so he doesn't let on. Can you blame him? God knows how often he has been abused when he said who he was.' I nodded, without knowing what I was confirming.

'I can put your mind at rest,' he continued. 'Our ideals are the same as your grandfather's. We want to act the way he acted, for the good of our country. People like him have taught us about obedience and loyalty. So remember:

if anything is wrong, you can always come to us. I'll do anything I can to help you.'

I saw Benoît many times during the summer. He never wore that blue Armani jacket again, probably it was too hot even for him, but whenever I think of him, I think of that jacket. Somehow or other it went with his eyes, which were incredibly bright, and blue like the flame of a gas burner.

FROM THE GUN shop, I walked to the small market square where lots of tourists sat in outdoor cafés. I unwrapped the painting and sat next to it on the pavement. Occasionally, small groups of people came past. They would notice it, enquire about the price and stroll on.

'Lovely,' said a young woman with a camera in her hand.

'Thank you,' I replied, barely opening my mouth. The heat seemed to radiate from the cobblestones more than from the sun. I sat closer and closer to the wall, because the area of shadow kept shrinking. I finished up sitting on the threshold of a small door which led to the kitchen of a restaurant. The door was ajar and a smell of roasting meat came through it in waves. Out of sheer boredom I peered in. There were six or seven people standing or walking about in the kitchen, all of them clearly Arabs, apart from the cook who looked like a real Frenchman. When the latter noticed me watching, he pushed the door shut.

Was I asking too much? As the hours passed, I felt my temper getting worse. I counted and recounted the money

I had on me, all my savings and some of the dollar notes my mother had got from her sale yesterday, but it was not enough. While I was concentrating on this, a smart elderly lady in slacks stopped beside me. She was carrying an umbrella to keep the sun off her face.

'Did you paint it yourself?' she asked in a lilting accent.

'Yes,' I said hopefully. But she, too, walked away. Around four, I wrapped the painting up again. Because it was quite impossible to climb the shepherds' path carrying the painting, I walked back along the road. At first, I met a few people. Cars drove past, and I could hear the shouts of playing children from the gardens behind the houses. But it became quieter the further I went into the hills. As I walked past the church yard wall, outside the town, lizards skittered among the hot stones at every step. The grassy verge of the road was overgrown with creepers. The barbed wire round the paddocks shimmered with electricity.

At the spot where the grassland changed into a rocky moonscape which sloped up steeply towards the convent, a woman was cutting out thistles with a hoe.

'On holidays again?' she asked. I put the painting down on one of its corners and said: 'I'm looking for a job.' She laughed. She knew me; I had come to her farm many times to buy eggs. She was younger than my mother, but they had been at school together, she in the lowest, my mother in the highest grade.

'A job?' she echoed. 'Aren't you supposed to be on holidays?'

'I need some money.'

'No jobs to be had here these days,' she said. She struck the soil with the hoe. A small cloud of dust rose. 'Every one of them has been taken. By illegals. They're cheap, and they've got strong backs. If you want any job at all, you'd have to work in a shop.' She half turned away from me, but for me the conversation wasn't finished yet.

'Did you know my grandfather well?' I asked bluntly. I couldn't think of a more gracious way to get her to talk.

She straightened her back, leaned on the handle of her hoe, and said: 'Yes, of course. He was my neighbour. It was really sad the way he died. It was a pity it happened like that, in the cold, in the middle of the winter.'

'And did you know him long ago?' I expected a sudden change in her manner—that she would start hacking awkwardly at the thistles, for instance, or start dishing up some feeble story. But she looked at me sympathetically and smiled.

'I've known him since the day I was born,' she said quietly, and nothing more.

About half a kilometre further along I met Caitlin. For a moment I thought she would just say hello and walk on. But she slowed her step.

'Is that one of . . . ?'

'My grandfather's.'

'Can I have a look?' I removed the paper which by now was torn in quite a few places. She examined the painting.

'Typical of him,' she said, 'with all that light.' I tried to look at the painting with fresh eyes. I had seen it so often, this one and all the other ones, which were very similar, and to me it was just an ordinary landscape.

'Can't you see?' she asked, looking at me intently. 'Just like an over-exposed photo, with all that white paint over the surface.'

'Yes,' I said stupidly. For a few moments, she didn't say anything, but kept looking at me in amazement, almost as if she was seeing me for the first time.

'You look so surprised! You really don't know anything, do you?' she said eventually. Her remark shook me up, because at first I thought she meant I knew nothing about art.

'Well, no,' I said because I couldn't think of anything else to say. She walked past me.

'I'm going to buy a soft drink,' she said. 'But when I'm back, I'll show you the cellars of the convent. Then you'll know what I mean.'

I wrapped the paper—what was left of it—back round the painting. 'There is a shorter way down to town,' I said as she was walking away. 'Along the shepherds' path.'

'I know,' she said. She disappeared. I continued my walk up the hill. My blood was banging in my head. My head felt as if it had caught fire, like a flaming torch.

Early in the evening, I screwed up my courage and ventured into the convent garden. I had sat waiting for a couple of hours for Caitlin to return, but hadn't seen her, and realised she must have come back along the shepherds' path. Getting into the garden I was more nervous than usual. I definitely didn't want to bump into Soeur, so I hid behind just about every bush I came past to listen for any sounds. A strange silence enveloped the convent, and I had no idea where to look for Caitlin.

Instinctively I went to the north side of the building, to the wing where the dining hall had been. As I passed the small graveyard with its white crosses, it suddenly became clear what Caitlin and Ruth had been doing the evening before: around five of the crosses they had hung wreaths made out of reeds from the pond. The wreaths had been skilfully woven and were decorated with small branches of ivy. I wondered how they had managed to make the reeds pliable enough, but I didn't allow myself the time to walk into the unfenced graveyard to have a look. I ducked down below the window where I had watched Caitlin dancing the first time and found that my instinct had been correct: Caitlin was dancing. Though I was dying with curiosity to see the cellars, I sat down close to the wall, my face against the gap in the shutters and kept still.

The dance was different this time, lighter and less incomprehensible. There were high leaps and twists when she snapped her legs apart and together again like a pair of scissors. This time there was music, and perhaps that made everything different. It was summery piano music that reminded me of foaming beer. She wore a white blouse with long sleeves, tight round the wrists, and over that a rather sloppy black sleeveless tunic, like the uniform of a schoolgirl showing off her rebelliousness. Around her, cats played with stalks of straw which had been blown inside.

For long minutes, I enjoyed the dance, and wasn't prepared for the sudden shift which followed, first in the music, which seemed to topple over like a tower and became low and intense and ominous, and then in her movements: she fell. She really fell. She fell and kept on falling. In between, she kept getting up in a movement which was a mirror image of her fall, flouting the laws of gravity, as if she was attached to the ceiling with elastic. She was like a ball which falls and bounces: the floor threw her back up. It was an amazing sight, like watching a film repeatedly stopping and reversing.

It was not beautiful to watch. I could clearly see that it hurt. It went on too long. She was panting too loudly; I could hear this above the music. The getting up became more and more slow and laborious. At last, she hit the floor for good. She stayed down, spread out flat on the floor. I jumped up, walked to the tall French window and pushed the shutters aside.

'Lucas!' Caitlin called out. She got up, supple as a cat, went over to the cassette player and turned the volume down. She rubbed her hand through her hair, and from her dreamy expression I could see that my arrival had forced her back to a reality she had been unaware of for a time.

'What are you doing?' I asked, upset. I was as disturbed by the fact that she could simply get up and walk to the cassette player as by her fall.

'Dancing,' she said.

'That's dancing? It looked as if you were hurt.'

'I am hurt.'

'I mean, it looked as if you wouldn't be able to get up. As if you were in a lot of pain.'

'No, it doesn't hurt. I can't help it. When I dance my own piece, I always feel as if I'm being sucked down to the ground. To dance, I have to fall.'

'When you told me last time that you danced, I thought of ballet, with dancing shoes and all that.'

'I am not a ballerina. I dance.'

'Modern dance?'

'Whatever you like to call it. I started out with the classical stuff. You know, *Swan Lake* and that sort of thing. I've worn out dozens of pairs of point shoes. Now I'm trying to create something myself.'

'Here? In the dining hall?'

'The floor is perfect. Ash wood, board on board and no concrete under it. It's flexible, and that's necessary if you don't want to break your bones. I have to be careful: my ankle hasn't quite healed yet.'

'What happened?'

'I was doing a piece with a group in New York, in public. I was doing a simple plié and felt a dry pain in my ankle. I could hear a sound like a cork popping. I just kept dancing, but by the time I went off stage, my ankle was twice its usual size. It's because of that bloody injury I missed the auditions for the dance school.' Her hair was damp with sweat. It was oppressively hot in the dining hall. When she saw that it was bothering me too, she walked into the passage to see if Soeur was anywhere near.

'I was going to show you the cellars,' she said. 'It's lovely and cool there.'

They were spacious, dry cellars, with windows high up in the walls here and there. Some of the panes were broken, and they were so dirty that one could only guess that the green glow behind them came from grass growing close to the walls. Although it wasn't dark, it was difficult to move about because of all the pieces of furniture, boxes and stacks of newspapers which cluttered the floor. As we walked, I felt vague memories, but didn't recognise anything. Only the cool smell of rising damp and stagnant air seemed familiar.

I had hoped she would let me discover the cellars gradually, space after space, with enough time to get used to the half-dark. But she seemed to be in a hurry. She opened door after door, switched on lights where there was electricity and kept walking without waiting for me. She didn't allow me to ask any questions ('Shush now, the kitchen is right above us. Soeur will be able to hear you!') or to touch anything ('She notices everything, even fingerprints in the dust.').

She moved fast, and from the unhesitating way she went for doors and light switches I could tell that she'd been here often before. I followed close behind her; together we resembled a pair of sniffing rodents in search of something edible. It was when we got to the furthest room, in the cellar that was a little higher than the others, with stone steps leading out into the garden, that I was startled by a sound near me. I saw a flapping shape rise up and fall down again. Frightened, I took a clumsy sideways step, getting my foot hooked in a ladder and bumping into Caitlin with my shoulder. It was like falling against a wall or a tree: she didn't move at all.

'What's that?' I asked hoarsely. An irregular, violent shaking sound came from behind a piece of fibreboard with a few pieces cut out of it. It was right next to me. I regained my balance, but didn't move another step: I was afraid I might stand on something soft and warm unexpectedly darting away from under my feet.

'The dove,' said Caitlin, and the next moment there was another movement of grey wings, a wide tail and blowing dust. It was a pearl grey dove, a large, old specimen with dirty looking feathers. It couldn't fly because its feet were tangled in a grubby tea-towel.

'She's been sitting here like this for four days now,' said Caitlin. 'I've been trying to catch her so I can release her, but I can't do it by myself.'

'How did it get in here?'

'I don't know. I only discovered her accidentally. She must have flown in through one of the windows.' She ordered me to stand near the steps up to the garden. Only half recovered from the shock, I did as she said. Clapping her hands, she chased the terrified bird in my direction.

'When she lands, grab her,' she said. I mouthed 'OK' silently so as not to scare the bird. She snapped her fingers. The dove took fright, flew up and landed a metre and a half from my feet. It was an elegant movement, like that of a lady in evening dress, but now that it was sitting so close to me, I could see that its legs were unstable under its body, like red, dry twigs, probably broken because of its violent movements. There was a fast pulse in its throat and a grey membrane passed over its eyes from time to time. It looked at me so wildly that I feared it would fly at me, at my throat or my eyes.

'What are you waiting for?' whispered Caitlin. I made a feinting movement. The creature flew up, flapping its wings, hurting itself on all sides in order to get away from me, and settled behind the racks. Caitlin sighed loudly. She waited a few seconds and then walked towards the bird again.

'Comecomecome,' she said as if she were talking to one of her cats. 'We'll undo the tea-towel.' We kept trying for a while longer. Things got worse. The dove became more and more panic stricken, started flying into things and banging its head against obstacles.

'We only want to help,' Caitlin called in a sing-song tone, but the bird was now so scared that the mere sound of our voices made it beat its wings wildly. She didn't say anything, but I know Caitlin blamed me. I could tell from the way she spoke to me when we suddenly heard footsteps in the adjoining space.

'Caitlin?' we heard someone call. It was Soeur, drawn by the noise. With a quick gesture, Caitlin urged me to disappear up the steps and through the garden.

'But my grandfather!' I whispered. 'What's this got to do with my grandfather?'

'Nothing,' she said curtly. Soeur was approaching. I walked up the steps and stood hesitating.

'Nothing, I tell you. Just get away!' I put my hand on the knob of the garden door. Last winter's rain had washed grit and leaves under the door. I pulled on the doorhandle with one hand, pushing against the doorjamb with the other and the door opened with a scraping noise. The evening heat fell on me like a layer of fur. The grass and the creepers were recovering from the sun. While I stood there letting my eyes adjust to the light, I began to suspect what had happened. She had put me through a test and I had failed. I left the garden and walked home. I regretted not having acted more decisively. I could have easily grabbed the bird. As a child I'd always handled my hamsters, and later my rabbits, so I had no reason to be afraid of the trembling life between my hands. It was something else that upset me: I felt she had used me. She had lured me into the cellar with the promise of telling me something about my grandfather, but that had been a pretence. She had just wanted me to help her catch the dove. That realisation had made me reluctant. I couldn't get away from the impression that she was in the plot, just like Alex and Benoît, the woman pulling up thistles, Nadine, my mother, Soeur and all the others. I walked through the house opening one door after another. But all I found were dusty rooms. The dove kept flapping about in my head.

NEXT MORNING I WOKE up full of great plans: I would open all my grandfather's cupboards, look through all his drawers and search the house from top to bottom for his things. I took it for granted that I would be able to discover for myself whatever there was to be known about my grandfather. The boxes under my mother's bed would be the key. I lay waiting to hear movement in her room. There was a brief rummaging in her cupboard, a chair scraped and finally I heard her door opening.

My mother walked slowly down the stairs, as if she was not very steady on her feet, and I suspected she had only just woken up and was on her way down to make coffee. But I had barely emerged into the passage when I could already hear her coming back, walking faster now, but quietly. I withdrew hurriedly. She went into her room without closing the door, and a moment later I heard her going down the stairs again, shuffling, as if she had gone blind and was feeling for each tread with her foot. The screen door out of the kitchen shut with a bang, a familiar sound that was usually followed by steps on the gravel. She walked into the garden. I saw a vague flash of her red shirt through the bushes.

The boxes had gone from under her bed. I searched her wardrobe and the blanket chest. In the passage I opened the wall cupboards where there always used to be boxes, and cases full of winter jumpers, but they, too, were mostly empty. I searched the attic, empty apart from a carpet of drying onions, the cellar and the living room. I must be overlooking something; the boxes I had seen just twenty-four hours earlier had vanished without trace. 'They're probably right under my nose,' I thought and went back to my room to look under the bed and in the cupboards there, too. All I found were paintings and knitted jumpers.

I gave up. I stretched out on the bed, my eyes on the ceiling, to think about how I would fill the rest of the day. Then the noise of a motor starting up sounded outside. Cheered up because something was happening, I pushed the desk under the skylight to see who it was.

I looked straight into the convent garden. With the sun now behind me, everything seemed even closer, so my instant reaction was to pull back my head and pretend to be busy doing something, checking the hinges or cleaning the top edge of the window. I looked intently at my hands, rather than outside, so I couldn't immediately work out who was in the car. Out of the corner of my eye I saw one of those old, wide, four-door cars you see quite a few of here in the hills, probably a Mercedes or Citroën. The engine purred and the car took off hesitantly. Cautiously, like a boat, it glided forward. It moved so slowly and quietly I could hear twigs cracking under the tyres. It swung wide, out of the courtyard and under the stone gateway, past the fence onto the road.

I caught a glimpse of the driver's profile. It was Caitlin. She wasn't eighteen yet. Her daring made my heart skip a beat.

Soon after, I rang my melancholy friend Arno. He was my best friend in the city, and when I had told him, still in a rage, that my mother had sublet our flat for the whole summer, he had shouted through the window of the departing bus that he would come to visit me no matter what. I spoke to his mother.

'Travel all the way out there? No, I don't know anything about that. I doubt if he is planning that, he would have told me.'

'But he promised!'

'Oh, you know Arno!'

I hadn't actually known him all that long. I'd met him by chance at a party I'd come to with some other friends. He was sitting apart from the others, listening to music through earphones. I went over to talk to him. To my bewilderment, he mainly talked about two operas he'd been to see that week, *Otello* and *La Bohème*. He spoke with an enthusiasm I'd only ever heard from reviewers on the radio. When I mentioned the few operas I could remember from my compulsory music lessons at school, I was convinced he didn't even hear me, but when we met again it was clear he remembered every word. 'I suppose you are bored here, too?' he had said. Since then, we'd been going everywhere together.

The next one I rang was Frederic, Fred to his friends, drummer in his brothers' band and hopeless muddler at school. There was no subject he could pass without help from his friends. He sounded delighted.

'Great fun out there in the hills, I suppose?' he asked.

'So so.'

'Look,' he said formally when I asked him when he was going to come, 'I know I promised. But I've pestered my dad to death. And now he's let me buy that Yamaha, but I have to work to pay him back.'

'I met a girl,' I said. 'You'd like her. She drives a car without her mum knowing.'

'Bring her when you come,' he said. He added a few things about some of our friends, but I found it hard to listen to him. He made vague noises about driving out here but not staying long. Having said something non-committal like 'Good idea', I hung up.

My last conversation was with Moumouche. He couldn't come because, after three weeks, he had finally managed to convince his flame Sabrina of his charms. 'I can't do it to her,' he said, 'she can't really do without me.' He added a haw-haw sort of laugh and I joined in to please him. I said I understood.

It must have been all those phone calls that made me feel the need to have a bath. First I filled the tub half full with tepid water, and after thoroughly washing and rinsing my hair, shoulders and armpits, I ran more water, right up to the rim, so I could hardly move without sloshing. I lay there for quite a while, till the water almost seeped through my skin, and thought. From time to time I put my head right under. Under water, all sound was reduced to the hissing of the plumbing, the scraping of my back against the enamel of the bath, and my breath escaping. I could just hear my heartbeat. I released the air from my lungs very slowly. From under the water, the bathroom looked like a large aquarium with a window full of fractured sunlight, a door, and a shower curtain with blue flowers floating around in it. I thought: 'I don't have to know. If they insist on being secretive, let them have their fun.' And I resolved not to ask anybody any questions about my grandfather, not to open another cupboard, and not to read any of his personal papers. I was overwhelmed by the deepest feeling of boredom I have ever experienced. Boredom, not because there was nothing going on, but because any desire to do anything whatsoever had drained out of me. A bit surprised with myself, I lay thinking about the day before, when I'd gone to the trouble of finding a gun shop to enquire about the possibilities. It now suddenly seemed even more improbable that I had walked all the way down into the town with that stupid painting of my grandfather's under my arm, and that I had actually stood in a hot marketplace with it for four hours. I had the feeling I would never leave this house, possibly not even this bathroom, for the rest of the summer. Even if a bomb were to drop on the town. There was nothing, but nothing, that could make me move.

Suddenly, a policeman stood next to me.

'Oops! Excuse me!' he said. Instantly I sat up straight. The water sloshed over the edge of the bath, washing away the plastic soap container which hit the floor with a clatter.

'Excuse me,' he repeated, visibly embarrassed. He wanted to get out again straight away, was already halfway out of the bathroom, his hand still on the doorknob, but kept making excuses. 'I could hear you talking, and when I called out you didn't answer. I thought that was strange.' I had to lean forward to see him; the flowery shower curtain was in the way and my eyes and ears were full of water. It was the man I had met by the garden gate a few days before. I remembered the way he moved like a tap dancer, and the lock of hair sticking out on either side of his head, giving his face a slightly comical expression. 'And with the things that have been happening around here lately . . .' He shut the door behind him, saying he'd wait for me downstairs.

Without bothering to dry myself properly, I put my clothes on. He was waiting downstairs, near the kitchen door which he had left ajar, with his right leg leaning casually against the drawer where my mother kept the pruning knife. He started excusing himself again: but the door had been open. That's what had started it all: the fact that, once more, the kitchen door had not been locked.

'I thought my mother was in the garden. And I don't normally lock it when I have a bath,' I said.

'Fair enough,' he said. 'But look at it from my point of view . . .' We understood each other. I pacified him with a can of iced tea I dug up from the bottom of the fridge and which I served him with a slice of lemon. He had wanted to speak with my mother, but as she was nowhere to be found, he would tell me: they were on the trail of the thieves. They had found a small warehouse with all sorts of items they suspected were stolen. That was all he could say. And could I tell him the exact make and model of the electric frying pan, the toaster and the two TVs.

'Is there a chainsaw there?' I asked. He had no idea. There was such a lot, and they hadn't done a proper inventory yet. As he told me all that, he kept repeating that he really wasn't in the habit of barging into people's houses. Because he was obviously bothered by it, I gave him another iced tea and let him tell me about his duties. The town wasn't what it used to be, with all those tourists and seasonal workers.

'Wherever you find wealthy holiday-makers, you find cheap workers,' he said, 'and vice versa.' He'd put his cap down on the table. The locks of hair now hung straight down by his ears.

'At first the problem only arose in the centre of the town,' he said, twisting his glass in his hands. 'But it's spreading. When there is nothing to be had there any more, they go and check out the surrounding area. Even in the tiny villages, those places where maybe a hundred or so people live, and the rest of the homes have been turned into holiday houses, they simply break in through the front door at night . . . They know there's nobody home, because if there are tourists in the house, there's a car in the drive. And off they go with the household gear. To their warehouse, and then into the delivery van. Half the Arab world eats out of our pots and pans. And there is no one around, of course, no one who sees or hears anything. The hills are deserted. Just look at this place, this side of the hill. How many people live out here?' He made a sweeping gesture. The sunlight lay in clear stripes across the tiled floor. I did a quick addition in my head.

'Five,' I said, surprising myself.

'Five,' he repeated theatrically.

I sat up. I thought I heard footsteps upstairs. The thermostat of the fridge cut in with a humming sound, and a blue fly landed on the table. Instantly, my dream of two nights ago flashed, bright as lightning, before my eyes.

'Five,' I repeated and squashed the fly with the flat of my hand. 'Four women and me.'

My mother hadn't left me a note, and her bike stood leaning against the smithy, so she couldn't be far away. I walked around the house. I noticed a column of smoke rising behind the trees, and went over. The smell of burning suddenly made me hungry for a waffle breakfast.

She was stoking a fire on the rocks in the far corner of the garden. I had to push through blackberry bushes to get near her. Because of the crackling of the wet twigs in the fire, she couldn't hear me coming. She was leaning on her poker. Her hair was pulled back with an elastic band, and she mechanically smoothed escaping strands behind her ears. She was wearing my grandfather's grey dust-coat over her summer shorts, and gumboots which protected her legs from the thorns, and she had the dreamy air of a child who had stopped in the middle of a game because she couldn't remember what she was playing.

'What are you doing?' I asked. Slightly startled, she turned. Her face was a bit swollen. The skin on her cheek was shiny from having been too close to the fire too long.

'Burning junk,' she said after some thought. 'That house is too cluttered.'

'The police were here.'

'The police?'

'They were looking for you.'

'What for?'

'They wanted a list of the missing items. They're onto something.'

'Oh, that stolen stuff. Do they have to bother me with that?' She pushed the poker into the fire, sending a cloud of ashes spiralling into the air. The exertion and the heat had made the veins on her hands stand out horribly. I went back to the house and opened a packet of cream wafers, which I slowly ate. When my mother finally came back, half an hour later, her hands and legs covered in black smears and dust, she didn't offer any explanation. She just said she was going into the town and asked me to fit the heavy bolt she had bought the day before to the side door. Then she left. She didn't say when she was coming back and didn't ask what I was planning. She didn't arrange for us to eat together, or to do anything.

She left like someone who didn't think it worthwhile ever coming back.

Feeling generally furious, I walked into the town. I was carrying the painting under my arm again, so I went along the main road, knowing from experience how hard it was to go via Challon's Bluff carrying anything. This time I was absolutely determined to sell it; I needed the money for the starting pistol. I listened to the faint echo of my footsteps between the cliff face and the low walls that edged some of the bends. I had locked all the doors of the house and walked around it to check that there were no windows left open. Every time a car passed, I strained to see the driver's face. I was walking quite fast. The bathwater that had soaked into my body was now coming out again through my pores and I could feel the back of my T-shirt getting wet and then drying again in the heat of the sun.

Like the day before, I went to the small market square which again was full of tourists and set myself up near the side entrance of the restaurant, right near the door to the kitchen where, as before, some seven people moved about. The cook, the one who looked more French than Napoleon, seemed to recognise me. He came and stood in the doorway, looked to the right and the left, and finally, as if surprised to see me there, smiled at me. It wasn't midday yet. Behind him, the copper pans and the knives shone. On the floor stood cardboard boxes with fresh vegetables. Soft piano music came through the walls, sounding more like scales than a melody, as if someone was practising for the evening's performance.

I hadn't quite unpacked the painting when I was surrounded by a group of Japanese bidding against each other. I watched their bickering like a game of ping-pong. I didn't understand a word they said. Suddenly, they were silent and the whole group swung across to the next stall.

'I think I'll buy it after all,' said a voice with a foreign accent next to me. It was the lady from yesterday. Like an ageing Mary Poppins she stood before me, smiling, her umbrella held high above her as if it was carrying her rather than the other way around. She held money at the level of my face, but when I went to take it she pulled it back and examined the painting very closely.

'It's not perfect,' she said, 'but perfection would spoil it. I think you're doing very well. When I come back next year . . .' She didn't finish her sentence. She put her finger on the name in the bottom right-hand corner.

'Stockx?' she said. 'That is your name?' For a moment I was so flabbergasted I didn't know what to say. She smiled understandingly.

'A pseudonym,' she said as if she had known all along. She picked up the painting, inspected the back, and scratched at the canvas with her fingernail. I stood away from her a bit. I quite expected her to start asking questions about the fixer or the kind of oil paint. The cook from the restaurant still stood looking around, waiting for customers who, in this heat, could think of nothing but milkshakes and iced water. I was moving over to him, trying to think of something to say, when she called me back. Could I please wrap it up? With some string around it, because it had to go on the plane as hand luggage. Of course I had no string, only that piece of paper, but the cook, who had overheard her, went inside to fetch what was needed. While we were waiting for him, she said: 'Something has happened to you.' I must have looked rather bewildered, for she rested her hand on my shoulder reassuringly.

'You don't have to tell me anything,' she said. 'But I have seen a great many paintings in my life. They are images of the soul.' She pointed at the areas of white in the painting. 'Someone who goes to so much trouble to bring light into his landscapes, has known darkness.' I nodded as if I understood what she was talking about and before she could go into it any further, the cook handed me a piece of string and some newspaper, which I carefully wrapped around the painting without saying anything much. I counted the money she handed me. It was a bit less than I had asked, but I didn't say anything. Carrying my grandfather's painting under her arm, she disappeared among the slowly moving tourists. Her colourful umbrella stayed in view until she had got to the other side of the square.

'Good sale,' said the cook.

'Yes,' I said, putting the money away.

'Easily earned money. If it's as easy as that, I think I'll take up painting.'

'I'm looking for work,' I said.

'Work? Do you need even more money?'

'Not really, I just need something to do.'

'There are too many people looking for work these days. Almost for nothing. In my kitchen, they get in each other's way. Drives you mad in this heat.' He looked over my shoulder into the street, at the people walking about the square in all directions, none of whom seemed to have a real destination. Then he turned back to me.

'You'd better go straight to the bank,' he said paternally. 'Best not to walk about with all that money.' While

I wondered what business it was of his, I said he was right. I hurled myself among the people. Around me I heard several languages. I looked at the things that were being offered for sale, the earrings, the books about the region, the handmade pottery, the sand paintings, but there was nothing that could hold my attention. My anger, part of which I had already walked off on my way into the town, now seemed completely gone. My wallet sat loosely in my back pocket, and I felt lighter, if only because I was no longer lugging that painting around. The wait in the shadow of the restaurant had slowed down my heartbeat. I sat down on a café terrace and ordered pineapple and mango ice-cream.

Sitting there, alone, but surrounded by people talking, passing the time, enjoying the sunshine and paying me no attention at all, I thought about things. That was a mistake. Thinking, I went around in circles, back to the same thoughts that I'd worried about in the bath: that I shouldn't have come this summer, that my mother had tricked me, that everybody lied to me and kept things from me. I thought: while I'm here, I'm like Caitlin's dove. There's nobody here. There's nothing to do. There's no light and no air. My feet are tangled up in something, but I don't know what. This town feels as if it's preserved in formaldehyde. The tourists stay for half a day, and by their next stop have already forgotten the fourteenth century castle, the remains of the old ramparts and the flavour of the regional dishes. While the air around me buzzed with activity, with the rapid movement of the waiters among the tables and the constant flying up and coming down of pigeons, all I could think of was my friends in the city.

LATER THAT DAY, I went to the gun shop. I wasn't really surprised when I noticed that Alex was there again. He was at the back of the shop, under the fluorescent light, with his back turned to me; he was wearing a baseball cap, so I couldn't see right away if it was him. When he turned round, I recognised the big head with the close-set eyes and the little moustache.

He immediately came over to me.

'Ah! Tintin!' he called. 'You've come back for your heater. Didn't we say so, René?' He looked at René, then back at me. 'René said you wouldn't come back. He thought you were one of those indecisive people who ask for infor-mation everywhere, but never buy anything. But we knew you were convinced. Benoît would have bet his mother's head on it.'

'Yes,' I said curtly. I hadn't come to talk to him.

'We were just talking about you this morning,' he said, 'when we heard about that gang of thieves.' I showed René the starting pistol I had decided on. He nodded his approval and muttered a few words about its quality. Alex leaned his elbow on the tabletop. He paid no attention to what we were doing, and just went on: 'They have recov-ered everything now. In a depot in a shed somewhere, they won't say where. The police raided the place. Just on suspicion, and guess what they found? The whole town's Lost Property.' René was rummaging in one of the deep cupboards behind him, apparently looking for a box or other packaging. The fan above us squeaked like an injured bird, and I waited.

'Now they're doing an inventory. Everything that's not claimed will be sold. It seems there are a lot of good things there.' René had found what he was looking for. He put a khaki-coloured leather case on the counter, took a small key from his pocket and, with deliberate movements, opened the glass door in front of the pistols. In a flash, Alex stood next to me. I put out my hand to take the pistol, but he got in first.

'Just having a look,' he said. He moved the pistol from his right hand to his left and back. 'The safety catch is only there to make it look real,' he said. 'Makes no difference. Look: you take its weight on the front edge of your hand, and when you pull the trigger, you move this finger in at the same time. For balance, you see. Lessens the recoil.' He took my hand and put the pistol into it. The barrel felt cool, but the butt was warm from his hand. He put my fingers in the correct position, but they remained stiff and unwilling. The joints didn't flex the way they should. I moved my wrist about a few times to loosen them up.

'Now aim at René,' said Alex. 'Right, good. Stretch out your arms. Here, look at this. Point at his chest. No, no, not at his legs, because then he'll know that you'll do anything to *not* kill him. Or at his head, between the eyes, like this, that's good, too.' I pointed the barrel at René's forehead. He looked at me as though it had nothing to do with him, and I felt a shiver down my back.

'Now, fire,' said Alex.

'Alex, for God's sake!' called René, alarmed. 'Not in the shop. Shooting allowed only in the sound-proof room!'

'Just fire, Tintin!' Alex repeated close to my ear. I didn't. I lowered the pistol and put it on the counter. René put it in the case, which he wrapped in a plastic bag. He showed me the instructions and the guarantee. I paid and went out.

Alex followed and walked next to me. I looked at him sideways. In the bright sunlight he looked different from just then inside. He seemed a lot older than me. His head sat massively on his body, which was rather small and thin, but with a muscular frame that hinted at great strength and stamina.

'I didn't ask what your name was last time. Stupid of me, because Benoît had told me to. But I got distracted by that painting. Benoît said to look for you until I found you. I looked you up in the phone book. Under Stockx. But that's not your name of course.'

'No,' I said and kept walking. I clutched the plastic bag under my arm to make sure the pistol wouldn't knock into something and accidentally go off.

'So to make things easier we decided on Tintin. Benoît's idea, you know. He's always giving people names like that.' The road sloped gently upward. Although I walked pretty fast, he kept up with me without any trouble. He managed to keep talking without getting puffed.

'He was convinced René wouldn't sell you the gun. He is always scared shitless, René. Good thing I was there.' He took his cap off and held it in his hand. His hair was so short I could see the pimples on his scalp.

'But what I really wanted to say is: you have to learn to dare.' There were sharp pieces of gravel on the footpath, presumably off a truck that had come from the quarry. I could feel them through the soles of my shoes. I kicked a few of them ahead of me, so they looked like insects darting away. He kept up with me, taking slower but longer steps.

'When René yells not to shoot, that's exactly when you should do it,' he said. 'Because that's the trick. Don't forget: they'll *always* shout that you shouldn't. And every second you hesitate is one too long. Your opponent throws something at your head, and that's it. You lose control. You'd be better off having stayed in bed.'

'This is a starting pistol, only to give a warning. I don't have to aim. I just have to make a noise.'

'Shooting is nothing to do with aiming. You have to if you're out in a garden or in the street of course. But usually your attacker will be standing in your living room. At five metres at the most; you can't miss. All you need is to dare. If you dare with a starting pistol, you'll be game to use a real gun.'

'I don't need a real one.'

'You have to practise. If you don't practise, you'll freeze. Your attacker will see that you've never handled a pistol before. Your heater may look as real as you like, but if you wave it about like an idiot, you'll be overpowered in no time.'

'I live in the hills. If I shoot, the neighbours will ring the police.'

'Silencer?' he said cryptically. He stopped, and I did too. He put his hand to his chin, an old-fashioned teacher's gesture, which made him look funny somehow.

'Have you got a bit of time?' he asked. 'A couple of hours a week?'

'Depends,' I said.

'We've got a sort of a club. A few friends. Benoît would quite like you to join.'

'A club?'

'Yes, you know, just some friends. We do things together. Keeps us off the streets, my father says.'

'Why does he want me to join?'

'Ah, that's Benoît. That's what he's like. He gets this thing about people. You should have heard him: Tintin this and Tintin that. Once he takes a liking to you, he *really* likes you. He wants to teach you things.'

'Like what?'

'Don't underestimate him. He's the best shot for miles around. There are people who would pay to get lessons from him, who would pay heaps.'

'I can't see . . .'

'Think about it. You're very busy, of course.'

'Yes.'

'I know your sort. Lots of hobbies and pursuits. You make friends all over the place. And reading, I suppose, non-stop.'

'Among other things.'

'What was your name again?' He began to move away from me gradually.

'Lucas Beigne,' I said. He walked slowly away from me until, at a few metres distance, he stopped and turned to face me.

'Sixty-nine Rue Machiavelli,' he said cryptically. 'That's where Benoît lives. Think about it. Absolutely no obligation.' He waved his cap and put it back on with an exaggeratedly broad gesture.

'Hey!' I said.

'What?'

'Something else.'

'Yes, what?'

'Why Tintin?'

He threw his head back and laughed. 'Your haircut, of

course!' he said, walking away. He turned into a lane which, I suspected, led directly back to the Route sur Mérinne, the road where the gun shop was.

So there I stood. Alone, some way from the busy centre of the town, in a residential area where tourists never go, clutching a starting pistol under my arm. I had some money left over. The police station happened to be nearby. I went in there, carrying the plastic bag casually so as not to draw attention to it, and asked if I could see the inventory of stolen goods.

'They're still working on it,' said the man under the 'information' sign.

'Oh,' I said. I didn't go away. The air-conditioning cut in noisily just as I was saying: 'And where is it?'

'What?' the man asked.

'The depot, where can I find it?'

He paid attention. He looked me up and down with his small, friendly eyes. He looked like someone who enjoyed the bustle around him. For a moment I thought he was focusing on the parcel under my arm. I hadn't taken much notice in the shop, but hoped the gun dealer's name wasn't on it. He bent over towards me. 'I can't tell you that,' he said, almost giggling, 'but, err . . .' He looked hard at me. 'I know you. Aren't you Stockx's grandson?'

'Ah!' he said, when I nodded. 'I knew you when you were a child. And now, your face, the way you stand! Exactly like Felix when he was young!' We talked for a few minutes, he about how sad my grandfather's death had been, I about my mother. He knew we had been robbed twice in succession; his colleagues had told him. I told him about the two TV sets and the other things. Policemen walked in and out constantly. They looked hot in their uniforms.

'Where is that depot they found?' I tried once more.

He went on smiling as before. 'I can't tell you,' he said. He tapped emphatically on the glass top of the counter at which he stood. Almost accidentally, I noticed that there was a map of the town under the glass.

'Oh,' I said, 'I'll come back some other time then.' I took a surreptitious look at the spot under his finger and left.

As I walked on, back into the town, I passed Nadine's salon. The door stood wide open and I poked my head in.

'Lucas!' she said. The salon was empty. She was reading one of the magazines which were there for customers. She fanned herself with a loose page.

'Getting used to your new cut?'

I pushed the fly curtain aside and went in. 'It needs to be shorter,' I said.

'What do you mean, even shorter?'

'As short all over as it is at the back. No long bit at the front or on top.'

'I thought you liked it the way it is?'

'It is always hanging down over my eyes,' I said. 'It looks stupid, makes me look like a girl.'

She got up and came over to me. I thought of the phone conversation she had had with my mother. Her eyes were clear and friendly. You would never guess that she was keeping things from me. She put her hand under my chin, smoothed my hair back, then sideways, and took a step back to get a better look at me. By pushing gently against my shoulder she turned me towards the mirror.

'Look,' she said. 'How about like this?' I felt deceived. She lied to me through her silence.

'Short,' I said.

'It will look very severe. Won't make you look like a nice boy, the way it does now.'

'Just cut it.' I put the pistol down carefully under the barber's chair, pushing it far enough to make sure she couldn't accidentally kick it. I sat down and stretched my legs. She took up her scissors and comb, twisting them in her hand a few times before coming towards me.

'Or did you want me to use the clippers?' she asked.

'Ye-es,' I replied as if she had offered me something really nice. The vibration of the clippers on my head relaxed the muscles in my neck. It gave me gooseflesh. For a moment I felt like letting everything be, like not asking any more questions and simply waiting for answers to come. But I recovered. I pulled my legs back, sat up straight and said: 'I've met Caitlin since.'

'Oh really?' she said, sounding genuinely interested for a moment. She spoke so loudly she seemed to give herself a fright. She cleared her throat and coolly added: 'How nice.'

'A lot has happened since. I have found out things about my grandfather.'

She didn't say another word.

'About the past, what happened. Nobody had ever told me anything about that before.'

'Really?' she finally managed.

'Most people know about it. You do, don't you?'

'Er, yes, I suppose so, sort of.'

'My mother has told me things.'

She lifted the clippers away from my head. They buzzed on in her hand. With her free hand she absently flicked hair from my shoulders.

'Your mother?' she said hoarsely. She struck my shoulder harder than necessary, almost as if she wanted to hurt me.

'Well, Caitlin first. She showed me the cellars. Now I know why my grandfather put so much light into his paintings.'

'Yes,' she said thoughtfully. She shifted her weight onto her other leg. She took a deep breath and seemed to relax for a moment. 'Yes. Perhaps. I've never thought about it that way.' She put the clippers back on my head, but pulled them away again, as if she had second thoughts.

'So what did she tell you?' she asked. I could see the suspicion on her face in the mirror.

'Everything, really,' I lied airily. 'She showed me news-paper clippings, too.'

'Oh, really?'

'There are a whole lot of things I understand better now. For instance why Soeur still breeds those geese. And why she never wanted me to play with Caitlin, when we were little.' That was all I said. Was all I could say. Anything more would put me on very slippery ground. Anything could happen now. I could say something wrong and have to own up. She could ask a question I had no answer for at all. We looked at each other in the mirror all the time, quickly and surreptitiously, for I didn't dare look into her eyes, nor she into mine.

'Well!' she said.

'Strong stuff, isn't it?'

'You can say that again. And all that time you knew nothing about any of it?'

'No. They thought it better that way. My mother feels I'm too sensitive for such things.'

'Yes, well, it is pretty shocking, of course.'

'I suppose so.'

Under the hairdressing cape I was rubbing my hands together so hard little flakes of damp skin were coming off. She was busy shaving now. My hair was already pretty short, so it went fast and I had to do something. If I left it to her to ask questions, I would run risks without finding out anything new. I tried to think of something, something neutral, something that wouldn't give me away. But she got there first.

'And,' she said, 'how do you feel now?'

'Cheated, of course,' I said. I felt relieved, this was going in the right direction.

'No, I mean, about your grandfather. Have your feelings for him changed?'

I stayed silent for an eternity. This was the hard question I'd feared she would ask. My feelings about what? What had happened? How could I worm it out of her? In the mirror I could see myself going red in the face up to the edges of my ears.

'Yes,' she said. 'I can understand why you want to be careful.' Her words reminded me of my conversation with Alex and Benoît. I reacted instantly.

'I'm not ashamed, no, if that's what you mean,' I said, congratulating myself. 'He believed in the interest of his country and in loyalty.'

'That's true, yes, you're right about that. People are responsible for their actions, but you can't always foresee the consequences. In the final analysis, all he did was expose an illegal practice, don't you think?'

'Yes, of course,' I said with conviction. 'That's all it was.'

'There was a lot of nasty gossip later.'

'Was there?'

'Yes. That business with Soeur Béate, naturally, the fact that she survived. The wildest assumptions: that she had been deliberately lured away, that it was an agreement with the soldiers. Don't believe any of it. Slanderers they are, all they're after is giving someone else a kick in the face.'

The shops were closing when I left the salon. I could feel the warm evening breeze directly on my still-damp scalp; it felt like someone stroking my head. Shopkeepers were taking flowerpots inside and putting up metal grilles over the windows. Cars started up and drove off. People walked back and forth in their gardens with hoses and watering cans.

The café terraces were practically deserted. The tables had been set out, with tablecloths and insect repellent candles. The sunshades stood furled next to the wooden wind screens. The smell of food hung in the streets, reminding me that I hadn't eaten a thing all day apart from cream wafers for breakfast and the pineapple and mango ice-cream. The food stalls in this area were expensive, so I decided to wait until I got to the Cercle.

The Cercle Meunier was like a gigantic evening market. There were people everywhere, walking, sitting about, playing. Doors stood open and furniture had been brought out into the street. In the gardens of the dilapidated houses, men lay resting on bedrolls they had dragged from inside. They had lit fires from wood gathered in the hills. There was music, and the scent of spices filled the air.

I walked on rapidly. The people who passed paid no attention to me. I was like them, was just another inhabitant of the town, just someone carrying a small parcel under his arm. There were children so absorbed in their game they didn't notice I wanted to get past them, and who only moved their bikes and skateboards out of the way after being asked directly. Someone stopped his car to ask me for directions. In some spots, hens and roosters crossed the road.

The Cercle is situated between the town centre and the hills. The further you go into the district, the more the road goes up. I came to places I'd never been before. I was looking for the most direct route to the north side and had to go through streets that were so badly paved you could barely call them streets. I reached a small square where there were three cars without wheels and a couple of advertising hoardings on wooden supports. I tried to visualise the map of the area, but I had absolutely no memory of any square, and realised I was lost.

There were fewer children in this area. Oil stained the footpath, and it was less crowded apart from some mechanics, with only their legs sticking out from under the cars. I thought I should try to find the back of the glue factory. It couldn't be far, because I'd seen the chimneys a few streets back. I crossed the road to get out of the way of a dog who started growling at me from behind a gate as if I had taken his bone away. Then I noticed a lane running behind the row of houses, a bit hard to find, but clearly a public right of way which led somewhere. There wasn't a living soul in the lane. At the end stood three police cars.

As I walked through the lane, I could feel eyes following me from behind the windows. Most doors were ajar. In a few places I could hear whispering. There were no lights on inside. The scent of evening meals was noticeably absent. Odd bits of rubbish blew around with every gust of wind.

The small building at the end of the lane had been cordoned off with an improvised barrier with coloured ribbon wound round it. I walked past and was about to step onto the loading platform, when four policemen and a man in plain clothes came out.

'You can't go there,' said one of the policemen, pointing at the barrier. I scanned their faces, hoping to see someone familiar—I was getting the feeling I knew the whole force—but they were all strangers to me. They had papers with them, and the last one, clearly the youngest, was carrying a carton of brass doorhandles, keys and jewellery.

'I've come to see if any of my things are there,' I said. The policemen looked at each other rapidly and exchanged significant smiles.

'That's not the way it works,' said the oldest of the four. He had his cap in his hand. His hair stuck to his head in tangles. He held out the papers he was carrying.

'You have to submit a description of the goods. Then we check that against this list.' While he was talking, the men behind him busied themselves with a heavy padlock. Before they locked up, the man in plain clothes poked his head inside and called out something.

'Buzz off now,' said the policeman, 'or we'll start getting funny ideas.' I turned to move behind the barrier, when a familiar voice sounded behind me. Smiling, and with the elegant step of a tap dancer, the policeman who had found me in the bath emerged from the building.

'Well, well, look who's here!' he exclaimed, sounding surprised. 'Dry yet?' As soon as he shut the door behind him, the plain clothes man stuck a lemon yellow strip across it with a couple of small red stickers like wax seals.

'How did you find us?' Because he was talking to me, the other policemen now turned to me as well. After a few words of explanation, they understood what I had come for. The oldest of the group repeated, in a rather more friendly tone this time, that I should submit a description of the stolen goods at the police station as soon as possible. I promised to take care of it. While they were getting into their cars, I went and stood behind the barrier like a model citizen. The man in plain clothes got in the back seat of one of the cars and they drove off in convoy.

I waited till they had disappeared from view, walked back and stood near the door. It was sealed, and the window had shutters nailed over it. I touched the doorhandle. Around me, the neighbourhood was silent, as if in expectation of a strong wind or a rain storm. I pulled my hand back. I have no idea what I was planning to do. Not a lot, probably. Go back home, perhaps, or go over to the window to see if I could look inside. Whatever it was, I didn't get the chance. Before I had even turned round, I could feel the street come to life behind me.

I stood in a dead-end lane, right at the end of it. I should never have done that, of course, coming to this place where I knew no one, particularly not just after the police had been there. It was my own stupid fault. Don't ever walk up a lane by yourself, not if it's just getting dark, and not if there isn't a single porch or doorway where you can hide at a pinch. And don't answer if someone speaks to you, don't talk to strangers.

'Lost something?' said a voice behind me. I turned. The doors of the houses had opened. Men had emerged, four or five of them, big fellows in moccasins, with dark eyes which don't look at you, but see you all the same. The man facing me had a small mouth, and eyebrows raised high, as if he was looking out into the world for the first time and was surprised. His shirt was open to his navel. I tried a joking tone.

'My TV set,' I said. My answer did not produce the effect I had hoped for. He didn't start talking to me. He waited. He let the others come closer and inspect me from top to toe. I was wearing shorts and a T-shirt, they wore slacks and white polyester shirts. I was clearly outnumbered.

'What are you doing here?' asked one of them, a discontented-looking character, who was not likely to put up with anything.

'Walking,' I said politely. I smiled, but they didn't notice, because they didn't look at my face, but at the most at my shoulders.

'Don't talk rubbish,' said the first one. They spoke a few sentences in Arabic. In an ordinary street, this would have been the moment to quietly walk away, in the opposite direction. But not in a dead-end lane. They stood around me in a semi-circle. Behind me, a few metres away, was the wall of the sealed-up building. I took a step forward, intending to walk between them, but immediately they moved in unison. As if an agreed signal had been given, a tremor moved through all their bodies, a barely perceptible straightening of backs and shoulders, and when I took a second step the circle closed around me. I couldn't get away.

'He talks with the fuzz,' said one.

'He's a skinhead,' a second one added. I knew they wouldn't talk to me any more, only about me. I shouldn't have come here, not just after having been to the hairdresser, and certainly not with a pistol under my arm.

102

'How come he is here?'

'He knew *they* were here.' They switched between languages. The change happened casually, as if it didn't matter which language they were speaking, but I knew they decided very precisely what I was allowed to understand and what not.

'They knew him.'

'He knew where the depot was.' The sun went down behind the houses and the hills. A soft light fell on the roofs, making it seem as if a glow like a smouldering fire rose from each building. I could have been home by now. I was hungry.

'Maybe he's running errands?' said the first man, the one with the surprised-looking face. 'Little errands around the place, a bit of information here, a little tip there.' I think that was the moment I became really confused. The man's face was now right in front of mine, much closer than I could bear, and I became terribly conscious of the pistol under my arm.

'No, really,' I said. I wanted to sound calm, but my voice went up oddly at the end, as if one of my vocal cords had come loose and was flapping about in my throat. 'A TV set. I was told you could buy TV sets here.' The man laughed. The weird red light of the setting sun made his eyes glitter feverishly.

'A TV set?' he said. I was wondering at the size of his feet. 'And how were you going to carry it? On your back?'

'In his handbag,' said the man right behind him. I didn't look, but I could feel him pointing. He had gone too far. And I had been dithering for too long. If I didn't do something now, there was no telling how much trouble there would be.

I'm still amazed at how calmly I put my hand into the plastic bag. They watched patiently, as if they expected to see a white rabbit emerge. With a rapid movement I unzipped the case. This is a bluff, I thought, pure bluff, and it shows. But before they know what is happening it will be too late. I'll stand there. I'll make a terrific amount of noise and force them to get out of my way. Anything would be better than being found by five nervous Arabs in this dead-end alley with a pistol under my arm in a plastic bag. From the shape of the case I knew at which end the butt was. I touched the metal. Because of the contact with my body it felt warm like skin . . .

And that, I think, was the end. The next moment I heard the man next to me call out. I saw his white teeth flash and felt the sound of his voice in my face.

'He's got a gun!' he yelled. Instantly, everything was chaos. Instead of moving back, all kinds of things were falling over me: arms, faces, shoulders, tattoos. I had one more thought: what if René made a mistake, and this is a real gun after all, with real bullets which can blow a real hole in a head? But it wasn't my problem any more. The gun was already on the ground with me next to it, beaten to a pulp, my consciousness in another world.

IT WAS THE police who found me. They put me on the back seat, among the raincoats and the white gloves. I had trouble breathing. They asked me where it hurt, but I couldn't decide; my whole body felt numb and stiff, like after a marathon swim. Having thought for few seconds I said: 'Nowhere.' Then I groaned and they smiled sympathetically.

'You've still got your wallet,' one of them said. 'Can you remember how much was in it?' He showed me the contents, and I saw that all the money left over after I bought the gun was still there.

'Did you have anything else on you?' he asked, as if he could read my thoughts. 'Camera? Watch?'

'No, nothing.'

'Then you haven't been robbed,' he said, pleased. The policeman behind the wheel—my old acquaintance, the tap dancer—started the car.

'We're off to the hospital,' one of them said.

They took the corners carefully. It was half dark and they had the headlights on, making the narrow streets of the Cercle look like a huge stage set. I tried to remember what had happened. The only thing I could drag up was a cool bath filled to the brim and a shower curtain with blue flowers. Then there were the phone calls to Moumouche and Fred. The rest was like trying to watch a scene behind a fogged-over window.

'No need,' I grunted laboriously.

The driver half turned round. 'You don't look all that fit.' His face was more serious than I had come to expect. We drove with the windows down. The evening air smelled of burning. A moss green blanket lined with plastic was spread beneath me to protect the seat from my blood.

'I'd rather go to my grandfather's doctor,' I said. I had to repeat it, because I didn't have the strength to raise my voice over that of a woman who was talking on the two-way radio about a speeding case.

'Are you sure?' asked the driver. The woman was passing on another message, something about a handbag snatcher. Her voice sounded more excited than before, as if she were cheering the thief on. The policemen paid no attention.

'Were you actually looking for a fight?' asked the other one.

'No, I was just walking, I think.'

'You came to look at the depot,' the tap dancer corrected severely. 'That was really stupid. We hardly ever go into that area ourselves, and certainly not on our own.'

'Yes,' said the other, 'really stupid.' I pursed my lips to try and locate the pain. The wound started bleeding more heavily and I covered it with my hand.

'Home then?' said the driver, the side of his face turned to me. I straightened myself as much as I could, cleared my throat and took a deep breath.

'Sixty-nine Rue Machiavelli,' I said. I was startled by my own voice. In the rear vision mirror I saw that I was actually smiling.

Benoît was all concern. He took my pulse, looked in my eyes and felt all over my body for bruises. He fired questions at me. I had to move my limbs and blow my cheeks out. He got sterile bandages and disinfectant from one of his kitchen cupboards and dabbed my lip. He talked non-stop, about nothing in particular, obviously to distract me.

'First aid courses should be compulsory,' he said. 'Just suppose your mother has a bad fall, and you don't know what to do. You'd never forgive yourself.' I was stretched out on a three-seater couch which stood against the central heating radiator under the window and obviously also served as a bed. The space was small. Rather tastelessly furnished with faded wallpaper and plywood furniture, but it was spotless and every square centimetre was put to use. In the

106

corner was a small kitchen, set up with grey cupboards and a sink with two dirty glasses on it.

Benoît's Dobermann Pinscher, Tascha, who had carefully licked all the blood spots I'd left behind me off the floor, now sat motionless, like a stuffed animal, next to the couch. It hadn't stirred since Benoît ordered it to 'sit!' On the small white table next to the wall stood a fairly new-looking fax machine. 'That keeps me in touch with all the newspapers in the area. I have all their fax numbers,' he said. He dabbed my lip with a preparation that smelled like urine. The used wads of cotton-wool he dropped in a small heap on the floor.

'You're a journalist?' I asked. He capped the bottle and put it back in the bread tin among band-aids and painkillers.

'Journalist? You could call it that, yes.' He smiled thoughtfully.

I was getting up to reach my glass of water.

'Stay there!' he said. 'I'll give it *to you.*' He handed me the glass and sat down on the chair next to me. As long as I didn't talk or try to move, I felt as though I was just having a rest after a day's wandering about the town. He asked me to tell him what had happened.

'And the pistol?' he asked after I had told him various things without mentioning the weapon. He saw the surprise on my face and said Alex had talked to him about it.

'Gone, I think,' I said. The light in the room was harsh. There was only a single overhead light and that was so bright it over-lit the place and caused eerie shadows in the corners. I opened my eyes as I spoke, but closed them again immediately. Benoît stood up and went over to a small cupboard which seemed to have a magnetic lock. He took out a small pistol, like some I had seen in the shop. He put it in my hand.

It felt delicate and alive, like a lizard which might escape any moment. I sat up straight. I tried to aim, but my arm hurt.

'This one is real,' he said, 'and loaded.' It sounded quite ordinary coming from him, not something to scare you, but rather reassuring. Yet my scalp turned ice cold. I put the gun down and looked at it without touching it.

'You can borrow it, for your mother,' he said. His blond hair had drifted over his face. Despite the heat of the last few hours, his shirt was immaculately white, even at the collar and under the armpits. He looked hard at me with his light blue eyes.

'I have to ring her,' I said so I wouldn't have to answer. He handed me the phone, a bright red one with a receiver in the shape of an upper lip, the most eye-catching object in this otherwise pretty colourless environment, and I rang to say I would be home later. She sounded as absent-minded as she had that morning, her voice raw from smoking. While I was talking to her, Benoît filled the dog's bowl with lukewarm water and called her over.

'Shouldn't you tell her?' asked Benoît when I had hung up.

'I don't want to worry her . . .' I said.

'That's what I like to hear,' he replied, filling our water glasses. He screwed the blue cap back on the water bottle with slow, measured movements. 'Is she the daughter of . . . ?'

I replied with a grunt. I could see her again, in my grand-father's grey dust-coat, the poker in her hand, her hair tied back. I couldn't resist talking to Benoît about it.

'She's ashamed,' I said. I wasn't sure if saying this was a good idea. But in my head things were as confused as a stack

108

of building blocks a child has knocked over. I knew what I wanted to know, but not whom I could ask. Benoît shook his head dismissively, loudly sucking in air between his lips, and waited for me to go on.

'She has burned everything which reminds her of it, boxes full, without saying a word to me.' He was sitting at an angle to me. I looked at him because I thought I heard him gasp, but he was sitting up straight, drinking from his glass and looking almost amused.

'Some people will never learn,' he said. The window behind me stood open. Now and then I could feel the soft net curtain brush my face as it was blown by the wind. I lay there, hoping he would say more. At the same time, I was terrified of the questions he might ask. He said: 'And then they are surprised when the town isn't what it used to be.' I couldn't see the connection, but didn't dare ask. For minutes, there was silence. A few times I opened my mouth to say 'What do you mean?', but I was terrified that he would look at me in surprise and say 'What do you mean, what do I mean? What could I mean?' So I was silent.

I had to approach it differently.

'What exactly did he do, according to you?' I asked. I spoke rapidly and rather softly, half hoping he would not understand me, or hear something different from what I said. But he was paying careful attention.

'You know as well as I do,' he said.

'Yes, of course, but *according to you.*'

'According to me? He reported those Jews because he thought that was the right thing to do. The kids in the school in town weren't getting enough to eat because the food was all going to those Jews. Illegal Jews, that is!'

'Yes,' I said cleverly. 'That business with the children was just the limit, wasn't it?'

'His own little daughter was one of them,' he said, pointing his finger at me as if it was my fault. My grandfather had only one daughter, so I played it safe, nodding and saying: 'Yes, my mother.'

He laughed. From the way he looked at me, his eyes twinkling as if he thought this was rather funny, I immediately realised I had got it wrong.

I thought fast. I must have overlooked something. I repeated to myself that my grandfather had only one daughter—and then I remembered. I could have picked up the pistol from the table and shot myself: the elder sister. Died at the end of the war. Of pneumonia; I could still hear my grandfather telling the story.

'My mother,' I tried to recover the situation, 'my mother has burned the lot.' There was another gust of wind. The curtain puffed right up and came down all over my head, a diversion I could use just then.

'Mm, nice and cool,' I said, much more cheerfully than I felt.

'Cool?' he said, amazed. 'I'm pouring sweat. This is an awful flat, right under the roof.' I can't have looked very convincing. The breeze from the window had brought me some relief, but I think my face was still scarlet, and all along I had been feeling dizzy not just from the knock on my head, but from the heat as well. He got up and opened the door wide.

'I guess we won't sleep much tonight,' he said. The curtains came to life again. First they were sucked outside and then flapped back, hitting me in the face. Benoît stood expectantly for a moment, as if trying to gauge whether I wanted to continue the conversation about my mother and my grandfather, but, as I said nothing, he went onto the landing to look down over the banister. I could hear his shiny, expensive shoes on the tiled floor. The sound reverberated through the stairwell.

'Fortunately, I've got the cellar,' I heard him say.

'The cellar?'

'I rent that as well. Costs me more than the flat itself, but I need the space.'

'For wine and that sort of thing?'

'No, no, not wine. Alex would turn it into a wine cellar, but not me. I use it for other things.' I recalled the conversation with Alex, about shooting practice and so on, and I wasn't sure that I wanted to ask any more. He didn't give me the chance. He came back inside, looked at me sharply and said: 'You look much too hot. Can you get up? We'll go downstairs, to the cellar. I've got a bucket of ice-cream there, and a few other things you'll find interesting.' He took two spoons from the kitchen drawer and stood next to me. 'Here, put your arm around me. We'll take the lift down.' I did as he asked, but we hadn't even reached the door when he stopped.

'You forgot the gun,' he said. He went back to pick it up. I stood by myself, a bit unsteady, not because my legs wouldn't carry me, but because things weren't quite back in order in my head.

'I don't think I need it,' I said.

'At least take it until you get a new starting pistol.'

I did have enough sense to say: 'But that's a real gun. Doesn't it occur to you that a real gun could cause real casualties?'

He went to the cupboard, took out a holster which he buckled round my waist; there was not much I could do. He carefully unloaded the gun and put it in the holster. 'Listen, Lucas,' he said, gently pushing me onto the landing. 'If they do something to my mother or my sister, I react like a madman. That doesn't make me a murderer.' His body was cool against mine, which felt dirty and stained. I didn't think his reasoning was logical, but was convinced that was my fault.

On the way to the cellar we met Alex. He looked at my damaged face and became all jumpy when I told him what had happened. Benoît kept giving him significant looks and finally told him not to speak so loudly as anyone could hear us from the landing.

'We're on our way down to the cellar,' he said.

'I've just come from there,' Alex replied. He was now speaking to Benoît, not to me. 'It was still touching the floor. I've re-hung it, further back. It's hanging OK now, nice and cool. I've cleaned up the bloodstains.' I noticed him watching me to see what effect his words were having. I remained perfectly still.

'You've had your hair cut!' he said. 'Nice and short.'

'It's better this way,' I said, 'less childish.' I noticed them exchanging a quick look. Next, Benoît gestured impatiently for Alex to stand aside. The passage to the cellar was so narrow we couldn't walk next to each other. He pushed me ahead of him.

'All right?' he said. 'Not going too fast?' I let myself be guided. After the events in the Cercle a sort of pleasant feeling of resignation had come over me. My head felt as if it was floating on water, separated from my body.

112

'Do you know why Alex wears his hair so short?' Benoît asked, sliding a key into the lock of a green metal door. He opened the door and manoeuvred me into the pitch dark cellar space. Even before he had switched on the light, I smelled the scent of forests and of blood.

'So they can't grab him by the hair in a fight.' They laughed uproariously. I laughed too, I couldn't help it. Their cheerfulness was infectious. With his right hand Benoît switched the light on.

At the back of the small space, head down and with blood on her flank, hung a young hind. Her eyes were wide open and reflected the light from the single bare globe on the ceiling. With her neck stretched out and her mouth half open, the hind seemed to be calling out. Benoît sat me down on the wooden bench opposite.

'Vanilla or mocha?' he asked. He opened the deep freeze and bent over it. I leaned against the wall. Its coolness did my body good, but the smell was making me nauseous.

'A bit of each,' I said without much enthusiasm. He put the containers down on the bench next to me and stuck the spoons in them. He sat down. Alex stayed on his feet and ate with his fingers.

'Did you . . . ?' I said after a while, pointing at the hind with the handle of my spoon. I didn't ask because I really wanted to know—my head was throbbing too hard for me to be curious—but because they were obviously waiting for it.

'This morning,' Alex replied.

'I thought the hunting season hadn't begun yet.'

'The hunting season?' said Benoît. He paused to swallow his ice-cream. 'Do you really think there are no animals around outside the hunting season?'

Alex giggled. The finger he used to scoop up lumps of ice-cream was red with cold.

'I suppose not,' I said. I found it hard to concentrate. I couldn't always work out when I was expected to answer. There was a buzzing in my head; later I noticed it was the freezer switching on and off.

'Such a large animal,' I said.

'Beautiful, isn't it?'

'I think it's strange . . .'

'What do you think strange?' Benoît quickly interrupted.

'That you can do that. I mean, kill an animal. Especially such a large animal.'

Alex looked at the floor. He stopped eating and dried his hands on his T-shirt. Benoît twisted his spoon around in the ice-cream, but didn't eat any. He cleared his throat.

'Look, Lucas, just as a man has to be able to save a life, he must be capable of taking a life.' The vanilla and mocha ice-cream slowly turned liquid. Nobody said anything. The longer the silence lasted, the clearer things seemed to become in my head. I looked around and saw the shelves with tins of food, the crates of mineral water, the potatoes. I was sitting in a cellar. I was sitting in a cellar eating ice-cream.

'Why am I here?' I asked. My voice sounded louder than I intended. Alex grinned again, his head still bent down as if something remarkable was to be seen on the floor. Benoît looked at me sharply. In the dim light, his pupils were so large that the blue had almost disappeared. He got up, covered the ice-cream containers and put them back in the freezer. Then he started calmly walking up and down in the small space. He held the spoon in his left hand, slowly rubbing it along his right arm.

'When I was eight, a blackbird flew against our kitchen window. I picked it up. It was still alive, but its wing was broken. I wanted to take care of it, but it was in such a panic it kept escaping from my hands. Our garden was full of cats and it was mid winter. After arguing with myself for hours, I killed it.' He looked at me kindly. I tried to think.

'Anyway,' he said suddenly, 'do you smoke?'

'No.'

'Nor do I. I have never understood why people smoke. I would be scared of that fire so close to my nose.'

Alex shook his head. He snorted, grinning. Benoît winked at him, and picked up the thread again, unperturbed.

'Sometimes, killing is necessary to preserve purity,' he said. 'You kill the weak so the strong remain. Refusing to do that threatens the future of the species. Just look at Tascha. She is a perfect Dobermann because her species was kept pure. And look at nature. Think about what Darwin says about the rights of the strongest.'

'When you walk through the town,' he continued, 'don't you ever look at our elderly, our mothers, the children in our schools?' He spoke slowly, with long pauses between words. 'Haven't you ever thought: how vulnerable they look?'

'Yes, at times,' I agreed sheepishly.

'And when you look at the country we've built. Don't you ever think: this must not be damaged, it must never disappear, for this is the way it should be?'

'I have occasionally.'

He smiled. 'You're a man of character, Lucas. A proper grandson of Felix Stockx. There should be more people like you.' I looked from him to Alex and back. The freezer hummed. The hind smelted of sweat.

'That,' he said cryptically, 'is why you are here.'

115

ALEX TOOK ME home on his motor bike. In the plastic pouch round my waist I had Benoît's gun. We were out of the town quickly: it was a powerful bike and it climbed the hill effortlessly. Only the last, steep stretch we took more slowly, as if in slow motion. The road surface was uneven, and every pot-hole hurt. I had trouble keeping my arms around Alex. The contact with his body was too hot and gave me a sick feeling.

He set me down by the garden gate. There was still a light on in the kitchen.

'She'll want to know what's happened to you, to your face,' said Alex. He was not wearing a crash helmet. ('On principle,' he claimed when I asked about it.) His face was covered in harsh shadows. 'But she'll get used to it.' He laughed briefly at his little joke. For the first time I felt there was something familiar about him, as if we had known each other for a long time and had been through a lot together. But his smile had barely gone before his voice was serious again.

'Benoît chooses his friends very carefully,' he said. He paused and silenced the engine while I hoisted myself off the bike. 'He's not just any old body; I've known him for four years now, and still I'm surprised every day. He has thought about everything. He has an opinion about everything. I remember what he says, word for word. And not just me. The others, too. You'll see, I promise you: you won't go to sleep without thinking about him, not tonight, and not any night.' There were sounds behind me: the murmur of water, women's voices, piano music. It was nearly midnight. The women on the hill were still awake.

116

'You'll do a lot for him, but you'll get a lot in return. He'll be eternally grateful to you.' His voice had a strange tone. It sounded as if he was promising something, holding out the prospect of something I was not aware of.

'What do you mean?'

'When you've cut down that tree, what else?' he said. A hard-to-read smile played on his face. He winked. At first I thought it was some weird joke, but from the way he swung his leg over the bike I understood there was something I didn't get.

'What tree?'

'Didn't Benoît talk about it? But that's what we had in mind. Strange. Perhaps he didn't get to it.'

'What are you talking about?'

'No, forget it. I haven't said a thing. He'll no doubt wait for the right moment.' From his bike, Alex pushed the gate open for me, because it jammed a little and the effort hurt me.

'And this club you were talking about last time,' I asked as I walked on. 'Who's in it?'

'Maybe "club" was a bit of an overstatement.'

'Who are they?'

He laughed sheepishly. His teeth shone in the dark. 'Benoît and me. And you.'

'Really,' I said, not meaning anything at all. Instantly, he became eager.

'Benoît will teach you how to handle a weapon,' he said quickly. 'Really, he told me he would. Didn't he give you that pistol?' I lifted up my T-shirt and showed him the holster.

'You see? Didn't I tell you? He'll make time for you. He has faith in you. Myself, I'm not so fond of guns. A knife is what I prefer. Just hanging on my belt, where they can see it. I think that's fairer. If they get difficult, they know what they can expect.' He slapped me on the shoulder, too hard for comfort. I took a quick step forward, past the gate, where I was out of reach. He started the engine, accelerated and raised his hand. I stood listening as he drove away, much faster than when we came, not bothering to avoid pot-holes or stones.

Dozens of photos were spread out on the kitchen table. My mother sat bent over them. They were photos of my grandfather and herself when she was a child.

'Someone bring you home?' she asked without looking up. She picked up a photo, put it back and picked up another one. It looked as though she was trying to remember their chronological order. She seemed to judge how old she was in each one by the length of her skirt and her plaits.

'What's happened?' she asked when I moved into the lamplight. I told her I'd sold a painting and then been attacked and robbed in the Cercle. As she listened, she lit a new cigarette from the butt of the old one. She listened quietly, blinking every so often. The ashtray among the photos was overflowing. I noticed that edges or corners were missing from some of the photos, as if they had been pulled out of a fire just in time. I looked at the photos as I talked. In some of them, she was standing next to my grandfather, others showed her alone, her eyes blank, not noticing the camera, looking over the photographer's shoulder.

She called me closer so she could examine the cuts on my upper lip. I bent forward and she put her fingers on my shoulder. She pressed gently to turn my face into the light. The holster of the pistol rubbed my skin under my clothes.

'And your hair is even shorter,' she said in a way that made me realise she only believed half of what I said.

'I like it better this way,' I said as casually as I could. She gave a long sigh, almost a groan. Then she looked at me, long and urgently. The cigarette smouldered between her fingers.

'Lucas,' she said, 'don't do it!'

'Don't do what?' I asked. My nerves tensed, as always when she forbade me do something.

'Anything,' she said hoarsely. 'Don't become like your grandfather.' With a slack hand she pointed at the photos showing him smiling, his hair still brown and his skin smooth. His expression was very different from hers: he looked straight into the lens, pupils like pin-points, not worrying about his appearance.

'What was he like then?' I asked. Raising my voice loosened something in my chest. My voice squeaked like a leaky accordion, and it hurt.

'You knew him,' she said. 'You know what he was like.' I had no idea what she meant. She sounded deceptively calm, as if she was suppressing something. If I hadn't known better, I'd have thought she was drunk, or at least extremely tired. For a while, we were silent. My eye fell on the photo of a young girl, seven or so at the most, with a toddler on her lap. The toddler was my mother. The elder girl had a sharp little face with big eyes, bigger than my mother's, but equally dark and dreamy. The harsh light behind her gave her a sinister appearance, as if she were bringing bad news.

'How old was your sister when she died?' I asked.

'Six-and-a-half.'

'What did she die of?'

'Pneumonia.'

'Can you die of pneumonia?'

'She was underfed when she caught it. It was war, you see, and everything was rationed. Now, they could fix that with vitamins.'

'And what did Soeur have to do with it?'

'Soeur?' she asked, startled. She straightened her back, as if someone had run a fingernail along her spine. 'Who have you been talking to? I can hear you've been at Nadine's again.'

'What's Soeur got to do with it all?' I insisted bluntly. She pushed her hair behind her ears with both hands. It was the same gesture as in the morning when she was standing by the fire. She looked down at the table.

'The nuns distributed the rations,' she said. 'From there, the food was sent to the school in the town, for the children. But they kept part of it. Your grandfather knew that.'

'How did he know? From Soeur?'

'He could see. From the skylight in his room. When the doctors said that it needn't have happened, your grandfather tipped off the Germans. He was sick with sorrow, Lucas. People suffering such sorrow do strange things.'

'Those rations went to Jews,' I said.

'Exactly. The nuns were looking after a group of fifteen Jews. So, of course, there was not enough food.'

'What happened, after that?'

'They selected five hostages. And put them up against the wall.'

Mosquitoes buzzed around my head, no doubt attracted by the scent of blood. I made no effort to drive them away.

'Soeur has never forgiven your grandfather,' she said with a sigh. There were no curtains over the kitchen windows. Behind them gaped darkness. All the lights were off in the convent. The sound of wind in the trees came to us. I was tired and wanted to sleep.

'And now you've burned everything that reminds you of it?'

She lowered her eyes and nodded. 'It's a relief that it's all gone,' she said softly. 'It's so clean.' She flicked her lighter until a long flame shot out. She turned it down and, seeing she had a flame, lit another cigarette.

'I thought I would be able to come to terms with him now that he's dead. But it didn't work.' My sleepiness disappeared instantly because of the resigned, intensely sad tone of her words. I didn't ask anything. I waited for it to come of its own accord.

'The logs of firewood have confused everything,' she said.

'The firewood?'

'The logs he always put out for Soeur.'

'What do you mean?'

'I started to ask myself questions all over again. Why did he give her logs? To ask for forgiveness? Or was there more to it? I've been carrying that question around for two days.' Her fingers fiddled with the gold-coloured pendant round her neck. She pulled it over her chin, stretched it and let go, so that it fell soundlessly back against her throat. The smoke was making the air between us solid. I stared at the burning tip of her cigarette.

'I looked in his boxes. I shouldn't have. I found this.' She took the bottom photo from the pile that lay before her. It was upside down, as if she had wanted to avoid looking at it accidentally. The back had yellowed and bore a message in graceful handwriting: 'For Felix, from Paula'. When she turned it over, a young woman with small eyes and a pinched face which meant absolutely nothing to me looked at me from inside the white borders.

'Who is it?' asked my mother. 'Do you recognise her?'

I tried my best, but my brain was stuck. My lip throbbed. I wished I could lie down and think.

'Paula is Soeur's real name. This is her before she entered the convent.'

When I got up and went up the stairs, I moved slowly and cautiously. My legs were heavy and my feet touched the ground reluctantly. I felt like a half-dead insect that keeps moving because its instinct tells it to, not because it wants to go somewhere. When I got upstairs, I looked back to check that I hadn't left a trail of slime behind me.

My mother had forgotten to tell me something.

'Caitlin was here,' she called from the bottom of the stairs. 'She came asking for you at least four times. It sounded rather urgent.'

'Caitlin?' I repeated as if I had no idea who that was.

'The girl from Sainte-Antoine, Ruth's daughter,' she said helpfully. I went into my grandfather's room and lay down on the bed, too tired even to get undressed. Sleep wouldn't come quickly. Here, too, there were mosquitoes, and the wound in my lip made it impossible to keep my mouth shut properly, so I was bothered by a dry tongue. The worst, of course, was that I couldn't stop thinking. Images of the past day kept flashing through my mind. I tried to turn over and relax. I thought about Soeur. I thought of my grandfather, in whose bed—his death bed—I lay. I thought of Caitlin and of my mother. My very last thought was of Benoît.

I PUT ON a cap to go and see Caitlin. I found her by the refectory wall, on a chair in front of a mirror. I arrived at an inconvenient moment: she had just made up her eyes like a fox, because she wanted to dance. When she saw me, she put her make-up gear on the ground.

'What's wrong with your lip?' She went ahead of me to the cellar, along the same route as last time, and equally hurriedly. A cat tried to follow us, but she chased it away.

'I expected you yesterday,' she said.

I told her a story about falling off my bike. She opened the cellar door and went in. She gestured for me to follow.

'It's the dove,' she said as soon as I stopped talking. 'We have to do something.' It took a while for my eyes to adjust to the darkness. I recognised the boxes and the furniture. The dove sat in the same spot, as if it hadn't moved in all that time. It looked carved in stone, its wings hanging down along its body, and I was surprised when a tremor passed through it and the membrane closed over its eyes. It hadn't touched the saucer of seeds which Caitlin had placed next to it. Its feathers didn't properly cover its body. In various spots you could see bare skin. Its legs were still tangled in the faded tea-towel which had since become heavy with its excreta.

'She is really getting on my nerves,' said Caitlin. 'When I lie in bed, I imagine I can hear her.'

'What do you want to do?' I asked. This time, I had good intentions. I would really do my best and seize the bird without being repulsed by the beating of its heart or the trembling of its wings.

'To kill it,' she said. I must have been visibly startled. From the way she lowered her made-up eyes, glancing at my hands, it was clear that she did not intend to do it herself. I laughed briefly. The bird made a small, frightened movement at the sound.

'I can grab it. We can feed it sunflower seeds,' I said quickly.

'It's too late. I've tried everything. She doesn't even try to get away any more when I pick her up.'

'I've never killed an animal,' I said.

'She's suffering,' said Caitlin. 'It's our duty. The pain is the worst, not dying. She doesn't know what dying is. Her fear is just instinct.'

We stayed still for a few moments, our eyes on the bird. It looked back fixedly, attentively listening to our whispering. It was sitting under a pallet that leaned against the wall at an angle and which had probably carried bags of cement or blocks of stone. I took a couple of steps forward, slowly, making reassuring sounds with my mouth. The dove was not afraid. It hardly moved and looked at me with only a little interest. It let me come quite close. I could have stretched out my hand. It would not have flown away. Its wings wouldn't let it.

I can kill spiders. Mosquitoes, certainly, and bees, too. Moths I find more scary because they have such thick bodies. They are hairy and look as if they would bleed. In the lamp-light you think you can see their hearts beating.

But I had never killed a warm-blooded animal. It was only because Caitlin stood behind me that I stretched out my hand. I was hot under my cap. The sweat on my upper lip burned in the cut. I gripped the pallet with one hand. I pulled. The centre of gravity shifted. The pallet fell. Pale dust flew up, and the sound of creaking wood filled the cellar. In my rib cage I felt again the white-hot pain I'd felt when I was knocked down in the Cercle.

Only the rear part of the dove was crushed. Its head and neck remained intact. For a very brief moment its beak pointed up, in surprise. The membrane came down over its eyes and shot up again. It made no sound. Even when its narrow head fell forward, its beak stayed shut.

Caitlin left the cellar straight away. I turned, and noticed how surprised she looked, as if someone had shown her something new and exciting. I followed. She shut the door behind me.

'I'll clean it up when it's dried out,' she said. She stood rubbing her hands on her clothes, as if something had stuck to them. She didn't look me in the eyes.

'And my grandfather?' I asked. 'Can you show me now what my grandfather has to do with these cellars?'

The beer cellar was one of the few spaces that had no windows. The other areas had high-up, oblong windows which only showed some grass in the garden, but at least they let in the light. Here, there was only a fluorescent tube, throwing an unflattering light on our faces.

'Sit down there,' she said, pointing at the empty beer crates. There were some bottles of soft drink, a sweetish kind of lemonade drunk by children, and Caitlin opened one of them by jamming the top against the door post, like a builder's labourer. It made a hissing noise. She took a few sips. When her lips let go of the neck of the bottle, a thin thread of saliva formed between her lower lip and the bottle.

'Here,' she said, giving me the drink. She sat down herself, on some hessian bags that lay on the floor, her back against the cool wall. She kept rearranging the bags and trying new positions. When she was finally comfortable, she folded her arms around her legs. So she stayed, quiet and patient, as if she intended to wait until the dove had decomposed.

'This is where they were,' she said unexpectedly, as if I had missed part of the conversation. Usually, I find I react too slowly. This time, I reacted too quickly. Perhaps it was because of the sounds. From the area where the dove lay, I could hear, every now and then, scratching and knocking sounds. Probably the boards of the pallet and the bags around it settling. Yet they sounded frightening because I imagined they were the spasms of a dying animal.

'This is where who were?' I said unthinkingly, but attentively listening to the sounds all around. I thought of mice, birds, rats. She looked at me in dismay.

'You don't mean it,' she said, irritated. 'Don't you even know that? Has your mother not told you anything at all? What good does she think that'll do you, for God's sake?' Because she reacted so vehemently, my brain shifted into high gear.

'Oh, yes,' I said quickly. I rubbed my hands together. They were covered in dust the colour of birdshit. I wished I could wash them. 'You mean the fifteen Jews.'

She relaxed. She rested her hands beside her on the floor and threw her head back a little.

'Aha!' she said, making it sound as if I had won some prize for giving the correct answer. 'You do know!' She looked at me as if she was about to say something more, her mouth open a little and her eyes focused on me, but said nothing. That was something she always used to do. You stayed silent and listened, but no matter how long you waited, nothing came. As a child, that gave me a feeling like hunger; now it made me feel I had failed.

'I'm discovering all sorts of things,' I said. 'Now that my grandfather is dead, everybody is beginning to talk.'

'Well, this is where they were. When there were strangers in the convent, that is. At other times, they could go anywhere, even near the windows. And very occasionally they could go outside. Then they played in the grass, while three or four nuns kept watch.' I let my eyes move through the space. It was large and empty, painted white, with electric wires running along the walls in a few places, carelessly painted over the same as the walls. The floor was uneven, and sloped towards the centre. A smell of damp hessian and stale beer hung in the air. I tried to imagine people in here. Mattresses on the floor, and corners where games could be played to kill the time, patience perhaps. But I saw nothing. The space remained white and empty, uninhabited, only usable for fermenting and storing beer.

'So what happened about it, later?' I asked carefully. I was afraid she would once again blow up at me about my ignorance, and I was right. She stood up to make herself taller. Her attitude changed, a sudden turn I couldn't see coming, which seemed to happen out of the blue. Her face was so pale she looked anaemic. She started talking. Without even wondering if I could cope, she turned her heavy artillery on me.

'Don't you know that?' she asked, almost laughing. 'Then I'll tell you. They were sent to a concentration camp. Driven to their deaths. Fifteen to Poland and five nuns against the wall, that is twenty in all. Not bad, is it, for one child who—just possibly—was underfed.'

'Yes . . . no . . .' I said, totally disconcerted. The lemonade was lukewarm and undrinkable.

'He could see into the convent garden, of course.' She didn't explain who 'he' was, and the impersonal word sent a shiver down my spine. 'All the nuns had overlooked that.' She started walking up and down from wall to wall, shifting her weight from one hip to the other, like a lioness in a cage. She was talking quietly now, being almost conciliatory.

'It doesn't really upset me, all that. I mean, it's a long time ago. It has nothing to do with us and our time. When Soeur starts going on about it, I snap at her. I'm sick and tired of the whole story. I don't need to hear it again.' She stopped, hand on hip, her lips moist. 'But you know what I can't stomach? That you seem to know nothing. You don't feel responsible. You're not ashamed. You're just like all other boys of our age: a clean slate with nothing on it yet. A chick that's forgotten the egg it has come from. And you can't help that, of course, nobody has said anything to you. What do you think of it yourself, anyway, that they've never told you anything?' Her lips were moist. The make-up made her eyes look even harder than she intended. Trying to talk and look at her at the same time, I stuttered.

'I . . . I don't know . . . Actually . . . I have no opinion about it.'

'Wrong!' she replied. 'That's where you're wrong! You've *got* to have an opinion. You have to make up your mind about it.' I made an effort. I was full of good will. But not quick enough.

'It's unfair!' she was saying already. 'You grow up as if nothing has happened. You don't have to listen to those stories. You don't have to live with those eternal discussions about how it could have gone that far, and why, and who is guilty. The question of who is guilty doesn't interest me any more than you. But if I have to listen to all the moaning, then so should you. You even more, perhaps.' I tensed my muscles. I didn't stand up, but straightened my back. From my movements, she realised I wanted to say something.

'I think . . . I don't think . . . that my grandfather was aware of the consequences. I mean. His daughter died. He reported them because . . . because it was illegal. Against the rights of the children of the town. He was law-abiding.'

'Spare me that bullshit,' she said nastily. 'He even painted for the Germans. He was a shining example for extremists. Right until his death, he denied the existence of concentration camps. And you saw nothing. You played with your grandpa. You cuddled him and loved him. While I had to listen to Soeur every day telling me what he had brought about.'

'He wasn't to know . . .'

'Don't say that. I won't even *listen* to people who say things like that.'

'You won't listen?' I asked. 'Then what is the point of talking to you?' It was a weak defence. I knew it, but I had the feeling that I couldn't say anything sensible until I had washed my hands. I felt an intense need to have Benoît near me. He would have defended us, me as well as my grandfather. She stood in front of me and pulled the cap off my head.

'You're just like him, Lucas Beigne,' she said, brushing her hand over my short hair. 'You don't know about anything. You don't even know that you're a cold person. The way you killed the dove . . .'

She said no more. She pushed the cap between my hands and turned. All I could see were her back and shoulders. She held her hands over her face, as if thinking very hard. Then she turned round, casually, as if nothing had happened, and walked to the door with a spring in her step. She held it open invitingly.

'Think, Lucas. If you want to talk about the rights of the children of the town. Those who lived in this cellar were children too, all between five and twelve. They were hungry, too.'

When I came home, the *Régio-Gazette* was spread out on the kitchen table. My mother had circled a short article with a thick red felt-tip pen. 'Skinhead on walk knocked out by Arabs' was the title. I read on: 'Yesterday seventeen-year-old L. Beigne from P. was attacked and knocked down by five Arab men while walking in the Cercle Meunier. The reason for the attack is not clear, but it can be assumed it was a case of robbery. The perpetrators have not been caught. L.B. was found unconscious. It was the third time in two weeks that he has been robbed by foreigners.'

My mother had underlined three words and added a question mark to each: *skinhead*, *unconscious*, and *seventeen-year-old*. I found the scissors and cut out the article. It was the first time my name had been in the paper.

A COUPLE OF days passed without anything happening. It stayed stiflingly hot. I cut the tree trunk into manageable pieces and stacked them on my grandfather's woodpile. Every day Caitlin walked past. Every day the pile grew. She knew what I was doing, but she never gave any indication that she noticed me. Usually she walked, sometimes she rode her bike down the hill, coming back soon after, walking the bike up the slope. I could never resist watching her. As always, it was the colours of her clothes that attracted me: one day she'd wear a light purple jumper with cheery floral pants, another something boyish and striped. I thought about our conversation. I did my best to work out what I should do next. One decision I made was to take Benoît's pistol from under my pillow and hide it, holster and all, in the chainsaw case in the smithy.

When I got too tired or too hot, I went and played patience in the living room with the shutters closed. Outside I heard cars approach, slow down for the bend and drive on towards Saint Laurent-en-Gatine. I managed to finish the game faster and faster, but I never ended up feeling I had won. Occasionally, my mother came and sat next to me. She cross-examined me about 'the attack', and I told her the story as it appeared in the paper. She wasn't really satisfied with it, but as I reacted in a very irritated way she left me in peace.

'I was quite startled when Caitlin appeared and asked for you,' she said once. 'I didn't recognise her. She's changed quite a lot. She used to be such a gawky, pale child, and now . . .' She didn't go on. We both sat and thought about her for a while.

A card from Arno arrived in the mail, and one from Moumouche. 'Be glad you're up in the hills,' said the first. 'It's unbearable here.' Moumouche just wrote 'Sunny greetings', but that was all I expected from him, not because he was usually short on inspiration, but because he always had to do everything fast, and I could imagine him writing the card while he was eating or watching TV. I stuck the cards on the wallpaper with drawing pins, but couldn't raise the energy to write back.

The third day, I went into Montourin. Everywhere I went I could feel people's eyes burning into me, and I was embarrassed to say my name. When I saw people I knew in the supermarket, I hurriedly moved away. If they recognised me anyway and called out 'Lucas! It's been a long time!', I avoided their eyes, because the strange feeling that they had known a lot more than me all along got in the way. In the street, I wore my cap and a pair of sunglasses I had bought with the rest of the painting money.

Climbing the hill, over Challon's Bluff, I made another decision. Before the sun had set, I went to sleep with my grandfather's old-fashioned alarm clock under my pillow. Its monotonous ticking helped put me to sleep.

Just after four, the alarm went off. I was woken by the mechanical rattle, but it couldn't be heard outside the room because it was smothered by the pillow and the weight of my head. Soundlessly, I got dressed, went downstairs, drank a couple of glasses of milk and did my best not to let the screen door slam. I stacked my grandfather's flat wheelbarrow with logs and pushed it to the convent.

Nothing stirred. I looked at the building in the half-light

and wondered behind which of the dozens of windows Caitlin slept. The garden was as lively as the convent was deadly still. The birds in the bushes only stopped twittering as I passed. I didn't hesitate for even a moment. I went straight to the pavilion at the side, a small, deserted building that was once used as storage space, and which, I knew, was now practically empty. I forced the worm-eaten door, spread out the piece of plastic I found on the floor and stacked the logs against the wall.

I don't know how many trips back and forth I made. I worked without stopping. After all those days of slaving in the heat of the day, the carrying in the cool morning air was easy. I saw the day breaking, and the first delivery vans go by. I stopped because I had run out of wood and because I thought Soeur would soon be getting ready for early Mass.

Around noon on the same day, a Saturday, the police came to say they had found a TV and a chainsaw in the warehouse that fitted the description I had given: a TV set with a picture but no sound, and a Stihl chainsaw, red with a black handle, well maintained, but without a chain. That same day, the TV was back on the kitchen table. The saw went straight into the smithy. I wiped it thoroughly clean with a rag. I fitted the chain onto the teeth to check if any part was missing, took it off again and studied the broken link. It was afternoon, about two, and around me hung the smell of molten tar, and, dominating everything, the twittering of sparrows squabbling on the roof of the smithy. Now and then you could hear the soft ticking and scraping of their feet and of the twigs that lay on the corrugated iron roof. The old radio, which had stood on a shelf above the workbench for years, was playing softly.

That morning I had intended to cut more wood with the axe, but now that I had the chainsaw back, and assuming it would be fixed pretty soon, I couldn't really be bothered with all that work. So I kept myself busy tying up bundles of twigs for kindling. I propped the smithy door wide open and walked busily up and down with pieces of string and bundles of kindling which I jammed under the rafters where they could dry. When I had finished, the floor of the smithy was covered with leaves, and while I was sweeping them up, my attention was caught by a program on the radio. It was a talk show called *Uproar*, and the idea was that people could ring the presenter and express their grievances about absolutely anything: rubbish in the streets, vandalised phone boxes, noisy disturbances at night, rude public servants, you name it.

I pricked up my ears when a woman said: 'In the Cercle! There's not just Arabs living there. We do, too, and we have to look at the ugly things.' At the word 'Cercle' I stopped in my tracks. But the presenter went on, and I relaxed.

'You are saying that the tram shelters in your area are less attractive than in the centre of town,' he said evenly.

'And the lights. In the centre they have proper lights, on nice standards, and with glass covers. Here, they're just those ugly fluorescent tubes that give you a headache,' the woman nagged on.

'Perhaps that is because where you are they'll only get smashed up.'

'See! You're setting it up. It's the same every time. If all we wanted to do was smash them, we could come down there and do it!' I swept the leaves outside, but as they stayed on the path and the wind seemed inclined to blow everything back inside, I pushed the dirt right under the lemon tree, which instantly released its pungent scent.

Later that afternoon I went into Montourin, looking for someone to repair the chainsaw. Before I left, I searched my grandfather's desk to find a receipt or some sort of warranty papers for it. When, after an hour's search, I hadn't found anything, I figured they had probably disappeared in my mother's fire, and so I looked in the Yellow Pages for places that sold chainsaws. I finished up with a list of three. I went to all of them.

In the first shop, they told me an estimate would have to be prepared, and the man who could do that was on holidays. In the second, getting the parts would take three weeks, and in the third they would only repair it if I could produce proof that it had been bought there. I went home with nothing to show for my trouble. As there was nothing else to do, I got to work on the TV, which still had a picture but no sound. I took the back panel off again, and tried to get into the part that said *Warning! Opening can cause serious damage. Only to be opened by a technician.* After I had forced the plastic cover and could see all the wiring, it still took me a full hour to find what the problem was. When, at last, I had sound, I couldn't find the screws that had secured the back panel and finally had to call on my grandfather's old duplicator once more.

I removed the plastic dust cover and searched for a screw of about the right size. There was one on the side, at the end of the ink roller, and, as I turned it, I remembered I had taken the screw at the other end out last time, that evening after I had been to Nadine's. So I wasn't surprised when the roller fell with a dull thud into the wastepaper basket. I screwed the cover back on the TV, but once I had finished work I felt a bit guilty about the duplicator being in bits, so I made another attempt at finding the small screw, lying flat on my stomach looking at the bits of fluff and dust under the bed for minutes on end, until I found it in a join in the linoleum. I got the roller out of the wastepaper basket so I could fit it back on the duplicator. As I was doing so, my attention was caught by the letters that I could see on it. I held the roller at an angle in front of my face, making the black ink more visible against the black roller, because the letters were shiny. They were in mirror writing, so I stood in front of the mirror. The large letters were clearest: *Auschwitz greatly exaggerated*. The text below that was partly illegible because I had touched it with my fingers, but, as far as I could see, the text dealt with the return of a group of Jewish children from the concentration camps. I could see the word 'Sainte-Antoine' and a date in 1945. I wrapped the roller in a towel I had been using to wipe my hands, held it carefully by the ends and went out.

I had no idea where I could find Caitlin. I thought the refectory was the most likely place, but was careless enough to take the shortest way via the goose run. Of course the geese started up, and I stopped so as not to make them even more agitated.

It was Ruth who appeared in the doorway. She was tall, and casually dressed. I nodded hello, but waited for her to approach me. I saw her looking at me through half-closed eyes—probably because Caitlin had already told her about our encounters, and she was trying to see if she recognised me.

'Lucas,' she said. Because of her very dark eyebrows, she always looked a bit as if she was telling you off, and I could remember the sense of being punished that always crept over me as a child when she was around. I didn't quite know what to say. She looked at the roller in my hand.

'Is Caitlin home?' I asked.

'Caitlin's been pretty cross with you,' she said.

'And I with her,' I replied quickly. She smiled through one side of her mouth. I could imagine what she was thinking: that we were condemned to each other's company here on this lonely hill where there was nothing to do, whether we were cross or not. She made a quarter turn, a movement that was characteristic of Caitlin, too, and said: 'She's working on the roses.'

I went in the direction she had indicated and found Caitlin by the climbing roses, a bucket by her side, cutting off the dead heads.

'Ah,' she said, glancing sideways and then carrying on with her work. I stood there, a bit helplessly, barely daring to move, because I didn't want to smudge the letters on the roller.

'I've got something,' I said.

'Really?'

'Here, in this towel.'

She lowered her arms. 'Oh yes?'

'It's the roller of my grandfather's duplicator.'

'Great.' She made me feel I had to get it all off my chest. This time I was prepared. I had hardly thought of anything else the last few days, and I had no intention of being slow or saying I didn't quite know. I knew perfectly well. I had first been ashamed of my ignorance, then of my grandfather. My new image of him clashed with what I had always thought, and that hurt. But the words on the roller changed all that. She was going to hear all about it. I spoke in a controlled manner, my voice steady.

'You said my grandfather drove fifteen children to their deaths. That is a lie. All fifteen of them came back.' For a moment she stood motionless, her back turned to me. Then she dropped the secateurs in the bucket with a crash.

'They *could* have died,' she said, her arms hanging by her side. 'Or rather: they *should* have been dead. It was the end of the war, Lucas. There wasn't enough time to gas them. Otherwise, they would have been.'

'So why do you say . . .'

'They were lucky! That doesn't undo six million other deaths.' Although she raised her voice, I managed to keep mine down. That in itself gave me the feeling she was admitting I was right.

'You're changing the subject, Caitlin. I'm not talking about those six million others. I'm talking about my grandfather. You've accused him falsely.'

'My God, Lucas!' she shouted. She came at me, yanked the roller out of my hand and ripped the towel off it. 'That's exactly what it's about. Your grandfather and his news sheet tried to create the impression that the return of those fifteen proved that Auschwitz hadn't happened.'

'He never said that Auschwitz didn't exist.'

'He made it sound like a minor thing. That's as bad as denying it.' She threw the roller into the grass in front of me. I calmly bent and picked it up. The air in the garden seemed on fire.

'That's exactly where you're wrong. You confuse putting things in perspective with denying. He sticks to the truth better than you: you make out that fifteen children died, and that's a lie.' In a flash I imagined Benoît hearing me and nodding in agreement. 'That's the problem with people like you. In order to make your point, you carry on as if everybody went to the gas chambers. You don't even want to see the people who came back.'

'Very many people went to the gas chambers. Your grandfather pretended there were just a few.' She was much more agitated than the last time we had argued. I wasn't. If someone had observed me from a distance, he would have thought I'd just happened to come by, carrying a roller from a duplicator.

'Many and a few are stretchable concepts,' I said. 'They don't get us anywhere. And certainly not if we lie about them.'

'I'm not lying.'

'You said my grandfather sent fifteen children to their deaths. That was a lie.'

'I meant that fifteen children ended up in a concentration camp because of him. If the war hadn't ended then, they would have been dead.'

'You didn't tell me they came back.'

'You didn't ask me about that.'

'Keeping silent about the truth is to distort it.'

'You're the ones who distort the truth, your grandfather and his mob. The concentration camps? Come, come, we don't talk about that any more.'

'I'm talking about it. Why do you think I am here? Why do you think I'm stacking the pavilion full of firewood?' I pointed the roller at the pavilion which we could see from where we stood. She turned her eyes away from me and looked at the little building, whose door still stood ajar.

'You're making the same mistake as my mother, Caitlin Meadows!' I called after her as she walked over to the pavilion. 'You keep silent about things! Everybody tries to make a fool of me. Nobody tells me anything. And then I get the blame.' She walked on through the tall, dry grass. She was wearing a tight, straight jersey dress, through which every one of her movements showed. Every step she took seemed to show a direct link between her shoulder and her hip.

'Why would anyone tell the truth if nobody wants to know it?' I heard her muttering. She stopped for a moment. She must have seen the tracks of my wheelbarrow in the soil. She peered into the pavilion, brushed both her hands through her hair and came back. When she stood before me again, she took a big breath, like a high-jumper before her jump.

'I thought,' she said softly, 'that it would make you feel less awful about what your grandfather did.' She bent slightly and picked a few petals from her skirt. Her voice was soft now, a little hoarse because of the sudden change in tone. 'But I've been worrying about it for a while. I had planned to come over to your place today. I don't want to hold you responsible for what your grandfather did.'

'Yes . . . no . . .' I said, thrown off balance.

'If you were like him, you wouldn't be here.'

I didn't reply. She confused me by saying things I hadn't expected her to say. She paid me a compliment, which made me feel relieved, but in the same breath she reproached my grandfather, which angered me. She stretched her hand out to me, touching my arm very briefly with two fingers. It was as if her touch caused a cool draught: the hair on my arms stood up and a shiver passed from between my shoulder-blades up to my scalp.

140

'And you've stacked wood,' she said. She bent over, retrieved the secateurs from the bucket and snipped off a few roses which seemed to me not to have really finished flowering. 'I suppose Soeur should be grateful. Although I really don't think you have any choice. Your family owes it.'

I was totally confused. I didn't know if she was playing a game with me. I wanted to go on talking about it, but her attention was distracted by Ruth who was waving at us from the patio.

'She's saying something,' said Caitlin, and ran off as if something had stung her. I followed. Ruth was coming down the wooden steps which separated the patio from the garden.

'I think I heard your mother calling,' she said. At first, I thought it was an excuse to get me out of the garden, but then I heard it too: my mother was calling my name, in high-pitched, long-drawn-out tones. I hurried home.

THERE WAS A phone call for me. I thought it might be Moumouche, to tell me he was coming after all. I went through the kitchen to the living room. It was Benoît.

'Tintin,' he said. A wasp had come in with me. I beat it away from me before I answered.

'Hello, Benoît,' I said.

'How's it going?'

'Good, good.'

'And your lip?'

'It's all right,' I said. It was odd that he was ringing me. I knew it wasn't to find out how my lip was doing.

'By the way, Tintin, there's something I wanted to ask you.' He paused and coughed. I knew that sound. In an odd way, Benoît, who always looked radiantly healthy, could often sound a bit sickly at the same time. 'I heard that that warehouse has been cleared, and I wondered if any of your things were there. Your chainsaw, for instance?'

'I got the saw and the TV back. The rest was gone.'

'Oh, good, your saw. That's what I wanted to talk to you about.' The wasp landed on my shoulder. I shook it off, but it promptly went for my head, which, with my short haircut, was very exposed.

'Yes?'

'I've got a job here that needs doing. A small tree that's in the way.'

'You want to borrow it?'

'You could say that, yes.'

'It isn't working. The chain is broken. The shops are closed, and tomorrow is Sunday.'

'Do you think you could get it to me here?'

'The chain is broken,' I repeated patiently. I was convinced he hadn't heard me.

'Can you get it to me?' he asked in the same patient tone. He seemed to assume in turn that I hadn't heard him.

'Are you going to fix it?' I asked bluntly. I didn't intend to sound rude. I just wasn't used to his manner of speaking, and half my mind was still with Caitlin in the convent garden.

'Listen, Lucas, I don't want to be difficult, but this is pretty urgent, you see. I can't really wait. I appreciate that it would be awkward for you to get here with that thing.

Alex has a motorbike. If all goes well, he'll be with you in half an hour.'

'Here?' I asked superfluously.

'If you could just get it packed up ready.'

'Yes, I suppose so,' I said. I needed more time. I always need time to grasp something. I can only think of the questions after I've had a few minutes to think.

'So you know someone who can . . .'

'Good,' he said without listening to what I was saying. 'I'll ring you this time tomorrow to explain what else is happening.' He hung up. I stood with the receiver in my hand. 'And Alex is already on his way?' I asked the dial tone.

I hardly had time to walk to the smithy before I heard the whine of a motorbike coming up the hill too fast. It slowed down in the curve and drove on as far as the garden gate.

'You can take it, but I want it back the day after tomorrow,' I said, watching Alex fix it onto the luggage carrier.

'The day after tomorrow?' he asked thoughtfully. 'Do you need it then?'

'I've got to get firewood ready for next winter,' I said.

'You'll get it back when we've finished with it,' he replied, his face rather close to mine.

'And when will that be?'

'The day after tomorrow!' He laughed when he saw my face. I realised he was trying me out, and laughed too. He swung his leg over the seat and turned the ignition key.

'Listen, Alex?' I said over the noise of the engine. 'Does Benoît have a garden?'

'No, not even a balcony. Why?'

'Then where is that tree that's in the way?'

He seemed surprised at the question. 'Didn't Benoît tell you?'

'No, he just talked about a tree that had to go. A small tree, he said.'

Alex shook his head. 'He is incorrigible,' he said with a thin smile which looked grim for a moment, but disappeared quickly. 'He wants to rope people in, but forgets to explain things.'

'Yes?' I said expectantly.

'But that's his style. When the time comes, you'll get all the information you need to do what has to be done.'

'I see,' I said.

'But I wouldn't worry about it yet.' He opened the throttle. As it took off, the motorbike barked like a nervous dog, changed to a deep rumble and disappeared down the hill.

The promised call from Benoît came punctually twenty-four hours later. I picked up the receiver expecting instructions, but they didn't come. He started talking about things that had no connection with our previous conversation.

'Human rights,' he said, 'does that mean anything to you?' He didn't wait for an answer. 'Everybody is talking about that these days. But there is one thing you shouldn't forget, Lucas Beigne, and that is: safety is a human right too. Every individual has the right to defend himself. Look at the law, and you'll see that I am right: someone who shoots in lawful self defence doesn't go to jail, right? Right?' He paused briefly. From where I stood, I could see a small corner of the garden. It was too hot for the roses. Because they opened, flowered, wilted and fell to the ground so quickly, their scent spread more intensely than ever. As

I said nothing, he continued: 'Exactly. And do you know the conclusion I'm slowly coming to? That we should no longer rely on the police and the politicians. They live comfortably in their villas, and when our lives are in danger, they're not there. We have to defend ourselves, Lucas, because no one will do it for us.'

He was in full spate when there was a soft knock on the kitchen window. I tried to see who it was, but the telephone lead didn't reach that far. A few moments later, Caitlin stood before me.

'And democracy,' Benoît continued. 'There's another fashionable term. Everybody is forever talking about that these days. Do you know what democracy means to me? That I can say what I want to. And people aren't ready for democracy, anyway: they drop litter all over the footpath, and cross the road against the red light. A strong hand is what is needed. Just as with children. A good role model, someone who shows how things should be done . . . 'He spoke so loudly I was afraid Caitlin could hear him.

'I have to go,' I said suddenly.

'What?'

'I have to go,' I repeated loudly, curtly.

'OK, I'll let you go. But do you understand what I mean?'

'I think so,' I replied. Caitlin was examining my grand-father's paintings on the wall, her hand on her back. I wondered if she was pretending not to be listening, or if she actually couldn't hear.

'That's the good thing about you,' he said, a curious tremor in his voice. 'You understand things. You know, Alex is my dear friend, but what I miss in him is the ability to think about things, to speculate. If you know what I mean.

Alex is no talker, he is a doer. And we need them, of course, desperately. But sometimes it is good to exchange thoughts about things. That's why I said to myself: let's give Lucas a call.'

'Yes,' I said, confused. I think I felt flattered. Most of my friends were younger than me. He was much older. He couldn't have been my father, of course, but my elder brother.

'Is it OK if I ring you? I mean, would you like that?'

'Yes,' I said again. It seemed a strange question.

'Good,' he said, sounding relieved. 'I'll ring you later, then. It's good to know you can always call on someone. It works both ways, but you know that.'

'Yes,' I said. He said goodbye and hung up.

'Hoi,' said Caitlin after I replaced the receiver. 'Sorry to disturb you. I just came by to tell you I've convinced Soeur that the wood in the pavilion is from one of the local farmers. If she asks you, you don't know anything about it.' We talked for a while, about nothing in particular, and when she left a little later, it was as if she took everything with her, even the table and the cupboards.

Two days later, quite early—I was still in bed—I had another phone call from Benoît to tell me the chainsaw was available again.

'You managed?' I asked.

'Yes,' he said, 'it's as good as new. You can come and pick it up.' I was about to ask about the cutting down of the 'little tree', but suddenly realised what he had said.

'Pick it up?' I said. 'Can't Alex drop it in? I have no transport.'

'What do you mean, no transport?' he asked, sounding surprised. 'So how do you manage? How do you usually come into town then? Not by taxi, surely?'

'On foot, over Challon's Bluff, that's the shortest way.' There was a silence, through which I could very faintly hear a woman's voice on a crossed line.

'OK, so you can't come and pick it up,' he said, considering. I felt he was trying to think of a solution and was flattered by his concern.

'Alex collected it,' I said.

'Yes, that's not the problem. Anyway, we'll see. I'll send Alex anyway. It's a pity, though, you would have been able to inspect the repairs first. Well, never mind. I'll send him over.'

About an hour later there was another call, from Alex this time. He said I'd better come in anyway: someone had punctured the tyres of his bike so he couldn't get away.

'You expect me to *carry* it up the hill?' I asked.

'I wouldn't worry too hard about that,' replied Alex. 'Benoît wants to talk to you about a few things first, anyway, and then we'll sort something out.' Even before I put the receiver down, I had already decided to ask Caitlin. Before I went to see her, I got all my money together, because I assumed the talk with Benoît would mainly be about that.

She was dancing. She was dressed in loose, yellow chiffon, and I could hear her counting with concentration. I stood in my usual shelter, but tried much less than before to keep myself hidden. So it was no surprise that she noticed me. She looked at me, smiled and danced on. Around her stood candles, small ones and large white beeswax ones, presumably from the chapel. As she moved, the flames moved with her.

'Here, Lucas,' she said suddenly, 'listen to this.' She bounced to the cassette player and pressed the start button. The sound was like that of a male voice.

'An oboe,' she said. She threw up her arm, making the other one follow. All of her torso bent like a reed, while her legs and hips did not move at all.

'Doesn't that happen to you?' she asked, looking back at me playfully, 'that you simply have to dance when you hear something like this? It releases the strangest things inside you, don't you think? A special kind of energy you never get from a piano or a violin.' I nodded, without having the faintest idea what she meant.

'I don't drive the car,' said Caitlin when I asked if she could give me a lift to pick up the chainsaw.

'But I've seen you,' I said.

'Have you . . .?'

'You don't have a licence.'

'Yes I do, I have an American licence. If the police stop me, I'll play innocent. I'll speak English and pretend I don't know that you have to be eighteen in this country.'

Soon after, we were in the car, with me crouched down on the back seat. She accelerated gently to avoid unnecessary engine noise. I couldn't see where she was driving, but from the sound of the tyres I knew we'd left the gravel drive of the convent and were on the main road. She slowed for the bend, and then drove quite confidently down the hill in second gear. I had a check blanket over me in case the police stopped us, and I was getting pretty hot. I could feel her concentrating.

'Do you drive often?' I asked. I wasn't completely at ease with the whole business.

'I'm not used to these gears,' she said. 'At home I drive an automatic.' The radio was on. It was the same talk-back program I had listened to before, and to my surprise I recognised Benoît's voice.

'Am I through? Are we on air? Yes? Well, what I wanted to say is, a friend of mine is a case in point here. I won't mention his name, you can't tell who's listening to this program these days.'

'No need to mention his name, sir,' said the man at the microphone, 'but you should introduce yourself. That's the rule on this program.' His voice sounded warmer, clearer and closer than Benoît's. It was as if his lips were very close to the microphone.

'My name? Do you really have to know that?'

'Certainly. We need your name. Without that we switch over. Yes? Can we switch to the next caller please?'

'Yes, no, wait. I have nothing to hide. My name's John. John Tureau, Johnny to my friends.'

I must have been mistaken. This man had Benoît's voice.

'Anyway, my friend wanted to go out on an errand. He's got a motorbike, you know. He went outside, and what do you think he found? Both his tyres slashed.'

'Oh yes,' said the presenter, to make it clear he was still there.

'To me, that proves one point: there are too many of a certain kind of people in this town. They land here like a swarm of flies for the fruit-picking season, because their backs are stronger than ours supposedly, and because they are used to heavy work. As if we don't have our own fit, strong-backed people! But look: our tyres get slashed, our bikes disappear, and just go into the Cercle . . . What do you see: anything up to thirty bikes in front of their apartments. Not even repainted!'

I listened with bated breath.

'What a load of primitive drivel,' said Caitlin, and, even though I was well out of her view, I dived deeper under my blanket.

'And what makes you assume that act of vandalism was the work of a seasonal worker, Johnny?' the presenter asked calmly.

Johnny ignored the question. 'Look, if we go to their countries, we are expected to fit in.'

'How do you know who slashed those tyres?' the presenter insisted. He spoke more loudly and slowly than before, irritation in his voice.

'My friend is an activist, sir. He stands up for his convictions. And why? Because he can see what is happening to this country. He *knows* the direction we're going. You must surely agree that it is immoral not to follow knowledge with action. So he reacts, and whoever reacts makes enemies. Those enemies slash his tyres.' A silence fell. The presenter hurriedly tried to fill it.

'Your friend is against foreigners?' he asked. Johnny coughed weakly, the way I had heard Benoît cough more than once.

'You misunderstand me,' he said. 'My friend is not at all against foreigners. He is against foreigners *who come here and think they can do anything they like*: nick bikes, burgle, slash tyres, you name it. He is for decency. For justice, respect and honesty. Old-fashioned values we've held for centuries and which are now under threat.'

Caitlin braked. I could guess she had reached the intersection with the ring road where she had to give way, but I thought she braked rather harder than necessary.

'How can they give that man air time!' she shouted when the car had come to a halt. 'Noise pollution!' She switched the radio off abruptly and changed into first gear.

From my spot on the back seat I explained the easiest way to Rue Machiavelli. Caitlin parked in the small parking area near Benoît's apartment. She followed me without asking any questions. It was the first time I had walked through the town with her, and even then I noticed how she seemed to immediately attract people. They nodded at her as if they knew her. Children instantly and surreptitiously touched her flaring yellow chiffon dress. She looked invigorating and exotic. Because I was with her, people held the door open for me.

I was getting terribly nervous. I realised that confronting Caitlin with Benoît was a crazy idea, and I had the feeling I would regret it. But I couldn't go back. The lift doors slid apart and she went in.

'Is this where your chainsaw is?' she asked as the lift rose, halting and groaning.

'A friend of mine has fixed it.'

'Is he a handyman?'

'He is handy,' I said, 'but he is actually a journalist.'

The lift stopped with a jolt. The door slid open, and I remembered just in time to let her get out first. Benoît was waiting for us by the door of his apartment.

'You've brought your sister?' he said when he noticed Caitlin. I was about to say: 'This is the girl who lives next door,' but she was quicker.

'I'm Caitlin Rose,' she said snappily, 'Lucas's friend.' She didn't offer to shake hands but gave a little wave. Since then I have often wondered what 'friend' actually meant to her at that moment. I looked up the meanings of 'friend' and 'girl-friend' in a dictionary, but only found literal translations. In my head, I could hear her repeat the word for days, as if she had pronounced a solemn charge, a challenge I had to meet. I remember precisely where she stood when she said it, the expression on her face, and how, immediately after, she looked at me and smiled.

'She has a car,' I added, as if I had to justify myself. He looked at me questioningly, looked back at her and said: 'That's a good solution then.' She walked ahead of him into the living room of his flat. I saw that he, too, was struck by the way she walked. He watched her as she walked over to the window, looked out over the surroundings and let the net curtain fall back again. He asked her to sit down.

Casually he poured her a soft drink she hadn't asked for. She took it from his hand and slowly drank it. Tascha sat in the corner of the kitchenette, whining with excitement but making not the slightest move. Caitlin made a smacking sound to try and attract the animal, but all it did was look imploring and rock from side to side a few times.

'So?' Benoît said to me while he poured me a glass too—in my case he *did* ask if I would like something. 'Your lip better?' I nodded silently. He looked at my mouth while he poured.

'A bit of a scar,' he said.

'That'll disappear,' I mumbled.

'Read the *Régio-Gazette*?' he continued.

Unnecessarily loudly I said: 'Thanks,' not so much to make him stop pouring, but to try and get away from the subject.

'The dog,' Caitlin said, pointing at Tascha. Benoît seemed to understand what she meant. He mumbled a word, and Tascha immediately came from her spot to lick Caitlin's hand. Benoît sat down where I had lain a few days before, on the couch in front of the window. The net curtain was again billowing in the wind.

'I just had an interesting discussion on the radio,' he said.

I stood up abruptly, pretending to look out of the window. 'Oh,' I said.

'What?'

'No, it isn't after all. I thought I heard an ambulance coming.' I felt totally ridiculous. I had grown up in the city, and ambulances have long since stopped drawing my attention. I went back to the couch. The static which had built up in the carpet crackled under my feet. I knew I had to say something right away to prevent the conversation from continuing.

'You had no trouble using the saw?' I asked. This time it was Benoît who didn't want to continue with the topic. He took a bag of crackers from the low cupboard next to him, struggled with the wrapping, and when he finally managed to open it, poured the contents into the bowl on his knees. Caitlin listened to our stilted conversation with mild amusement, stroking the dog. She leaned against the wall. Sunlight, filtered by the curtain, fell on her face and shoulders. She looked from Benoît to me, from me to Benoît, clearly waiting for whatever was going to happen. After a fairly long silence, filled with Tascha's panting and the sound of cars slowing down and taking off at the traffic lights below, Benoît got up. He pulled on the belt which held up his loose cotton pants and said: 'The saw probably works fine. Only, we don't really know an awful lot about those things. Someone will have to try it out.'

'Ah,' I said. I wanted to know more before showing any real reaction. He turned to Caitlin and drew her into the conversation by saying: 'Isn't it true, Caitlin, that Lucas is a bit of an expert on chainsaws?'

'I don't like chainsaws,' she said sharply. 'Trees should stay where they are.'

He shifted his weight from one thigh to the other and looked at her through half-closed eyes. 'You are sentimental . . .' he said, articulating carefully with his small, thin mouth. She wanted to reply, but he got in first: '. . . sentimental and sensual.' His words didn't confuse her. She laughed and shrugged her shoulders as if she didn't think it worth her while reacting to his innuendo. He kept looking at her. She became serious and didn't avert her eyes. It was a trial of strength which I interrupted by saying: 'But it has been fixed?'

'It's been fixed and it's in the cellar.' He stood up and went to the door. 'You can come, if you like.' I stayed in my seat. I did want to go, but I was worried about the hind. It did not seem like a good idea to let Caitlin see that dead hind. But he stood waiting so emphatically that I couldn't do anything but get up. When Caitlin also started getting up, Benoît said to no one in particular: 'Actually, I'm expecting an important phone call. One of us should stay here.'

'OK,' said Caitlin. 'I'll stay here.'

THE HIND HAD gone, of course. Alex was sitting there in the half-dark, reading a comic, leaning against the wall. He had obviously been waiting for us for a while.

'Got your tyres fixed?' I asked by way of greeting. He was totally absorbed in his reading and seemed quite confused for a moment.

'Tyres? Oh . . . my bike? Yes, just finished, five minutes ago.' He moved his arm, as if he wanted to show me the evidence, but there was nothing there. The cellar floor was swept clean. There was some dirt in the dust pan in the corner, but that could not have come from a tyre.

'Where have you been all this time?' he asked Benoît. 'I'm getting cramps from all this waiting.'

'He had someone with him,' Benoît replied.

'Oh!'

'She's upstairs.'

'So?'

'She'll wait for a while.' I looked from one to the other. They were very different, but had the same way of talking without looking at each other. When they spoke, they always seemed to be concentrating on something else, something more important. I went and stood closer to Alex, away from the door and more in the light. When I enquired about the hind, Benoît pointed at the freezer to my left. He went over to one of the shelves and took down a tall carton which proved to contain my chainsaw.

'How much do I owe you?' I asked, convinced that that's what it was all about. Alex laughed conspiratorially, without looking up from his comic.

'Nothing,' said Benoît. 'For friends, we do everything for free, don't we, Alex?'

'The bill goes to our non-friends,' said Alex. He sniggered, and so did Benoît.

'Alex is a real comedian,' he said. 'When we do something together, he always manages to sound cheerful. That's what makes it such fun to work with him.' He tore open the box, clearly showing the chainsaw. I knelt and examined the chain. It had a new link, and had been oiled.

'How did you manage . . . ?'

'With a bit of help from the experts, of course.'

'What do you mean, experts? When I asked, they said it would take three weeks.'

Alex kept making noises behind his book.

'We know people,' said Benoît. 'That's the difference.' He wiped his hands clean on a rag.

'But now we want to ask you a favour in return,' he said. I waited. 'There is a tree which stops us having a clear view of a building. It needs to be cut down; we need to be able to see who comes and goes in that place. You can keep the firewood for yourself.'

'I don't actually need any more firewood. I have a couple of trees which I'm . . .'

'Need? Need?' Benoît said in a dry tone. 'I don't quite see the connection. Alex, did you hear me ask him if he needed firewood?' Alex shook his head. He sat leaning forward, the light on the top of his head rather than on his face.

'Exactly. That's not what I asked,' Benoît went on. 'I asked you to cut down a tree. Or even better: to cut it just far enough so that it will have to be cut down. That would be perfect: somebody else will actually do it for us. Not far from here, near the factory building in the Cercle, there is a linden tree, not too old, only ten years or so. It's in the way.'

I knew the place. I knew the tree, too. It was a crooked, neglected tree; it was self-seeded and had never been pruned or looked after. It stood in a small square, the rest of which was occupied by illegally dumped car wrecks. I knew the tree because it stood out: it was one of the last in the Cercle. It was surrounded by suckers, and its trunk was full of scars left by young knife-throwers killing time in the square.

'But that tree is on public property,' I said.

Benoît smiled resignedly. From the way he reacted—calmly and without any sign of irritation—I realised he had prepared thoroughly for this conversation. He had foreseen my objections.

'What do you think the people in the Cercle will do when we pull that tree down? Call the police?' Their appreciation of each other's humour was mutual. Alex laughed in an exaggerated way.

'Well, no,' I said, caught off balance. 'It's still illegal.' A silence fell. It went on, shimmering between the walls. It made Alex uncomfortable. He shuffled his feet along the floor and didn't look up. Benoît calmly put his hand in the inside pocket of the lightweight jacket he was wearing over a bright T-shirt and produced a strip of aspirin tablets. He pointed a limp hand at the crate of Perrier water on the shelf.

'Alex, my boy,' he said, 'do me a favour and open one of those bottles for me. I need an aspirin. It must be the heat. You can't believe how debilitating a headache like this can be.'

'You are very welcome to borrow the chainsaw,' I said while he extracted a tablet from the foil. Benoît didn't look at me. He watched Alex get a bottle from the crate and remove the cap with a screwdriver.

'I hate having to explain things twice when I have a migraine,' he said, almost in a whisper. I realised I had moved out of the light and leaned against the wall with my arms crossed over my chest. I pressed my back into the cool brickwork, as if hoping to disappear into it.

'Listen, Lucas. Two things: if friends ask you to do something, you don't ask yourself, do I approve? It shows a lack of trust. If you choose your friends right, you can assume that they know what is good or bad.' The foil strip made a crackling sound between his fingers. He looked at it, and put it back in the pocket of his jacket.

'If there is anything I dislike, it is half-heartedness. I like people who are committed. Integrity and directness are great qualities. People who prevaricate make compromises. In the end, they achieve nothing. I prize action. Doing what has to be done quickly and efficiently.' He waited for me to say something. I couldn't think of anything. I wanted to get out of that cellar. But I knew that the longer the silence lasted, the harder it would be to get out of the task. If I didn't go on resisting, I was lost. I took a deep breath.

'It would have to be done fast,' I said in a voice which was pitched higher than I wanted. 'Alex is stronger than me.' Benoît drank from the bottle. His Adam's apple moved up and down, steady as a heartbeat. There was a sucking noise when his lips let go of the neck of the bottle. He put the half-empty bottle on the floor, straightened himself and came and stood right in front of me.

'Alex is my right hand. I have total faith in him. But you have to know he has had bad luck a few times in his life. It wasn't his fault, it was the fault of the weaklings who couldn't control themselves. Ever since, he has been the scapegoat. If a young guy gets beaten up somewhere at night, he is the one who's done it. The police drag him out of his bed twice a week.'

'General whipping-boy,' Alex interjected.

'Friendship doesn't just happen, Lucas, you know that. Have you ever had a good friend? Take Alex, for example. He is a good friend. I don't pay him for things he does for me, and he doesn't pay me. We call that returning favours. You know what that means, Lucas, returning a favour?' I could hear my blood throbbing in my head. It was so loud I couldn't concentrate on my thoughts.

'How would you feel if you refused to do this for us?' he continued. 'You would leave this cellar and say to yourself: is this comradeship? They fix my chainsaw for me and when they ask me for something, I tell them to get lost.' He looked at me with eyes that were as bright and transparent as a magnifying glass. 'That wouldn't make you feel good about yourself, would it?'

'Yes . . . no,' I said.

'You are your grandfather's grandson.'

'Leave my grandfather out of this,' I said loudly, glad to have found something to say, 'and don't compare me with him.'

He grinned briefly. 'Lucas, how did you know that man? As a traitor? Or as an idealist? Exactly. He was a man you could rely on. Yet everyone accused him, so that even his friends left him. Do you find that honest or fair? For God's sake, don't let yourself be so confused. Think for yourself and protest. Gossip it is, nothing but gossip and slander.' He threw his empty bottle into the bin. It landed with a clink.

'By the way,' he said. 'I saw it the first time I met you: you are like him, really. You're a person of character, someone who knows what is good and correct and says so. That's exactly why I want to get you involved in this. We are fighting for a noble cause. We are not doing this for ourselves. The people of this country are asking for it. I know it's not all necessarily terribly obvious. So it's only fair that I leave you by yourself for a while and give you a chance to think about it. Not too long, of course; I'll be back in half an hour. And whatever you decide, I'm pleased that we have fixed your chainsaw.' He disappeared from the cellar. I stayed behind with Alex who, for a while, kept on reading as if nothing had happened. I sighed to draw his attention.

'Just do it,' he said suddenly, chewing on his gum and without looking up from his book. 'You don't really have much choice. It's either that, or leave your saw behind for good.'

It was more than an hour before Benoît returned. He was carrying a pair of blue overalls, dust goggles and heavy work boots which looked like Doc Martens.

'Here,' he said, 'these are for you.'

'Where is Caitlin?' I asked immediately. I had gone upstairs earlier to look for her, but everything was deserted and locked up.

'Don't worry about her,' he said with a smile. 'I've taken her home. I explained to her that the chainsaw wasn't working properly yet, but that we'd take her back. A gorgeous girl, Caitlin. She's even allowed us to use the car.' I looked at him in surprise, hoping for further explanation. He winked and said: 'Of course, you really owe her now. Fortunately, a few barrow loads of firewood will do wonders.' He held the overalls up in front of me so I could step straight into them.

'Why wouldn't you let her see the cellar?' I asked while I pulled up the overalls.

'Only the landlord knows I rent this cellar. It's not on the lease. I need some privacy. If they come to do a search, all I have is the studio with a harmless fax machine.' He put a cap on my head, and told Alex to put one on too. He held out the boots. I put my feet into them. He did them up, and instantly I felt far too hot.

'We'll drive with the window down,' he said. 'Then it will feel better.'

'We do this without carrying weapons,' he said while we walked down the narrow passage. 'Remember, Lucas: there are things you do unarmed by definition. Carrying a gun at the moment would be an unforgivable mistake.' Once we got to the lift, he remained silent until we were inside the car.

WHILE WE SAT in Caitlin's car, waiting for darkness to fall, Benoît and I drank cola and Alex beer. The car stood in the shade and we had all the windows open. Benoît talked constantly, I said hardly anything. He was talking about politics.

'Politics is at the centre of everyone's life: you see that things are going wrong, so you do something about it. A person who is not active isn't worth the cost of a bullet in the head.' As he talked, he toyed with the small items lying on the back seat: a furry dog, a nail file and a whole lot of loose beads from a broken necklace. He spoke quietly, as if all we were doing was killing time with nothing to do but spend the whole summer in idle chat. Nothing showed that he was up to something. Every now and then he tried to make us laugh by telling a joke.

As the evening progressed and the sun turned more and more orange, Alex's eyes became brighter. He was constantly, rapidly, looking around, on the alert, and no movement in the street or the square escaped his attention.

'Knowledge which does not lead to action is immoral,' Benoît said, as if he was not aware of the rising tension. 'Our actions will change the political situation, Lucas! You cut down a tree in the forest, and nothing changes. But just make a deep cut in this tree here and everything changes. Not immediately, of course, but after a few days. We're making the neighbourhood safe again.'

There were hardly any people anywhere. I suspected that the spot had been carefully selected for this, and that the quiet all around us was no coincidence. When a few girls came by, they took absolutely no notice of us.

Around nine o'clock, Benoît wound up his window. He got out, stretched his legs without going far from the car and looked over the fence of the house in front of which we were parked. He smiled at something behind the fence—I thought he must have seen a child or a dog there—and came back to us. He poked his head in and said: 'There are stacks of car tyres behind this fence. Alex, can you imagine how much smoke it would cause if they caught fire?' Alex whistled through his teeth. He laughed much louder than the joke warranted. He got out, too, and inspected the surroundings. They stood talking in whispers a few metres away from me, and, though I tried hard, I couldn't make out what they were saying. Alex said something, and Benoît patted him on the shoulder encouragingly. At that gesture, I felt a shiver, and I knew I was a bit jealous.

Seconds later they were back in the car, Alex at the wheel and Benoît next to me on the back seat.

'Time for a drive,' he said to Alex, who immediately turned the key in the ignition and got the car moving. They wound their windows right up now, and I automatically did the same. Benoît stretched himself right back in the seat. When he noticed I had my face near the window, he asked me to move to the centre a bit.

I remember how a strange kind of excitement overcame me. This slow, almost soundless gliding through the practically deserted streets leading to the Meunier set all my muscles and nerves on edge. The memory of my walk of a few days ago came back vividly. I felt as strong and untouchable now as I had felt weak and vulnerable then. My senses were so alert that I noticed the blades of grass between the stones and the moss on the walls. The red light in the sky was reflected in the car's bonnet. Nothing could have induced me to swap this ride for a barbecue in Moumouche's garden or anywhere. Montourin seemed different, more threatening, but also more exciting, a bit like the brightly lit and over-crowded streets full of cinemas and dance clubs in the city. Although I was uncertain and suspicious, I was overcome by the excitement of belonging, of having a mission: I had to cut down a tree.

'You are not to cut the tree down,' said Benoît. 'All you do is make a deep cut, enough to damage it irretrievably, but not so deep that it falls over. The noise of the saw will bring people out of their houses. They won't know what is going on and will crowd around you. You will say nothing, and work very fast. As the cut deepens, people will stand back. You'll switch the saw off for a moment, and then on again. That will be the sign for us. We'll drive the car right up to you. You get in and we disappear instantly.' I wanted to ask why. All through the ride the question was on the tip of my tongue, but I didn't ask it. I felt that if I put it into words I would become an accomplice. I would become afraid, and the mystery would disappear. The excitement would collapse like a house of cards, and I wasn't prepared to risk that.

It had become dark. Benoît told me to pull the overalls on over my clothes. As we drove through the town with the lights on, I vividly remembered the painful ride on the back seat of the police car with the plasticised blanket under me. The memory of how that had felt brought me back to reality.

'What if something goes wrong?' I heard myself ask. My voice was shaking with excitement. Benoît was not put out by the question. To him, every objection was routine.

'For every undertaking there are basic rules,' he said flatly. 'Alex knows them, but you don't. What are the basic rules, Alex?'

Alex, who was concentrating on the road, quickly glanced over his shoulder.

'The basic rules?' he echoed. 'Rule one: if you're caught, you've been acting on your own.' Benoît smiled approvingly.

'Exactly,' he said. 'There was no one with you. You were acting without any plan. You had been watching a violent film on TV and were bored. And rule number two, Alex?'

'Rule two: if one of us is hurt, eliminate the danger.'

'. . . is hurt, eliminate the danger,' Benoît said, almost simultaneously. 'Stay with the victim. You hear that, Lucas: stay with the victim. You know from experience how dangerous this neighbourhood is. People here are capable of hitting a man with a broken leg until he has two broken legs and ten broken ribs. You only start running once the police are in sight.'

I did what I had been instructed to do: I got out, walked over to the linden tree and pulled the starter handle of the chainsaw. I stood still for a moment to feel which way the wind was blowing. I studied the way the roots were anchored in the soil and the shape of the trunk. It was partly hidden by the many suckers which grew all around the base. It was a healthy, solid trunk, very different from the lightweight pine I'd cut down earlier in the week. I thought of the motions my grandfather used to go through before starting to cut. He would bend forward, as if in greeting, and dig his heels into the soil. The saw whined. I put the blade against the bark at an angle, the way I had always seen him do it. The first touch sent a shock right through me. I needed all my strength to stop myself being thrown backwards. But as soon as I was through the bark there was just a throbbing cloud of dust and a trickle of sawdust which formed a small cone on the ground. I made a cut at a clear angle, pulled back the saw and made a second cut at a sharper angle. The saw lay steady in my hands, and not even for a second did I have the feeling that it might slip out and end up in a dangerous spot. I saw no light coming on in the houses around the square. I saw no doors opening or people coming towards me. I was wearing dust goggles, not for the dust, but to avoid being recognised.

I made a cut as deep as I thought necessary. It was guess work, but for some reason I felt quite confident. Although I had never done this before, it felt like a routine job. It was a tricky decision, because the tree stood at a bit of an angle. The whining of the saw made me feel calm. Feeling just a little sorry that I couldn't go all the way, I pulled the saw back. I sniffed the scent of freshly-cut wood: the scent of forests, resin and camp fires. Only when I switched off the saw and noticed Caitlin's car coming towards me did I become aware of the movement around me. There were people in the square. They were carrying children in pyjamas. They were talking and pointing at me. They moved back when I started the motor again.

The number plate of the car was covered in a grey plastic bag. An invisible hand opened the door. I switched the saw off again and, while it was still vibrating, got into the car. Our departure was quiet, without screaming tyres or suspicious swerving. The wipers made a knocking sound against the windscreen every time the car went over a pot-hole. Nobody spoke. We drove out of the town and up the hill. Once we were among the trees we opened all the windows, and I rinsed my mouth out with cola.

It was Alex who first suggested we should go back. He stopped the car on the narrow shoulder between the road and the rock face.

'I want to know what's happening,' he said. Benoît shook his head.

'It's dangerous. We're absolutely covered in evidence.' But Alex insisted and got his way. We wrapped the goggles, the overalls and the saw in the grey plastic bag, hid the lot under a bush we would be able to find easily in daylight, and did a U-turn. We left the car outside the Cercle, in the parking area of an apartment building where it would not be obvious. We walked casually to the square. Most people had gone back inside, a few still stood around talking. Alex went into an all-night shop and bought a few cans of beer and soft drink and at least ten sausage snacks. While we were eating them he told us the shopkeeper had said that someone had rung the police, but they had said they would come and have a look in daylight.

'This is a free area,' said Alex. 'You can do what you like, the police are terrified of coming here.'

I was tired. I wanted to go and sit in a pub, but Benoît thought it wouldn't be a good idea to be seen anywhere that evening. So we stood about for a while near a bus stop with a seat and a few ill-lit posters, unable to make up our minds. More than anything, I wanted to go home.

Suddenly I got a shock. In the distance, leaning against the graffiti-covered small monument with the fountain, stood a group of young men, one of whom I thought I recognised.

'What's the matter?' asked Benoît who instantly realised that something was wrong. I didn't answer immediately. I kept looking hard at the man, trying to see his face. While I was standing there, I broke out in a cold sweat, and if I'd followed my instincts, I would have walked away right then.

'What's the matter? That man? Was he one of them?' asked Benoît, fast but calmly. I wasn't sure. It could be the man, but might just as well be his brother, or someone who looked like him. They all looked like each other, those Arabs, and they all wore moccasins and short-sleeved white polyester shirts.

'Which one?' said Alex. 'That one? That guy on the left, with his hands in his pockets?' Because we were looking at them so intently, they started to look at us. There were six or seven of them, against the three of us. The way they stood there, waiting, brought back the pain in my ribs. They were obviously talking about us, gesturing in our direction. There was no lamp post near them, so all their faces seemed to have the same, dark expression. But there was a light on in one of the houses behind them. When the man I was staring at stepped back, he stood in front of the lighted window, and I recognised his profile.

'Yes, that's him,' I said. Instantly, something changed in Alex's and Benoît's attitude. I can't describe it very clearly now, but it was something in the air around us, a sort of vibration. Their breathing changed. They were breathing like young race horses closely confined behind the starting barrier.

'No, don't go near them. He'll recognise me.'

'Not go near them? And what about your split lip?'

'That's just about healed.'

'They're forcing us, man,' said Alex. 'Can't you see that? They're challenging us, and I tell you: let them get away with provoking you just once, and they'll never stop. Any harassment has to be nipped in the bud.' As we moved in their direction, the group fell silent. They watched us in the dark as we moved to a different corner of the square, not that much closer to them than before but with a better line of approach. We stood still, and they were laughing and smoking. I don't think they were afraid. Yet suddenly they were gone, swallowed up by the dark.

'Hell, where have they got to?' asked Alex. 'What are they up to? Are they being smart-arses?' The question seemed to be addressed to Benoît. Before we realised what we were doing, we were walking in the direction they had disappeared, into an unlit area, away from the square and the people.

'They think they'll catch us in an ambush,' said Benoît. He ordered us to move apart, one ahead, one following behind, one on the other side of the narrow street. Walking like that, by myself, more than ten metres away from Benoît, made me more scared than I would have been prepared to admit. I sped up to reduce the distance, and before we knew it we were walking together again.

'There's one,' said Alex who obviously had the sharpest eyes. Along the footpath at the end of the street a young man approached. He was quietly walking in our direction, apparently hardly aware of us. As he came closer, I could sense Benoît next to me and Alex ahead becoming tense. The boy was younger than I expected, fourteen at the most, and the curly hair sticking out from his head gave him a friendly look. He was still more than five metres away from us when Alex started talking.

'Here comes something walking along our footpath,' he said. The boy didn't seem to realise it was aimed at him. Without taking any notice he stepped off the footpath to let us pass. He didn't look at us. His thoughts were obviously somewhere else. But Alex wouldn't let him pass. He jumped sideways and deliberately knocked into him. The boy was frightened and stopped.

'Wouldn't it have been better to stay with your friends?' Alex said.

'My friends?' I recognised his way of mechanically repeating what the other said. It was a way of gaining time. It gave you the chance to think and find a better reply.

But usually, by the time the right reply occurred to you, there was a new question to confuse you even more.

'Yes, your friends. Don't you think it's dangerous here all by yourself? Take my advice. It would be better to stay with them. It's not clever to allow yourself to be separated.'

'I have no friends around here. I'm only here by chance.'

'Hear the cock crow,' Benoît said sharply. Of course the boy didn't get the allusion, and looked around, listening.

'So what are you doing here, out in the street at this hour of the night?'

'Walking.'

'Walking in the dark is dangerous, don't you know that? Hasn't anybody ever told you that walking in the dark is dangerous? You never know what other people are up to, do you?'

'No,' he said. All this time he had a friendly smile on his face. He must have thought we were joking, or had had a few too many.

'This is a bad neighbourhood, you must have heard that. Old people get robbed here, and women raped. Animals are sacrificed here. You must have heard about that.'

'Eh, yes.' He wanted to walk on. He had to get away, and thought we were a minor obstacle. He thought we were just playing games because we were bored. He had no idea how angry Benoît had become. He couldn't very well know: Benoît had a friendly expression on his face, and his voice was calm, almost soothing.

'The police are here, too, or at least they should be. They could ask you questions. They could ask for your residence permit, for instance, and see if you're actually legal.'

'Yes,' said the boy. I was pretty sure he had no idea what Benoît was driving at. I stood and watched, my arms by my side. I wasn't much older than the boy, I could see. I had lied about my age, and had started to feel older since then. But as the dark-haired boy stood awkwardly before us, I realised how misleading that feeling was. I knew I would have been exactly as awkward. I was no longer interested in what else was going to happen, but couldn't see a chance to disappear.

I took a couple of steps back. But Benoît signalled with his finger and Alex put his arms around my shoulders and pushed my head towards the young Arab.

'You see that lip?' asked Benoît. Alex had me in a kind of head lock, and I couldn't get myself free. 'You see how ugly and damaged and swollen it is? You see that scar? You know how that happened? That happened because he walked through the Cercle by himself. In broad daylight! You'd think it was safe in daylight!' The boy looked at me for a fraction of a second, but he wasn't interested. He wanted to walk on. Alex let go of me abruptly and stood a few centimetres in front of the boy. The boy turned his head away. He was about as tall as Alex. He tried to step sideways to get past him but Alex moved with him. I could hear him snorting.

It went on for too long. The distance between their bodies was too small; something had to happen. The boy must have felt so threatened he did something stupid: he moved his elbows forward and pushed Alex. That was very stupid.

'What's this?' said Alex. 'Hitting me?' He made the same movement and pushed back, harder, and the boy had to take a couple of steps backward. It was as if they were linked together. As soon as the boy moved away, Alex followed.

Every push he gave, he got back. Alex was wearing boots with reinforced toe-caps. The Arab boy was wearing moccasins with leather soles. He lost his balance on the cobblestones which were probably a bit slippery with oil or grease from cars. It was an awkward fall: he tried to grab hold of the only thing near him, which was Alex, who kicked him in the ribs as he hit the ground. The kick made almost no noise at all, at the most the sound of a small leather ball bouncing. The boy didn't groan, but grasped the spot where he had been hit with both hands. Alex pulled his leg back and kicked again. The boy tried to parry the kick with his arms, but he was too late and the tip of Alex' boot hit him in the small of the back. This time a sound came from his throat, like a suppressed burp. The boy writhed in pain and made a crooked uncoordinated attempt at getting up. Alex gave him time. I saw him look at Benoît. Benoît stood off to one side, turned to me, rather than them, looking as if he had nothing to do with what was happening. He watched the scene with a cool glance. He gave Alex an almost imperceptible nod. Alex lashed out again and kicked.

The polyester shirt came out of the boy's jeans—jeans of the same brand Moumouche swears by . . . , and against the exposed dark skin of his lower back I could see a strangely shaped birthmark, slightly raised, dark red. It was the size of a hand, the shape of a heart. As I stood looking, I became conscious of a thought that has not left my mind since that day: that life is intolerable. It hurts on all sides, and no matter how you wriggle, you can't escape the blows. You have to make choices, and every choice is the wrong one. I stood in the Cercle, and could not choose. So I stood, waiting till it was over.

'You know what makes me more angry than anything else?' said Benoît when the boy had stopped moving. 'It's the fact that they always force you to use violence. I hate violence. I never use violence unless I am provoked. Some people ask for it. He asked for it. That makes me furious: that they can drive you so far. They deserve a beating just for that.'

'He is bleeding,' I said weakly.

'That's nothing,' said Benoît, guiding me away from the place. 'A split lip and a bit groggy. It's no more than what they did to you that time.' We walked out of the street. Behind us we heard the boy calling out one word which he repeated over and over. I assumed it was a term of abuse. Only much later did I learn that he was calling, in Arabic, for his mother.

MY MOTHER HAD no idea what was going on. With hindsight I blame her a bit for that: I came home late at night and she didn't bother finding out what I'd been up to. She could have stopped me. But she seemed very self-absorbed. She moved my grandfather's paintings about and rummaged around in his cupboards. As soon as it became sunny, she put jugs of herbal tea on the warm tiles of the terrace to brew in the sun, put tomatoes on the windowsill to ripen, and pinched the dead heads out of the rose bush with her fingernails. I saw her walking about in the garden from the kitchen window, and she waved, but didn't come in to ask me why I had come home so late last night.

The *Régio-Gazette* was on the table. Listlessly I flipped through it, vaguely expecting that there would be something in it about our action. And so there was. It said that the half-cut tree was a danger to the old presbytery in the square and that the council officials intended to cut it down altogether for safety reasons. There had been some controversy about the presbytery, and the journalist mentioned that the builder who was in charge of its refurbishment had said more than once that the tree was in the way. It was suspected that he had hired someone to damage the tree. The second theory was that it was a senseless act of vandalism.

There was no mention of a fourteen-year-old boy being beaten up.

As if I had to atone for something, I decided to start cutting the firewood right away. With my baseball cap pulled low over my eyes, I walked to the spot where we had hidden the plastic bag and retrieved the saw, leaving the overalls and the goggles. As unobtrusively as I could, I carried the saw home. Then I hurled myself at the thickest parts of the pine trunk.

Still my mother said nothing. She didn't ask how I'd got the saw repaired, nor did she forbid me to work with it; she was only too pleased I wasn't hanging about any more, sulking and bored. While the pieces of pine fell with a gentle thud into the carpet of needles underneath the sawhorse, I wondered what had happened to the Arab boy after-wards. I imagined that nobody had found him and that he had bled to death. When you die, so much effort suddenly seems to have been wasted. Take all those mornings the boy had got up, reluctantly because he hadn't had enough sleep, struggling out of bed though he had nothing in particular to get up for. I fantasised that I, too, was dying and my mother and Caitlin were weeping for me.

I got a fright when I suddenly found Caitlin standing next to me. She had been drawn by the sound of the chainsaw.

'So it's been fixed after all?' She stood with her hand on her hip. A brightly coloured ribbon was tied round her wrist. 'The car still isn't back, so I thought . . .'

'There were complications,' I said.

'Your friend is a bit unusual, isn't he?' I had no idea whether she meant that in a good or a bad sense. No matter how hard I was trying to appear normal, I couldn't make myself look her in the eyes. I pretended I had no time to lose.

So what should I have done? I thought to myself. Tell them to stop it? She kept hanging about, examining the flowers and shrubs as if they were rare and exotic.

'I've told my mother I lent the car to a friend who had to take his old grandmother somewhere. That sort of thing always works.' She laughed out loud. I was deeply ashamed and wished fervently that she would go away. Until she actually waved at me and disappeared. Then, instantly, I missed her.

In the afternoon I saw Caitlin's car coming up the hill. Like last night, Alex was driving with Benoît in the back. They parked in front of my grandfather's house and came into the garden. I kept myself out of sight in the smithy, hoping they wouldn't find me, but they must have seen me as they drove up, for they walked resolutely in my direction. When Benoît called my name, all I could do was to come out.

Benoît was wearing white slacks with an even whiter polo neck jumper, making him look like an apparition in this messy corner of the garden.

'Good afternoon, my dear friend,' he said. 'How's it going?' Alex stood just behind him, in a grubby T-shirt as usual, and in boots which were far too heavy for that time of the year.

'Good, good,' I said without looking at them. I was covered in grease and sawdust. As I had done with Caitlin, I pretended to be very busy, but Benoît didn't let it throw him.

'Nice little work area you've got here,' he said, pointing out the junk in and around the smithy. The lemon tree, which was now in full flower, gave off a sharp scent. Benoît snapped off a twig and held it between his teeth. With his hands behind his back he walked into the smithy.

'Ideal for messing about, isn't it?'

I nodded, grabbed a broom and started sweeping away the pine needles which covered the ground.

'Just what you need, Alex!' Alex interpreted this as an invitation to have a look around inside. From where I stood, I could see how they inspected the shelves, looking at the paint tins, reading their labels. Benoît came back outside and pointed at the chainsaw.

'You wouldn't happen to have a bit of extra petrol?'

'Petrol?' I asked. I had a bit left in the bottom of the jerrycan. I'd filled the tank of the saw that morning and decided I had just enough. I assumed he wanted to reimburse Caitlin for what he had used by filling up her tank.

'No, no, not for the car,' he said as if reading my thoughts. 'For something else. I don't need a lot.' I pointed out my grandfather's purple jerrycan. Alex picked it up, shook it and grinned.

'Well, that's actually rather *too* little,' Benoît said, laughing.

'What do you need it for then?' I asked. I was being

wary. I knew this sort of question could change his mood suddenly. He remained friendly and calm, but the muscles in his jaw betrayed his annoyance.

'Listen, Lucas,' he said. 'You did first class work yesterday. You've proved brilliantly how carefully you work and how aware you are of your responsibility.' He looked briefly at Alex, who nodded as if his head had come loose. 'The tree has caused no damage and is being removed by the authorities. All according to plan.' His eyes glittered in the sunlight. His fair hair fell softly along his smooth face, and for a moment I thought how nice it would be to look like that.

'But, of course, that was only a beginning,' he went on. 'We can now get a good view of the presbytery, and the real work can begin.' I said I didn't understand what he meant, which was true. He exchanged a quick look with Alex and moved a corner of his mouth up and down.

'We need some for our cocktails.'

'Cocktails?'

'We're having a party!' Alex said snappily. He waved his arms as if he was dancing. Benoît remained dead serious.

'A bottle of petrol with a fuse, that's what I mean. We'll . . .'

'Molotov cocktails?' I interrupted my sweeping. The sun shone straight in my eyes.

'That's the limit!' Alex said in an affected voice.

Benoît looked at him severely and said: 'Can I go on?'

'Sorry.'

'We'll prepare them so we've got them handy, not to use them.'

Suddenly, I felt utterly desolate. It was as if I was standing in the middle of the hills, without a living soul for miles around, and with nothing but scorched grass and sand around me.

'Isn't that a bit . . .' I said uncertainly. Benoît turned to Alex.

'Lucas is still very young,' he said quietly. 'He is intelligent and learns fast. But he is also suspicious. I think he actually believes we are planning to use violence.' He turned back to me and continued: 'We are against violence. Whoever uses violence sullies our name. Okay, okay, yesterday we got carried away a bit. Alex was drunk and a bit nervous. He shouldn't have overreacted. He's terribly sorry about it, and so am I.' He went across to Alex who now leaned with bowed head against the warm corrugated iron of the smithy. Benoît put an immaculate white arm around his shoulder.

'But in a way I can understand him, too,' he said. 'He's frustrated. He has been out of work for months; all those brownskins have work.' Alex lifted his head so he could nod.

'They shouldn't provoke me,' he said, aggrieved. 'Whoever provokes me will piss blood.' Benoît patted his back encouragingly and detached himself.

'Look, Lucas, a man has to be prepared. In case something happens. Or are you one of those boys who lets everyone walk all over him? Over himself and his house and his land and his family?' I had to say something, but I was unprepared. All the creative ideas I had worked out while I was cutting wood had disappeared.

'Why?' was all I could think up. There were wasps buzzing around, attracted by the scent of the roses.

'Because we are waiting for a decision by the Council. That decision will be made soon. Possibly, we will have to take some action then. It's not certain, but it is possible. You have to look at it like this: Molotov cocktails are a cry of alarm. They're a way of saying: this can't go on. They are a shout of protest. I promise you, there won't be any casualties, just some fire damage here or there, and that's paid for by the insurance—paid for so well that usually the building is better after than before.' He turned on his heels and turned his face to the sun. It was the movement of someone without a care in the world.

'And, okay,' he said, 'I must admit, throwing a Molotov cocktail is a kind of violence, you're right about that. Even if we don't endanger anyone, it is still violence. But sometimes violence is justified. If you can't express your ideas democratically any more, what do you do? Let them walk all over you? Our violence is no aim in itself, it's a means to an end. And we don't do it for ourselves. We want to achieve what is good for our people. You mustn't forget: our country is at the moment being occupied by a foreign people. A bit like the Germans during the war. With this difference: they brought civilisation with them, while now we are regressing into barbarism. If you look at it that way, we are simply in the resistance. You wouldn't want us to be collaborators?' For long seconds I stared at a greasy carton on the shelf.

'It's dangerous,' I said, but he misunderstood me.

'That's exactly why,' said Benoît. 'If *you* buy the petrol, it doesn't attract attention. We both live in a flat. If we as much as open a jerrycan the fire brigade is at the door. You've got the smithy, and the excuse of your chainsaw.' I kept sweeping like a maniac. The path was well and truly clean, but I kept going.

'I . . . I don't want anything to do with it,' I uttered with difficulty. I was worried about what I'd said even before I finished speaking. I realised I was putting our friendship at risk. It was a relief but it hurt at the same time.

'You don't have to, my friend,' said Benoît softly. He took hold of the broom handle, forcing me to look at him. His eyes were bright and friendly.

'Take my word for it: you'd do us a tremendous favour. You'd show that you know what friendship means. But your help is not indispensable. We'll get hold of petrol one way or the other. We've got plenty of friends who can get it for us. But if it comes from you, it means you understand what loyalty is. You need petrol, anyway! Look, your jerrycan is practically empty! And that's all you *have* to do. You don't have to be involved in anything. Above all, I want you to be true to yourself, and only to be involved in things you really believe in.'

I stood, totally confused. I no longer had any idea what I should do. I looked around as if I expected to find an answer among the shrubs or in the joins between the bricks in the path. Benoît must have noticed my desperation, for he sent Alex off home and asked me to show him the garden.

'Is your cousin here?' Benoît asked unexpectedly after we had walked about the garden together for half an hour, talking about the power of the chainsaw, small-game hunting, our plans for after the summer and the political leanings of the regional radio stations. He had been cheerful and even talked confidentially about the friendship he felt for me. ('Sometimes you dislike me, don't you?' he had said. 'That's good. Real friends make you want to strangle them occasionally. That's how it should be. Friends must arouse emotions, otherwise their company is worthless.')

'My cousin?' I asked.

'That girl with the American accent, what's her name? Caitlin? She's your cousin, isn't she?'

'She's my girlfriend.'

'No! Really? Don't tell me you're living here with your girlfriend?'

'She doesn't live here.'

'No? So where does she live? In a tent in the garden perhaps? I did drop her off in front of the door last night.'

'In the convent,' I said, pointing to the edge of the roof, the only bit that was visible from where we were.

'A novice?'

'She's on holidays.'

'So the car has to go back there?' he asked.

'It should, really,' I replied. I wiped the sweat off my head with my handkerchief. 'If you bump into her mother or anyone else there, you'll have to say you needed it for your crippled grandmother.'

He stopped. Crickets were chirping by our feet. He studied my grandfather's house, and, sounding as if it really mattered to him, asked: 'Which room is beneath that skylight?'

'My grandfather's.'

'Can't you look into the convent garden from there?'

I was bewildered. 'Eh . . . I wouldn't know. The window is pretty high up. I've never tried.'

'Come on. I want to see that room. I want to see if we can look into the garden.' I went in ahead of him, and upstairs. Inside, the sickly smell of insecticide hung in the air. All the shutters were closed, and there was only an occasional bar of sunlight on the floor. Benoît followed me, looking at everything. Now and then he stopped at a painting, pointing out things in it. I was surprised to realise I'd never even noticed most of them before.

'So this is Stockx's bed?' he said when I pushed open the crooked green door to the room. He went over to the duplicator, touching it with both his hands. 'And this is where he produced his pamphlets.' Here, too, Benoît studied the paintings. The mirror in the wardrobe door rattled with every step he took. He tried looking through the window.

'The window is too high up,' he said accusingly, as if it was my fault. He looked around quickly.

'That desk, can that be moved?'

'Yes . . . no, never tried. Pretty heavy, I think.'

With a gesture he got me to stand on one side and lift the desk with both hands. He lifted the other end. I pretended not to know where he wanted it, but he made it clear by pushing with his thigh until it stood exactly under the skylight. He took his shoes off and stood on the desk.

'Wow!' he said. 'What a view. Look, there she is, our princess. Carrying buckets of water by the looks of it. The way that girl walks! She's like a panther among all those cats.' He was silent for a bit, as if he wanted to give himself time to absorb the scene. I stood next to the table, my hands in my pockets.

'What a gorgeous girl,' he said. I couldn't understand why, but the fact that he admired her pleased me.

'I'll go and return the car. Does it bother you if I visit her? You're not jealous, are you?' He let himself drop off the desk. The mirror on the wardrobe rattled.

'No, no,' I said. He put on his shoes and left the room. I went with him as far as the screen door, but as soon as he had turned the corner I went back to the room. I climbed onto the desk and saw him start the car and drive to the convent. He got out, leaving the door open as if he was planning to take off again immediately. As nobody stirred, he walked up and down in front of the main wing of the building a few times. The geese cackled as if they were being plucked alive. Caitlin came running out. She was wearing short plastic boots and rubber gloves which she took off hurriedly when she saw there was someone there. I watched them talk to each other. Passing birds were reflected in the windows of the convent. The conversation was short and seemed friendly. Then Benoît took off down the hill on foot. I could have gone out to tell him it was quicker down the shepherds' path, but I didn't.

WHEN MY MOTHER came home, I asked her if she had any idea what important decision the Council had to make soon. She looked surprised. She was wearing a white sailor's cap with a turned-up brim because the sun always gave her a headache.

'I've only been here as long as you have,' she said.

I asked Caitlin the same question. We were in the pavilion together to see how much more wood would be needed. She held her head at a slight angle and said thoughtfully: 'A Council decision?'

'Is it anything to do with that linden tree they cut down?' I tried to prompt her. She clapped her hands together like a little girl who has suddenly seen something wonderful.

'Oh, of course,' she said. 'The presbytery. They're going to decide about that. Whether it's going to be a shelter for refugees.'

'Refugees in that presbytery, in the Cercle?' I said. 'But surely that's irresponsible?' She misunderstood and said: 'They'll renovate the building. Plumbing and electricity and all that.'

'That's not what I mean. I mean: surely it's asking for trouble?' I added that I thought such a decision would be stupid, and I meant it.

'Those people have to go somewhere,' she said, without the slightest trace of indignation. 'The Cercle is not the best place, but it's the only neighbourhood where they wouldn't be driven away by protests.'

I bent to straighten a few blocks of wood that looked unstable. My clumsy effort dislodged one of the blocks that held up the pile, and instantly the whole lot keeled over. With a dark, dusty rumble, like remote thunder, the hundreds of blocks of wood landed on the tiled floor. We jumped back with one movement. The whole space was instantly filled with a thick cloud of dust which rose from the floor and formed ochre-coloured columns in the sunlight from the windows.

'Shit!' said Caitlin.

Speechless at my own clumsiness, it occurred to me how the collapsing woodpile reflected what had happened to my thoughts in the past few moments. I sincerely believed that foreigners could make much better progress in their own country. I had dozens of arguments to prove that refugees would be out of place in the presbytery, and wanted to tell Caitlin, but I was afraid of her counter arguments, her reproaches, and my arguments had collapsed with the woodpile. The dust irritated my throat and made me cough. She pulled me out of the door by the tail of my

T-shirt, to where the sun was shining and a slight breeze stirred the escaping dust. The pavilion looked as if it was on fire.

'Smart work!' she said teasingly. She'd forgotten about the presbytery. Peering in the direction of the convent to see if anyone had noticed anything, she pushed me into the shrubs in case Soeur looked out or came our way. She giggled, and I shrugged with a grin. We stood around for a while, waiting for the dust to settle. Then she put her head inside. She turned and said: 'We'll have to find another tree. This will never see her through the winter.' I interpreted this as a sign that I could come out of my hiding place. The woodpile looked a lot less impressive than when it had been properly stacked against the wall.

'But I'm out of petrol,' I said. I tried to pronounce the word as neutrally as I could. She stood behind me and dusted off my shoulder.

'Then we'll go and buy some,' she said.

Carrying my grandfather's purple jerrycan in her hand, she followed me, first through our garden, then down the mountain path.

She was in an exuberant mood, delighted with the unexpected beauty of the path. She overtook me and went down the slope quite recklessly. The way she walked radiated an animal strength. She leapt and slid.

'Careful,' I said. She turned and stopped. Her attitude seemed suddenly defensive—her head pulled down between her shoulders, her lips pursed—as if I had told her off.

'Yes, I know: I should be careful of my joints!' she said. 'But I'll never get in anyway. I'm not good enough. I may just as well sprain my ankle. Then I'd know why I wasn't dancing.' I smelled the warmth of her body.

'I'm glad they didn't let you into that school,' I said.

'Why's that?' Her mouth was dry from the effort.

'Otherwise you wouldn't be here.'

'Oh, you idiot! If you knew how much I want to go there!' A dreamy look flitted over her face. I regretted what I'd said. 'And then do my own choreography. I want to create a piece in which I dance myself to pieces.'

Right at the end of the garden, near the road, we found a tree trunk which had probably been there for a while, but I'd never taken any notice of it before. It was pretty dry and wouldn't be hard to cut up. The climb back through our garden would be too cumbersome, so we decided to carry the blocks of wood up to the road just a few metres above us, and then pick them up in the car.

It seemed like a perfect idea. It was an innocent idea, full of good intentions. How could we have even suspected that it would turn out to be so disastrous? I clambered up the big rock at Challon's Bluff and held my hand out to her. She put hers in mine; it was cool, as if she had just held it under the cold tap. Her fingers were supple, almost like a monkey's in the force of their grip. With a dancer's strength she pulled herself up along the smooth rock face. We came to Monsieur Orchamp's garden; I was excited, more reckless than usual. Without looking properly, I walked past Orchamp's strawberry patch. She followed me unsuspectingly when suddenly the old man stormed out of his house, waving his stick, followed by a yapping, rusty brown mongrel dog. I grabbed her by the arm and dived into the dry ditch. With a small cry she fell down beside me. For a moment I was amazed to feel her so close. Then, giggling like school kids, we walked up the street.

'That man yesterday, Benoît, I think—what's he like?' she asked as we walked along the low garden walls.

'Benoît is a friend of mine,' I said emphatically. 'A true friend. At home I've got friends, too; I have fun with them. With Benoît it is something else. He's much older. As a journalist, he's really involved in life, and that makes him so interesting.'

Perhaps it was a premonition, I don't know, but when we got to the petrol station I didn't want her to come in with me.

'I'm thirsty,' I said. 'Why don't you go to the super-market and buy us some soft drinks.' She returned carrying two bottles of cola, covered in pearly condensation. She held out some money.

'Here,' she said. Her forearms were covered in short, fine hair, darker than that of most other girls I knew.

'What's that?'

'For the petrol.'

'It's my petrol.'

'It's for *our* firewood.'

From the window of my grandfather's room I observed Benoît visiting Caitlin every day. The first time I saw him coming I thought he was coming to see me. But the next time I already knew better. As soon as I saw him go past I went inside and stood on the desk. He walked into the convent garden like an old friend. Ruth and Soeur came out to greet him, a bit standoffish the first time, but friendly and relaxed from there on. I couldn't work out what was being said. Caitlin sometimes walked in the garden with him, showing

187

him the roses and the pond. Other times he went inside and emerged with his jacket draped over his shoulder.

One afternoon, after I had been working on the tree trunk for hours and had stacked the wood neatly by the roadside, I couldn't resist talking about him. We were together in the car, Caitlin driving without her mother's knowledge, and me in shorts on the hot vinyl seat next to her.

'What do you think of Benoît?'

'Benoît? Why do you ask?'

'No reason.' She took the bend carefully. Even the most experienced driver would be wary of that one. I wasn't worried or scared: the pile of wood wasn't far away, less than five hundred metres from the convent entrance, and the chances of being stopped by police here were minimal.

'He scares me,' she said.

'Scares you?'

'There's something about him. I don't know what, but it's violent. I have the feeling I could fall violently in love with him. He is intelligent. He is curious about everything, a journalist through and through.' She pressed the accelerator, but quickly changed her mind, as the road sloped downward quite steeply now. She shifted her foot.

'Shit!' she yelled, 'the brake isn't working!' She pressed the pedal again, harder this time, and now the car slowed so abruptly that I was thrown forward and fell with my hands against the dashboard. The engine spluttered and we stood still.

'God, sorry,' she said and turned the ignition key.

'What was it?'

'I don't know. It was a weird feeling. It felt as if the brake wasn't gripping. How can I put it; there seemed to be 'no resistance.' She engaged first gear and we were moving again.

'But he's dangerous, too,' she said as if nothing had happened. It took me a moment to realise she was talking about Benoît again. 'He's so persuasive I don't dare raise any subject with him because he's prepared for any topic. And he's challenging.'

'Challenging?'

'He pushes you. Don't you ever feel that? If you're sitting down, he makes you stand up. If you're walking, he makes you run. He makes your blood run faster. He can shift your mood.' We had arrived at the stack of wood. She steered the car onto the shoulder of the road on the outside of the bend.

'Am I challenging?' I asked.

'You? No, no, you're not challenging. You're engaging.'

'Oh.'

'Once, when he was having a go at the Arabs, I asked him if it didn't upset him to see how little they had. You know what he said to that?' I waited for her to go on.

'He said: we've worked hard for what we have.' She didn't go on and kept looking at me meaningfully. It was really too hot to sit in a stationary car, even with all the windows down.

'I hope it was a joke. But people who say things like that scare me,' she said. 'He maintains we have a lot in common. I want to make the world a better place and so does he. He calls it being involved. He says the greatest danger for this country is not the political refugees and that sort of thing, but the lack of involvement.'

'He could be right about that.'

'I don't know, Lucas. He talks too cleverly and too much. He has instant answers for every question and every argument. It takes me a bit longer to form an opinion.' She opened the door and lowered her feet to the pavement one at a time.

'Yes,' I said dully, 'I feel a bit like that too.' We loaded the boot and drove back. When I got home I looked up the word 'engaging'.

Once, I saw from my window how Benoît put his hand on her shoulder. Caitlin stayed motionless and looked away from him as if she didn't notice. He left, and I saw him going down the hill, the tail of his bright white shirt flapping. Caitlin stood in the courtyard for a little while longer. She had her hands behind her back. She was as still as a bird by the water, and I was completely enchanted by her. All the perspective lines of the convent building seemed to converge on her. She coloured the landscape yellow.

Then something happened which I should have expected. She turned her face in my direction and, instead of ducking instantly, I stood motionless. She saw me. Her worried face broke into a smile. She couldn't have noticed from where she was, but I blushed violently. I waved back.

'Hello!' I called stupidly. That only made things worse. My mother heard me calling and came into the room. When she saw me standing on the desk, she flew into a rage.

'What are you doing on that table, for God's sake?' she asked. 'That's an antique! And with your shoes on!' Her fury was out of all proportion and I couldn't think why, until I remembered the earlier incident.

'Grandfather himself stood on it,' I said triumphantly.

'That's not true, Lucas. You're only saying that to justify yourself. Your grandfather did *not* stand on that desk.'

She was so furious she slapped me across the face. It was a strangely exciting experience. I could not remember her ever hitting me before.

ALL THAT TIME I was using and spilling petrol. I deliberately left the jerrycan open. Every day the level went down. I found half of another tree trunk—obviously left or forgotten by an earlier woodcutter—and cut that up too. When Caitlin heard my chainsaw she would come over, usually followed by a few cats, invariably including Copernicus. She came not only because she thought she should, but because she couldn't concentrate on her dancing anyway because of the noise of the saw. Occasionally we walked into Montourin, just to do something different, or to go and sit in the pizza shop which was air-conditioned. But we never stayed long. We went back to continue working. With the strength and stamina of a small donkey she carried the blocks of wood up the steep slope to the edge of the road.

We were a bit further away from the road now, more towards my grandfather's smithy, and we could easily have taken the wood there, and then to the convent in the wheelbarrow. But we didn't. We had developed a taste for using the car; we could take a lot more at a time, and it was much more exciting. It was already near the end of August. We worked among low bushes which gave off sharp scents. One of them was covered in berries which attracted flocks of greedily twittering birds. They flew off in fright whenever

I started the saw, but returned as soon as I stopped it. Caitlin brought iced tea in a thermos and we sat down together to drink it when we got tired.

Was it jealousy that made me? I filled the cup we were sharing and started talking about Benoît again.

'I heard him claim recently that Auschwitz was just an ordinary prison,' I said, 'where people sometimes died.' She was startled.

'Did he really say that?' She thought for a few moments. 'I should have known,' she said at last. 'He's managed to fool me. But I was beginning to suspect. People like him want to forget Auschwitz so their racism can be acceptable again. They're not ashamed of what happened, on the contrary, they're even proud of the fact that the Germans managed to organise those mass deportations. They know that as long as people remember the mountains of human hair and shoes, their racist propaganda doesn't have a chance.' She stretched her hand out to the bush behind us.

'I think he had an unhappy childhood.' She popped a red berry into her mouth, and that took some courage: I had tried them and they were incredibly sour.

'There's an anger in him,' she continued. 'Anger I find wonderful. You can do beautiful things with it. I'm angry, too, and it's anger that makes me dance. Only I feel he misuses his anger. Instead of doing something with it, he nurtures it. He doesn't want to build, just to destroy. He doesn't quite know who, but he wants to make someone pay for everything that's going wrong.'

'He is good to his friends.'

'Of course he's surrounded by friends. They're brought together through their hatred. I can make friends like that, too: just look for a disaffected young man who's unemployed. He has no money and no love and he wants to belong. He has no political convictions. You persuade him that the guest workers have robbed him of his birthright, his flat, his job and even the most beautiful of the white girls. Once he swallows that, you tell him the latest myth, the one about the Jewish plot. All our problems stem from a Jewish plot to dominate the whole world. It's so easy. There's nothing to it.' I sat speechless. There was too much lemon in the iced tea and not enough sugar.

'I would like to know how he would react if he found out I'm Jewish.'

'You are Jewish?'

'You know that.'

'Caitlin Meadows isn't a Jewish name.'

'Jewishness comes from the mother's side,' she said. 'And my first name was chosen in case history repeats itself.' She picked up Copernicus who came walking past and put him on her lap. 'I think I'll go and talk to him,' she said. She stroked the cat's fur. It was a patient, wise sort of movement. As I watched it, I drank down the sour tea.

Benoît turned up next morning, as if he had sensed that something was wrong. He had brought Tascha who jumped all over me as soon as I appeared in the garden.

'She loves the forest,' said Benoît. 'She can let herself go here.' I was still in the boxer shorts I slept in. I hadn't washed or had breakfast.

'Have you read the paper?' he asked. He pushed the *Régio-Gazette* under my nose. All I could see was a photo of a racing cyclist and an article about flooding further south.

'No.'

'Well, read it. How can you *not* read the paper? Aren't you interested in the world around you?' I gestured him into the house and poured him the coffee my mother had meant for me.

'The Council has decided,' he said. 'The presbytery will become a reception centre for refugees.' I buttered some toast and chewed it slowly. It was the wrong decision. It would lead to nothing but problems. I could see it in the way Benoît looked at me.

'Have you got the petrol?' he asked. He produced five empty Perrier bottles from his bag and arranged them in a straight line on the table. I looked at them silently.

'You know how it's done: fill them with petrol, soak the fuse thoroughly, preferably put in a cork while they're being transported. When they're ready, they have to be brought down.'

'And what are you planning to do with them?' I asked, trying to keep my voice as normal as possible.

'Listen, Lucas. Think of the consequences for the Cercle. Ghanaians, Chinese, Brazilians, all together, all in the one place. Now there is an explosive mixture for you. They've got no money. They don't speak the language. Just what the neighbourhood needs. I can show you the statistics: near reception centres more cars get stolen, more property gets damaged, more gardens get trampled.' He tapped the edge of his cup with the teaspoon and took a sip without making even the slightest slurping or swallowing sound.

'That's all fine, but what are you planning to do with them?' I repeated.

'The presbytery is still empty right now.' His lips were damp and shiny from the coffee. I was endlessly amazed at the calm he exuded. All he moved was his hand and his mouth. I was glad I was still groggy with sleep: it prevented me shuffling my feet.

'Into the presbytery? Are you going to throw the Molotov cocktails into the presbytery? But that's dangerous!'

'If we wait any longer, the damage will be greater and there will be casualties. Surely we don't ever intend that? It's a scare I have in mind. I don't want to hurt or injure anybody. Just scare them. A little bit of material damage in a good cause. Then they'll go away of their own free will.'

'It's still dangerous. For the people in the neighbourhood, the passers-by.'

'You shouldn't reverse the roles, Lucas. You're going on as if *they* are being threatened. That's not how it is. *We* are in danger. Our people and our country are threatened with being overrun. You had a beating in the Cercle, but you are young and strong. Imagine if that had been your grandmother, or your sister. We men must shoulder our responsibility.' He pulled a tissue from the box on the table and dabbed the corners of his mouth.

'And, please, don't tell me I hate foreigners. Other cultures fascinate me. I have tremendous respect for them. But their different character cannot be fully developed here. Can you imagine: Africans in jeans, Indians in runners? That can't be what we intend? We must protect them from Western influences and send them back to the land of their birth. Here, they'll only be miserable. In order to integrate, they'd have to give up their own individuality. Farewell customs, farewell tradition. Surely that would be a terrible shame?' He put both hands flat on the tabletop and got up. His cup was still nearly full, but he asked me to come to the smithy with him. He gave me three of the bottles and carried the other two himself. He held the screen door open for me, and while we walked through the garden to the smithy I thought rapidly. Tascha followed us excitedly, dashing off now and then to dig an imaginary rabbit from its burrow.

'I don't think I want to do this,' I said before entering the smithy. It was still early, but already it was hot and I was surprised at the number of flies buzzing around. Benoît put his bottles down on the damaged workbench and I put mine next to them. I opened the chainsaw box and got out the jerrycan. It was half empty.

'Your dithering is making it all much worse than it need be. Do you want to force me to wait until there are people living in the place?' he asked, bending over the box. He noticed the small gun in the bottom and pointed at it.

'I'll teach you how to handle that gun. I promise.'

'You'd better take that away,' I said. 'I don't want to learn how to handle it. Why should I? Seeing you don't believe in using violence . . .' He interrupted me.

'Lucas,' he said, putting his hand on my shoulder the way I had seen him do with Caitlin, 'take the advice I give you as a concerned friend: don't sell yourself short. Defend yourself. See that you're armed and that you stay master of any situation you get into. Otherwise you live in fear. I'm prepared for everything. My weapon is my strength. I know what you want: you want justice and peace. But the world isn't like that. The world is threatening. When I go anywhere, I assume that anyone who approaches me does so with ill intent—until he proves the contrary.' He shook me by the shoulders as if he was trying to wake me up. It made my head rock. I had no idea what to say, so I said nothing.

'I'm terribly sorry for you. You're my friend, and that makes it even worse. You'll always be a loser. You're not prepared for aggression. You always smile politely. You cannot believe what others are capable of, because you're not capable of it yourself. You have no feel for danger. You can call it innocence, I would call it naivety.' He pushed the jerrycan into my hands, but I put it down and went outside where I stood in front of the door.

'Okay, okay, so you won't do it,' said Benoît. He unhooked my grandfather's old apron from its nail on the door and tied it on over his clothes. He looked around until he found a funnel and filled the bottles with petrol. He tore pieces of cotton into strips and twisted them into fuses. Tascha kept wandering in and out, sniffing the air which hung heavy and suffocating in the confined space.

'Give me a carton to put them in,' he called to me after a few minutes. I stood motionless. If I had been my mother, I would now have calmly lit a cigarette. Benoît didn't let my attitude bother him. He looked around and found a suitable box.

'We still have to get them down, of course. That'll be the hardest part,' he said. 'Perhaps I'll ask Caitlin if she'll do it.' The mention of her name alarmed me more than I wanted to show. I put my head in through the door and faced a row of completed Molotov cocktails.

'Keep Caitlin out of this,' I said quickly. He clicked his tongue as if I had said something that was quite wrong.

'I've already had many long talks with Caitlin,' he said. 'More and longer than you think. I know her. She's on our side.'

'Forget it, she'll never do it.'

'Of course she won't know what she is carrying, smarty! It'll just be a few expensive bottles of wine in a

197

sealed carton. So long as you don't spill any, or she'll smell it straight away.' He pushed a large roll of sticky tape into my hand. He must have brought it, for I had never seen it before. Benoît took off his apron and put it back on its hook. 'I'll go and explain to her right now. About our party—you know?'

'Yes,' I said. 'Just go.' My tongue felt thick and numb, like after a visit to the dentist. I walked with him as far as the gate. He crossed the road and I went inside to go and stand on the desk.

The cats scattered in all directions when Tascha stormed into the convent courtyard. Benoît knocked on the small wooden kitchen door. It took forever for someone to open it. As he persisted, Caitlin finally emerged. They talked for a while. Caitlin looked agitated. She waved her arms. He said something back. She looked him up and down. She started at his feet, and gradually moved up until she examined his face. Then she turned around, went inside and shut the door in his face.

Benoît came back, walking angrily. He went towards the smithy. I went downstairs and, from behind the kitchen window, watched him go in and emerge with the box in his arms. Then he walked carefully down the hill, Tascha in his wake and the sun straight in his face.

That evening a fire broke out in a tyre dump in the Cercle. It produced a spectacular column of black smoke which was clearly visible from up the hill. I stood watching it from my grandfather's garden and worked out that it must be the place where Alex, Benoît and I had waited that evening when we cut the linden tree. I later heard from Benoît that this had been a 'warm-up exercise'. Alex had a different version. He said it was because Benoît had discovered that morning that Caitlin was a *filthy Jew*.

A few days passed without anything happening. I cut more wood, and tried to use up the petrol. The chapter of the Molotov cocktails was closed as far as I was concerned. I thought I'd made it quite clear to Benoît that, no matter how much I valued his friendship, I had no intention of following him to the bitter end. Caitlin came to help me but didn't mention him except once. After we had been carrying armfuls of firewood for half an hour, all the time talking seriously about things we wanted to do later, she said out of the blue: 'I'm only intolerant of intolerance.' Then she worked on and it was as if the words had escaped her accidentally, not meant for my ears and not carrying any message.

That was in the morning. In the afternoon when, by a lucky coincidence, she had just gone back to the convent to do a few jobs for her mother, Benoît and Alex came up the hill, much more cheerful and excited than I'd come to expect from them. They saw me from the road and their gestures made it clear they wanted to talk to me.

'This is something for you, Lucas!' they shouted from a distance. Alex had a can of beer which he drank from a few times and then threw into the shrubs. 'You're in favour of non-violence and democracy. Here's your chance to show the local politicians what you think.' They walked around the house and came into the garden. All the time they kept muttering to each other, and occasionally bursting into laughter so wild it actually stopped them moving. If I hadn't known better, I would have thought Benoît was a bit drunk, too. Every now and then he almost folded double, slapping his thigh, laughing so loudly I thought I could hear his voice echoing from the surrounding hills.

'What do you call a Turk in a rubbish bin?' was the first thing Alex asked me when they reached me. I knew no answer was expected. He was laughing so hard it took a while before he could finish his joke: 'Selfish, because there would be room for more Turks.' I smiled because I thought it was funny and because I didn't want to spoil their fun. Benoît roared, after which he immediately apologised, wiping his mouth with a handkerchief. 'Sorry,' he said, hiccupping a few times. They were red in the face, and their eyes watered. Half supporting each other, they sat down on the grass.

'Not in the sun, not in the sun,' said Alex, twisting around like a dog trying to find a good spot on the grass, 'or we might turn *brown*!' They sat down in the shade of the low shrubs. For a while they said nothing, but burst out laughing every time they so much as looked at each other, something I'd only seen girls do before.

'Well now,' said Alex. And again: 'Well now.' They shifted around until even their shoes were in the shade.

'We actually came to tell you there's a demonstration tonight,' Alex said finally. At the word 'demonstration' they both turned serious, really deadly serious. It startled me.

'What for?' I asked.

'Against the presbytery.' With his long fingers, Benoît started pulling grass stalks from the ground. They were tough and dry; he arranged them side by side in his hand.

'What do you really think about that, Lucas? Do you think it's a good idea to put the refugees there?' It was a tactic they had used before: they asked a question and let me talk myself into a corner.

'They have to assimilate,' I said quickly. This I had thought about. It was a conclusion I had come to. I had a number of arguments for it.

'Can you change a man into a woman?' asked Alex. It sounded like a trick question, too obvious to answer. Actually, I thought it was the beginning of another joke. 'Well, you can't change an Arab into a European either.' Benoît sat patiently, plaiting the grass stalks.

'That wasn't the question,' he said softly. 'The question was whether you thought it a good idea to house refugees in the presbytery in the Cercle.'

'No,' I said.

'What have you got against it?'

'I think it will cause even more problems in that neighbourhood. It's a difficult enough area as it is. The city can't afford the costs that would result.'

'Exactly,' said Benoît, suddenly looking up. 'We have to pay twice for those blacks: once in the form of foreign aid—for a hungry continent. And then again when they come here. You have to ask: what is happening with all that money? Why do they come here while we are sending dollars over there?' He paused to look around, shading his eyes with his hand. 'But that's how the Council want it. It's a democratic decision.'

'The people in the Cercle haven't been heard,' I said. 'They have no representatives on the Council.'

'Bingo!' shouted Benoît. He lifted one side of his mouth in a grin. 'The government of the city forces its inhabitants to live together with people we know are a threat to our safety. That's dictatorship, isn't it? The boat is full. They don't realise this, that the boat is already full.' He threw the stalks of grass on the ground. He rubbed them with the sole of his shoe, until all that was left were some brown stringy threads.

'We can't let just anyone into the country,' said Alex. He seemed to have a special attraction for insects. They sat on him without him noticing. 'Only a whore leaves her front door open all the time.' I noticed that I was nodding.

'They must assimilate, and the boat is full,' I repeated in confirmation. Benoît got up, brushing the grass from his trousers with both hands. He waited for Alex to get up, too.

'So we've come to tell you about this demonstration,' he said. 'This is your chance. You've said you're seventeen.' He paused as if he wanted to give me a final chance to admit my lie. 'Next year you'll be an adult. It's time to take your life into your own hands, man, to take risks, to do something. You can't sit on your behind all your life and hope someone else will fix things.' The sun reflected off his watch.

'These are bad times, and we're the only ones who can do something about it. We are the first generation who can't count on things being better for us than they were for our parents. It's no coincidence that we are also the first generation who have to share everything with the Muslim brethren.'

They told me where they would be when. I didn't promise I'd be there. I left it vague to give myself a chance to think. About an hour later, when I went to the far end of the garden to carry up some more wood, I noticed that the stack I had been working on for three days had gone. I asked Caitlin if she had collected the wood, and she said she'd intended to, but that her mother had been out in the car all day. I remembered the many wood fires in the Cercle and felt myself getting angry. It was this new theft that made me decide to go to the demonstration.

ALEX WAS AT the agreed spot. He had been to the hairdresser. His hair was now terribly short, so short it seemed
no more than a shadow on his white skull. He appeared to
be neatly dressed, but I noticed he had cut the frayed bits off
his cuffs. He was carrying a motorbike helmet.

'I thought you were against those,' I said, pointing at the
helmet.

'I'm against a helmet when I'm riding,' he said, 'but in
favour of it when I'm demonstrating.'

He was surrounded by a number of boys and rather
fewer girls, whom I hadn't seen before, and who stood
talking excitedly. When Benoît arrived later, all heads turned
in his direction.

The mood was friendly. People talked to me as if I were an
old acquaintance, and the way they stood with their hands
casually in their pockets, telling stories without looking at
each other, reminded me of my friends at home. A brown-
haired boy came and stood between Benoît and me. He
handed cigarettes around until his packet was empty.

'Watch out for the press,' he said, to me as well as to the
others who stood listening around us. 'These days they call
you a Nazi if you simply love your country. If you see a journalist, clobber him one. If you don't know what for, he will!'

'Hey, hey,' Benoît shouted, acting indignant, 'mind your
words. I'm a journalist, too!' The boys around us laughed;
I couldn't work out whether they were laughing at Benoît
or the boy. More people kept arriving. Some had flags
and banners. A few were selling magazines, buttons and
stickers.

When the group started to move, the mood changed. At first I'd seen nothing but relaxed faces, but now there was a feeling of rhythmic tension, reminding me of military music and of the pulse of a metronome. We marched in rows. Nobody had asked us to do that, it just happened. Somebody was counting time. His voice became louder and louder, creating a feeling of tremendous strength, as if we were a heavy locomotive rolling forward, unstoppable. It wasn't aggression, but determination. I was amazed at the energy that was being released in me and the others, perhaps because we had shed the burden of a hot day. Some boys were chanting: 'Love your country or get out!' over and over, until the phrase sounded as familiar as a nursery rhyme. People stood on the footpath watching our war dance. They were silent, and some waved. I was walking between Alex and Benoît and wondered why Benoît had chosen me among all his friends to walk next to him.

'It's working!' said Benoît without turning his head to me. 'Our method is working. Just look: so many people and not a single Arab in the street. They're scared.' There were people ahead of us, tens, perhaps hundreds. At first I thought: we're stamping our feet to get the feeling there are more of us than there actually are. But when the road sloped upward and we could see the front of the march, with the flags and banners sticking up above people's heads, I realised there were more than a thousand people in our demonstration. The ones in front knew exactly where we had to go. I just had to follow. It gave me the confidence I needed to join in the chanting.

Alex was beaming. He carried his helmet on his hip and walked jauntily, but with restraint, like a nervous horse. He was in the outermost row. He didn't join in the chanting, but looked around eagerly. Like me, he swung his arms, in the same rhythm, as if our wrists were joined with rods. At first, he apologised if he accidentally bumped into someone. But he soon stopped that.

We had a police escort. They walked alongside us but had trouble keeping up. They gestured at the people on the footpath to move back. Just past Mercier Square, unexpectedly, a different type of police were waiting, younger men with grimmer faces and carrying batons. At first I thought their presence was pathetic, because I was convinced this was one of the most exemplary demonstrations ever. But when we swung round and came past the bend, we saw, down the Rue Tivole which runs to the town hall, a group of counter-demonstrators. Their presence didn't seem to surprise the people around me. They looked a miserable lot, in their chaotic formation, with their banners on which the paint had run. With their flaming torches and unkempt hair they looked like cave dwellers.

Again, the mood around me changed. We lost our rhythm; some marchers started stamping their feet, the chanting turned to shouting. Instantly, I could smell sweat, on myself as well as on the people around me, as if we had become a single body reacting as one organism to the new stimulus. Among the counter-demonstrators were some Arabs. They waved their identity cards—just scraps of paper faded through constant handling—to prove they were citizens.

'Coming, Lucas?' I unexpectedly heard Benoît asking next to me. Above our heads, the windows of the derelict building we were passing were being opened.

'Where to?'

'A special mission. We have to get to the square before the other protesters.' Something fell. It came from above us, from a window. Somebody was throwing things. Benoît ducked and pulled me down by my shirt. They were eggs. They hit the pavement with dull thuds and left a glistening trail behind. When I thought they had stopped, I stood up, but a new volley came down and an egg hit me on the head and neck. It didn't really hurt. I shouted more in fright. The yolk felt warm, as if someone had held the egg in his hand for a while.

'Merde!' yelled Benoît when the muck dripped off me. Automatically, he pushed me away from himself to avoid getting it on his clothes. The demonstrators milled around looking for stones to throw through the windows of the building, until there wasn't a single one left unbroken except for a tiny toilet window that was too high up.

In the confusion, amid the pushing and shoving and slipping on egg yolks, I suddenly saw Caitlin among the counter-demonstrators. She was wearing her striped fisherman's jumper with the hood. Benoît didn't see her, and she didn't see us. I doubled up and ducked into the side street opposite. As if I'd given a signal, Benoît and Alex followed me, with three others I didn't know but had seen talking to Benoît earlier.

'Good on you, Beigne!' Benoît called in a muffled voice, while the distance between us and the demonstrators grew. I started running, probably mainly to calm my nerves, because I'd had a terrible shock. I wasn't heading for anywhere in particular, and it took me a while to realise I wasn't leading. Benoît and Alex ran a couple of metres ahead of me, and they turned up streets and lanes where

I'd never been, deeper and deeper into the Cercle. Looking back, I don't know why I followed them. I think I was looking for more of that earlier, good feeling of not having to decide, of being allowed to drift with the current. I was moving easily and fast, better than the boys with me, who had trouble running—cans of beer in their jacket pockets banged against their thighs at every step—and after a while they had to let me get ahead.

We arrived at the square in front of the presbytery. Somehow, the group split up, Benoît towards the bus shelter, the first boy into a side street, and the other two towards the presbytery. Dusk had fallen, and I was confused by the strange half-light from the sun which had just disappeared behind the hills. I intended to follow Benoît, but Alex made me walk into a van behind which he was hiding. The way he was lurking was contagious: I started behaving like someone who didn't want to be seen, though I had no idea why. Alex opened the rear door, threw the helmet he had in his hand onto the seat and gestured at me to get in. I hesitated on the step. He followed me and shut the door.

'How did you know it was open?' I asked.

'Everything has been thought of,' he replied. He had the same alert expression on his face as he'd had that evening we cut the tree. He sat motionless, looking out through the tiny window in the door, talking all the while, not particularly to me or to himself, as if it wasn't important for someone to listen, but he just wanted to reassure himself that he was there.

'Let those red ants crawl over our shoes,' he said. 'It won't slow our steps. They're ugly cuckoos, making themselves comfortable in the nest we have built. Dungbeetles, I'd call them.' He giggled briefly. 'Only Benoît won't allow that.' He pulled the knuckles of his fingers until they cracked, eight times, four on each hand.

'It's their own fault,' he continued. 'They shouldn't have come here. If there were no foreigners, there wouldn't be any racists.' Meanwhile, I was wondering what I was doing here. When my eyes had adjusted to the dark, it became clear: on the floor stood the carton from my grandfather's smithy. I knew what was in it, and kept myself motionless like a child that has dirtied its pants.

'Why doesn't Benoît do this?' I asked, my mouth feeling like sandpaper.

'Benoît does the thinking. You can't expect him to do everything.' He picked up the helmet from the seat and put it on.

'And anyway,' he added, 'it's a privilege to be able to work for him.' He looked at me through the visor as if something was hurting him. I tried my best to believe him.

'Is he really a journalist?' I asked.

'Benoît's profession is being a *son*; his parents have money, you see.'

I nodded and asked no more. I knew I could get away. The door was open and I knew the way. But I stayed out of curiosity. I wanted to see what exactly would happen and how it would work out. My decision became irreversible when Benoît opened the door and got in.

'Everything's going to plan,' he said to Alex. He looked at me quickly, but seemed to hardly notice. He sat down on the bench opposite and crossed his arms over his chest. I had only the vaguest notion of what we were waiting for, and perhaps that's what made it so exciting. I didn't ask because I was afraid the spell would be broken and this would turn into just a vulgar attack with Molotov cocktails. But I did have another question, a much more pressing one.

'How come you're so certain that this is right, Benoît?' I asked.

'What?' he said, looking up, annoyed.

'How can you be so convinced you're in the right?'

He sighed as if his patience with me had run out. 'Look at me,' he said softly. 'Look at what I do. Doesn't the fact that I am prepared to put my life on the line in this business prove that I'm right? Do I look like someone who would give up his life for a lie?' It didn't really sound like a question, but I felt I had to say something. But at that moment I heard a whistling sound in the distance. I wouldn't have paid any attention if Benoît and Alex hadn't reacted so compulsively. They slid towards the door. Alex jumped out of the van, and Benoît grabbed for the box and hurriedly removed two cocktails which he passed to Alex. Alex disappeared, and Benoît gestured for me to get out too. The fresh air outside suddenly made me dizzy.

'Here, Lucas, you stand over there, and you throw this bottle through that window,' he said, emphasising 'there', 'this' and 'that'. I stayed where I was.

'You can't pull out now,' he said, sounding concerned rather than threatening. 'You can't just leave the sinking ship. You've chosen. You've come part of the way with us and you can't go back. You know too much. Not that I bear grudges or am looking for revenge. I'm mainly thinking of Alex. Alex is very sensitive about people who first put their trust in us and then turn away. I'd call it changing one's mind, but he calls it treachery. I can't guarantee that he'll keep his calm if he hears that you've run out on us now. And you know what he's like. He's quite capable of throwing rocks through all your windows. Loyalty above all is his motto.' He followed my glance.

'That house is a slum,' he said. 'It's inhuman to make anyone live there. It's not that we don't want those foreigners to have a good life. It's just that they shouldn't live here. It's a matter of geography, not racism or anything.'

I still stood motionless. It was going on for too long. People could see me. It was making Benoît nervous.

'You're not responsible. *I* am responsible. You're carrying out an order.' There was a sound of breaking glass. Simultaneously we turned our heads in the direction of the presbytery. For a moment, there was nothing to be seen, but then a yellow glow appeared behind one of the windows, faintly lighting up our surprised faces.

'Take that cap off, Lucas. You can't work like that. You'll lose it if you have to run.' He pulled the cap off my head and threw it into the van. I walked towards the presbytery, up to the window he had pointed out, on the other side from Alex's window, and hurled the cocktail inside. It made an awful lot of noise, more than I had expected, and I was embarrassed by the racket. At the same time I felt untouchable. I stood motionless because I was fascinated by the vulnerability of the building. And I had a problem: I thought I could hear someone calling out behind the wall. I knew it was impossible; the building was dilapidated and empty, but I heard a voice. I only started moving again when Alex ran past and dragged me away from the square.

We had to run again. This time in the opposite direction. Alex was in front of me, and up ahead I saw a bat-like shadow which could only be Benoît. I was running on a bitumen road, but it felt as if my feet were sinking centimetres deep into shifting, warm sand with every step. When we reached the edge of the Cercle, we changed to a fast walking pace. For a while, there was just our panting. It was several minutes before anyone spoke. Then Alex shouted 'Yoohoo!' or something. It sounded like a war cry. Benoît gestured at him to be silent.

At the fork in the road into the hills, he stopped.

'This is where we separate,' he said. 'Alex goes back to the demonstration via the park. I'm going via the Rue Gallant. And you, Lucas, are walking home.' He pointed at the dark woods and fields up the hill.

'Thanks,' he said, patting my back in a fatherly way. 'Now I know I can count on you.' The pine trees on the hill rose into the sky like pointing index fingers.

'Just one other thing, Lucas,' he said as I was about to take off.

'What?'

'Caitlin has deceived me.'

When I heard him say her name, I braced myself. 'Caitlin?' I said.

'She's been playing games with me. I'm looking for a way to pay her back.'

'You leave Caitlin alone, Benoît.'

'She said some things to me that I didn't like at all. To be precise: she said some really nasty things about me. I am not in the habit of just taking that sort of thing. And particularly not the underhand way she did it: first pretending to be on our side, and then thinking she can really put me in my place.'

'Don't lay a finger on her,' I said. I think my voice was shaking.

211

'I saw her just then, with those counter-demonstrators. She's one of those who keeps giving and giving in. A crawler and a weakling. A multicultural rat. I have to get back at her. In a way that really gets to her. I don't quite know how yet. But you know where she is vulnerable.'

His words gave me the courage to do what I hadn't dared do all that time. I grabbed him by the lapels and held his face right close to mine. He didn't budge an inch. 'You touch her and I'll shoot you down with your own gun,' I said harshly. There was a sob in my voice. There was nothing I could do about it.

'I thought you were against violence,' he said and coughed. With a small movement, he pushed me away from him.

I let my arms hang loose by my side. Alex, who stood watching us from a distance, said with a sneer: 'You're shouting!' He looked relaxed, obviously having been through all this before. I thought him pitiful, like myself. We're in the same boat, he and I, I thought. We've gone along with Benoît step by step. We've thrown Molotovs. Now we're both being sent in opposite directions, he to the demonstration, me home. Benoît put his arm round my shoulder as if nothing had happened.

'My boy, control yourself,' he said softly. 'I quite understand you're angry. You're in love with her. You don't know yet that friends are more important than romance.' I slapped his arm away. Without saying goodbye, I walked away, up the hill. When I got to the stone garden walls, I ran my hand along them to make sure I wouldn't walk into anything, as if I had gone blind. Higher up, I entered the woods. Repeatedly, I thought I saw a striped jumper moving among the trees. 'My cap,' I thought suddenly, 'my baseball cap stayed behind in the van.' Although I knew the way home like the back of my hand, I had real trouble not getting lost.

ONLY AFTER I'D had some sleep did I begin to realise just how desperate my situation was. Sounds which I used to barely notice now seemed to make the house feel strange, unwelcoming. The walls no longer offered protection. The dirty dishes on the sink, two of everything, were a trick to make me believe that my mother and I were still the only people in the house. The rooms seemed full of explosive scents. Nothing was what it seemed, or what it had been. I sat down to breakfast, but didn't touch it. I watched the column of ants crawling up along the kitchen cupboard, over the draining board and towards the fridge, slowly invading the whole kitchen.

When my mother came back from her shopping, I asked her if she'd bought the *Régio-Gazette*. She appeared rattled, as if someone had pursued her on the way back.

'No, why?' she asked, panting. 'Are you expecting important news?'

'Not really.' I got up to help her unpack, but changed my mind and went upstairs to stand on the desk. Caitlin was watering the potted plants. She saw me, but pretended not to notice. The white road separating our gardens crawled up like a snake. The sky had changed. For the first time this summer it looked grey and threatening.

I went to the smithy, intending to remove all traces of the cocktails. I would smash up the remaining bottles and burn the rags from which Benoît had torn strips for the fuses and which he had used to wipe up the spilled petrol. But I didn't get the time. I had just gone inside the smithy when I heard someone approaching through the long grass. Frightened, I threw everything into a bucket. It was Caitlin. When she came in, I nearly burst into tears. This had never happened to me before, but her strolling in so carefree, laughing, in her light dress, really affected me. She was so vulnerable. She stood before me and said: 'Murderer!'

'What do you mean?'

'It's written all over your face.' She had a piece of chewing gum in her mouth which flashed pink between her teeth as she spoke. I was totally bewildered. I gasped. I wanted to say something but had absolutely no idea what.

'God, Lucas, don't look so desperate,' she said, exaggeratedly gentle. 'There's a corpse hanging off your head, that's all.' I brushed my hand over my forehead and looked at my finger. A squashed mosquito was hanging from it. She laughed her tinkling laugh, and nudged me playfully, but I felt numb, and it was as if her arm passed through me like it would through a shadow.

'What are you doing?' she asked casually. She didn't mention that she'd noticed me watching her, and that confused me, too.

'Cleaning up,' I said truthfully. I felt gloomier than I can describe. And disappointed, although I couldn't say with whom or by what. She was unaware of all this, and started talking about Soeur's store of firewood, as if that was of any importance.

'I've come to tell you I'll need lots and lots more wood,' she said mysteriously. She interpreted my blank look as surprise, and explained: 'It's just possible that the convent will be chock-a-block this winter.'

'What do you mean?' I said, without feeling any interest in what she meant.

'All sorts of things are happening,' she said, almost in a whisper. 'But nothing has been decided, and it's still top secret. It has something to do with the presbytery that got burned out yesterday.' I couldn't speak.

'I went to the demonstration yesterday. I came past to ask you to come, but you had gone already. I'd hoped to see you there. Whereabouts were you?'

'I was there,' I said hoarsely, looking away from her. 'I was . . . at the end.' I was afraid she would ask more, but she went and leaned with her behind against the workbench, resting her weight on one leg, drawing circles in the dust with her other foot. She was wearing low black espadrilles.

'Oh, and you haven't heard the funny bit yet. You know who went off with our stack of wood? My mother! She came past it in the car and thought: that would be nice for Soeur this winter! and loaded up the lot.' I tried to force my face into a smile, and found to my surprise that I could do it.

'It's perfect, really,' she went on. 'Soeur couldn't possibly object to her bringing the wood.' She looked around sniffing, shifting her weight.

'Did you fill up the saw? There's a terrible smell of petrol in here.' I nodded. If she had asked me, at that moment, if I had been throwing firebombs, I would probably have nodded, too. I would even have been prepared to admit that I had heard someone calling out in the presbytery.

'I'm so excited,' she said. 'I have to do something with all this energy. I tried to dance, but I can't concentrate. A bit of manual work is what I need. Can we . . . ?'

I picked up the chainsaw and followed her outside, to the tree trunk which had already kept us busy for a few days.

I really slaved. I worked hard and fast and sweat poured off me. When I had finished with the saw, I put four blocks in Caitlin's arms, picked up six myself, and we walked together up to the road. While we went up and down, each time carefully waiting for each other so we could walk together, she began talking about the demonstration again. My exertions had numbed me, making her voice sound as if it came from a distant radio somewhere.

'The racists say they steal. And they make the neighbourhood unsafe. But why is that? What have we taught them? What are the values of the Western world?' Her mouth had become dry from exertion; the road was a fair way up, and the slope was steep. She swallowed before going on. 'Make lots of money. That's the lesson you learn in this country. How you do it, nobody really asks. You know, the people here with their restaurants, the farmers with their seasonal labour, the rich women with their foreign nursemaids, they're all breaking the law. They make their own rules, and nobody will ever be any the wiser. Well, those Arab boys are doing the same. They make their own rules to make money. So they steal and fence. Of course they take our bicycles and cars. But we steal their dreams first. They wanted to be teachers or shopkeepers. But because they couldn't, they set up other kinds of businesses. With stolen goods. Everyone is forever talking about *competition*. *Equality* and *solidarity* have become dirty words.' Her hair fell over her face as she bent down. She brushed it away, leaving black streaks next to her ear.

'Do you know why those guys are so racist? It all revolves around fear. All people's lives revolve around fear. You're afraid you'll fail, that your mother will become ill, that your bike will get stolen, that you'll die one day. You're afraid of everything you can't control. That's how it is, that's how we are made. The trick is to learn to live with it. But the problem with a lot of people is that they can't bear fear and uncertainty. So they make their own certainties: they make new rules, they want the death penalty brought back, they want to keep out anything that's new or different. They demand power. He who has power need not fear. And power is centred on itself. Me, me, me, and the rest can get lost! But get this into your head: it's not the Arabs who threaten our existence, but those men with their firebombs! They want dancers, writers, homosexuals and journalists in jail too. *They* scare me, not the black boy who takes off with my bike. If there's anything I've learned from my mother, it's this.'

I stacked my pieces of wood on the shoulder of the road, in the usual spot, where the grass had already straightened itself after being flattened by the previous stack. Then I helped her stack. She squatted down to help me, and when she sat down to take a break she took a long look at me, as if she suddenly noticed a strange colour in my face.

'My mother has forbidden me to tell anyone, but I think you have to know this,' she started. I was hearing everything through a screen of static. Her voice crackled and I had to really focus to understand her. 'She was one of the fifteen Jewish children here. Some of the food that was meant for your mother's sister went to her.'

217

'Oh,' I said.

'Swear you won't tell anyone, but this is so exciting it's beyond words: Soeur wants to do it again.' She clapped her hands.

'Do it again?' I asked stupidly.

'She says it's in the tradition of the convent. She wants to take in the refugees.'

'No!' I said, feigning disbelief. I believed everything, every word. Nothing surprised me.

'They're families, two from Zaire and about three from Chad. They have children, some very young. I've seen photos. Now that they can't move into the presbytery any more, they have to come here as soon as possible. Soeur is discussing it with the mayor. Can you imagine, Lucas?' She threw her arms up into the air as if she could already see them coming. 'That's why we need lots of firewood,' she said, suddenly moving her head intimately close to me.

The rest of the afternoon she could talk of nothing else. She went on about the atmosphere in the convent, and about the fact that it had been years since children had played in the garden. She speculated about the languages, and the kinds of music. While I listened, the message I wanted to give her became more and more urgent. The more she told me, the harder it became not to talk about it. When, quite a while later, she sat down again, this time to open the cans of cola she'd brought, I stood behind the boulder she sat on. With my left hand I raised the can to my mouth, while I put my right hand on the nape of her neck, which felt dry and warm. When she turned her head, I could feel the vertebrae in her neck move under my fingers. They felt quite fragile, like the bones of a bird.

'What are you doing?'

'Drawing your attention,' I said.

'Why?'

'Because I want to say something.' She shifted around on the rock, as if looking for a more stable position.

'So say it.'

'Don't have anything to do with Benoît.'

'I don't.'

'No, I mean: have really nothing to do with him.'

'That advice goes for you too. He's just as dangerous for you as he is for me!'

'It's not the same. I'm a boy. He can't dominate me; we're on the same level.'

'He can't dominate me, either,' she shouted, flushing with indignation. She shrugged off my hand. 'He's a fungus. He thrives on misery: on desperate situations and terrible conditions. And he does nothing to improve them.' I put both hands around my cola can and let the cold seep up through my arms.

'That's not true,' I said quickly. 'He does things, but they are the wrong things!' Thick clouds were appearing on the horizon, turning the sky a strange colour.

'A few days ago,' she said, 'I told him exactly what I thought of him. You saw it. I saw your face behind the skylight.' I blushed violently.

'Weren't you worried, just for a bit, that I had fallen for him?' she asked, almost laughing.

'No . . . yes,' I replied.

'Don't worry,' she said, getting up and walking away. 'I don't fall in love easily.'

THEN IT STARTED raining, from the clouds we barely even remembered existed. The change happened in just a couple of minutes: the sky turned purple, then grey, and cones of sunlight appeared through gaps in the clouds. Then the sky turned black, and the rain came, in floods.

When the sky started clouding over, Caitlin left 'to get this wood inside in time'. She went to fetch the car. While she was gone, I used the opportunity to remove any traces of the Molotovs. I had to be quick. I found a box of matches, lit one and threw it into the metal bucket with the gear.

That was a mistake. I hadn't reckoned on Benoît's carelessness. He must have spilled more petrol and soaked more rags than I thought. In my hurry, I broke the first match and this fell burning onto the ground. Instantly, the dust and dirt on the ground caught alight. The fire ran away from me like a small animal and jumped at the rags near the door. From there it spread to my grandfather's apron. What I hadn't dared do with Caitlin's dove I did now: I jumped at it and grabbed it with both hands. I fell on my knees and beat at it furiously. I particularly remember my fury, how I felt that my blows were meant to punish the fire rather than put it out. I was angry about the bad timing: I knew Caitlin was on the way with the car. She would be waiting for me, unable to understand why I had gone into the smithy, let alone why it was on fire.

The door caught fire. It started with the draught strips my grandfather had fixed on the jambs. Running up, fire consumed the pieces of paper attached to the doorjamb: the notice about rubbish collection days, the safety instructions for the chainsaw, a calendar with Swiss mountain scenes. I had no extinguisher and no water. The newspapers on the shelf next to the door caught, then the shelf itself. On it were bottles with 'flammable' warnings. And spray cans. Momentarily, I just stood. My hands didn't hurt. My actions were having some effect. I managed to extinguish some of the smouldering objects, and to get the fire out of the corner, so that it ran out of fuel. My best decision was to open the door. I dragged it open with one hand, using the other to pull at the wooden set of shelves until it fell over. As the shelves came down, the fire intensified, stimulated by the rush of oxygen and swirling dust. Then I pushed the whole lot outside where the hissing rain put it out.

They say a misfortune never happens by itself. In retrospect, the fire wasn't a misfortune, or even an accident, but just an incident. If nothing else had happened that day, I probably would have remembered it for a long time, a story you tell your children years later. But because, immediately after, something much more terrible happened, something that totally disrupted my life and abruptly put an end to my youth, it seems like something trivial, hardly worth remembering.

While I stood in the pouring rain, with my palms lifted up, I saw Caitlin's car coming down the road. She had her headlights on. I don't know what went wrong. Was it the terrible rain? Faulty brakes? The bend where, all through the summer, dozens of cars had slowed and perhaps lost drops of oil? The car slipped. I saw it happening. I saw the wheels slide inexplicably sideways and hit the shoulder. I saw them slide over the shoulder which had become sandy and weakened by the prolonged dry weather. The car was like an animal scrabbling about. It lost any grip, yet the wheels kept turning desperately. When the left wheels were suspended above the slope, the car seemed to throw its weight backwards and try to dig itself into the earth with its right wheels. But then it gave up and tilted over. As soon as it started falling, it went without any restraint. With its full weight it let itself slide into the gully, stiff and stretched out like a warrior in armour. In passing, it touched the tree trunks and boulders covering the hillside. It nudged them and let itself be dented. It threw itself upward again and slid deeper into the gully until, front first, it hit the bottom and planted itself there. Its fall caused a series of faint noises, damped by the rain. For a moment, the car stood helplessly, as if trying to find its balance. Then it caught fire.

I stood maybe fifty metres from the wreck. Before I was conscious of what to do, my body was already moving towards it. I think I shouted something while I ran, hoping help would come. I made slow progress over the cobblestones which were now slippery with mud. I was still moving when the car slowly settled back on its wheels, like a dog settling itself after some deliberation. A shower of sparks flew up, flaring briefly and then disappearing.

'Caitlin!' I yelled when I reached the wreck. The front of the car was smashed in. It was so deformed I had trouble finding the driver's seat. I went to the nearest door. I saw the back of a head with Caitlin's hair. Below, a suggestion of the flower pattern of her dress. The window was so dirty I could see little else. It was a few moments before I realised that it wasn't only the mud on the window that stopped me seeing in; sparks came from the splintered dashboard and thick smoke began to fill the car. I tugged at the door, but I couldn't pull hard enough with my burned hands and it wouldn't open. Flames shot out of the engine which had been pushed backwards. The rain had lessened to a thin drizzle now, hissing in the fire.

The window of the rear door was open a little way. I forced my hand through the gap and tried to open the door from the inside. That wouldn't work either, so I grabbed a piece of rock from the ground and threw it through the window. Immediately, a cat jumped out, hissing. Its pupils were wide, its claws spread in fear. It took off through the trees.

After the cat came the smoke. I could see so little I had to open the door by touch. Then I tried to wrench open Caitlin's door. She didn't get in the way. She was slumped sideways and didn't move. I could only hear her breathing and coughing now and then, like someone caught under the blanket in his sleep. I didn't see any blood. The door suddenly gave and fell off its hinges onto the carpet of pine needles. I pushed it out of the way to give myself space to lift Caitlin out of the seat. I squatted down to get at the right level to see what to do. Her upper body was slumped at an angle over the passenger seat. I would have to pull her towards me by her left arm. But she was still caught in the safety belt. The heat was unbearable. The bark of the tree jammed up against the engine started to hiss and burn.

I pulled on the belt like mad. The catch was caught under the seat, and the only thing to do was to pull the shoulder strap around her. Which still left the lap belt. I kept pulling, but the belt didn't budge. I was leaning right over Caitlin now, and the uncontrolled, jerking movements of her body made me desperate. Sweat covered her face like a glaze, and a rattling phlegmy sound came from her throat. I put my arms around her thighs, thinking to bring her legs round first and then slide her out from underneath the belt, but she

223

was caught fast. Her head fell back against my shoulder. In the corner of her mouth, the pink piece of chewing gum was stuck, linked to her tongue with threads of spittle. Quickly, I removed it and threw it away.

The thump of buckling metal sounded from near the petrol tank, followed by the hiss of petrol overheating. I put both hands on the horn button, hoping to call for help, but the battery must have been destroyed and the electrical circuit wasn't working.

How did I come up with the idea? I don't know; it was an act of desperation. I ran the fifty metres back to where I was standing when the accident happened. As I ran, I tried to remember Benoît's basic rules. The second one was: 'If someone is hurt, eliminate the danger.' But what was the first? Ring the ambulance? Stay with the victim? Mentally, I heard a clock ticking. I grabbed the chainsaw and ran back—much more slowly now, for the chainsaw was heavy and, with the skin gone from my hands in a few spots, I could hardly lift it.

I nearly died of fright when the first tyre blew up. When the second one went, I didn't react as much, even though I was closer and was beginning to fear not just for Caitlin's life, but also for my own. I started the chainsaw and bent over her. The heat inside the car was inhuman. I tried to protect myself by hiding my face behind my shoulder. My skin was stretched taut with the heat. Foaming fluid was coming from the radiator.

I cut the safety belt. It was quick and effortless, just one short pull and a few sparks flying when the saw touched metal somewhere. Some fell on my arm and my hand, but I felt no pain. The upholstery of Caitlin's seat began to burn.

Again, I tried to lift her, bending her body more forward this time, for she was free now and I could slide her along the seat. I'd assumed I'd be able to pull her free easily if I could bend her leg. I was wrong. I leaned right over to see what the problem was; her left foot was caught under a rod, some sort of shaft which had been pushed up through the floor of the car. Coughing from the smoke, I straightened up. Then I saw that the edge of her dress had caught fire. Instead of beating it out, I grabbed the chainsaw.

Having cut the safety belt, it seemed as if I had crossed a threshold. It was easy. It worked. I could save her life.

There was nobody to ask for advice. The fire didn't allow me any time; it was roaring in my ears and coming at me, hissing furiously. I felt infinitely alone and knew that, no matter what I did, that feeling would be with me for ever.

I could see the rod clearly. I knew the saw wasn't designed to cut metal. I was aware of how great the risk was that the chain would break, leaving me with nothing to free her. The tip of the saw was wide and hard to position. Her foot lay immediately below the rod, almost bent around it, her toes in the black espadrilles pointing upwards. Around me hung the smell of scorched flesh.

I think I did try. But there wasn't enough space. I had no room to manoeuvre. The shaft was too deeply embedded in the buckled metal. It was too hot. What exactly happened? I don't know. Did I slip? Could I no longer bear the hopelessness? Did I choose a terrible reality above the uncertainty? Was I afraid my hesitation would make things worse than necessary?

I couldn't cut through the rod, so I cut through her left leg. Then I dragged her out of the car. She fell across me on the ground, her hair in my face. I didn't look at what I had done, just extinguished her burning dress. I was screaming.

⅃

I SEEM TO remember shouting incessantly at the ambulance men: 'The foot, you've got to take the foot.' One of the three orderlies told me a few times that everything would be all right, that I needn't worry. Finally I heard him say something to a policeman who came and put his hand on my shoulder and led me away. But I didn't want to go away. I wanted to see. I think I wrenched myself free and went back.

The medic put an elastic tourniquet around Caitlin's leg. He tightened it with a movement that made me think of my grandfather tying up a bundle of branches. I saw disconcertingly little blood; it had soaked into the pine needles and the rain rinsed it away. A second medic slapped Caitlin on the cheeks. I saw her eyes open for a moment and then roll back, as if she was falling backward into a fathomless depth.

'For God's sake keep that guy away from here!' the first medic yelled at someone behind me. Caitlin was taken away, sirens screaming. The departure was chaotic because there were too many people standing around and because the mud, pouring down the slope, made every movement difficult. Near the wreck I found the pink chewing gum I'd pulled out of her mouth. I picked it up. The fire brigade smothered the wreck in a white powder, until it looked like a piece of experimental art. On the small parking area next to my grandfather's house stood a few cars, their headlights on.

The policemen took me to the blackened smithy and quickly questioned me. They were technical questions which I can't exactly remember. I had to tell them what had happened and what I had done. I was thirsty.

'We'll take you to the hospital,' they said, after they had measured things up in the rain and were back with me.

'Me? There's nothing wrong with me,' I said. The man pointed at my hands.

'I'll look after that myself. I'll rub some butter on them.' The policeman laughed sympathetically.

'You're coming with us,' he said. 'You're in shock.' I remember how his words totally amazed me. I didn't feel at all different from usual, and was under the impression that I was behaving in a normal, calm manner. Sweat was pouring off me, but that was from my physical exertions.

I remember nothing of the trip to the hospital, whether I was asked questions, or whether I answered. I do recall all the time scratching with my right thumbnail—the only one that wasn't burned—at the bloodstains on my jeans, as if I hoped they would peel off like bits of skin. I also remember that the image of the hissing cat pursued me into the hospital ward, where a pale-faced nurse gave me an injection to deaden the pain. Pain I didn't feel at all.

'Does anything else bother you?' she asked when she had finished. She had to repeat the question several times because I couldn't understand her properly. There was a whining noise in my head that only stopped occasionally.

That same evening, the hospital ambulance driver took me home. I asked him questions about heavy bleeding, infection, gangrene and coma. I questioned him about Caitlin, but he seemed to know next to nothing about her case, which made me impatient and suspicious, because I assumed he was lying. My mother, who had come after me on her bike in the rain, sat behind me. Although I was speaking calmly and clearly, she kept whispering at me to keep calm.

'Think about something else,' she said, the way she did when I was a little boy and called her because I was afraid in the dark. Like then, I felt like hitting her.

The first person to call me after my mother had made me comfortable on the couch with cushions was Benoît. It was late, nearly eleven, and it sounded as if he had tried several times before.

'Aha!' he said. 'Congratulations!'

'You've heard?' My bandages made it hard to hold the receiver.

'Yes, of course, it's been on the radio.' The kitchen smelled strongly of the piece of lamb my mother had put in the oven just before the accident. She had taken it out two hours late. The smell of scorched meat stung my eyes.

'Brilliant work, Lucas, I'm proud of you. I think I've already said this to you: you're a man of solid character.' I was dumbfounded by what he said. To me, my character seemed hollow.

'You know of course what I want to ask you. But I won't worry you with it now. I'll ring you in a few days about the practicalities. Things have to go on, the world doesn't stand still.'

'What are you talking about?' I asked.

'Doing this has proved your loyalty. I know I can now safely call on you for even more important matters.' I don't think I had the vaguest idea what he meant at the time. Yet

I began to feel panic rising in me. But I was so confused that I ignored it. My mother sat next to me, rocking, trying to work out who had rung from what I was saying. I hung up before she could figure it out, and the wondering expression stayed on her face for the rest of the evening.

The roast lamb had finished up in the rubbish bin, so she brought me a baguette and cheese. I was hungry. I put the piece of pink chewing gum that had been stuck behind my teeth for hours next to my plate. As I ate, one thought kept going through my head: Caitlin is in hospital, and here I am, comfortably lounging on cushions, eating a baguette and cheese.

THE PAIN IN my hands and my racing thoughts kept me awake all that night. My sleeplessness had the quality of a nightmare. The film of the past day constantly replayed itself before my eyes. Alternative versions kept offering themselves: I freed Caitlin's foot by lifting her up and turning her leg back ninety degrees and then pulling, or I put out the fire and let the firemen free Caitlin, or I cut a piece out of the floor of the car and dragged her out with that stuck around her leg, to be removed later. I tried thinking about something else. But my brain resisted. I couldn't switch off the replay function, and had to helplessly suffer the film on my retina rewinding itself and starting again.

Not long after midnight I got up, stood by the phone in my bare feet and dialled Moumouche's number with my right thumb. He was still up and asked, a bit surprised, how I was.

'Fine,' I said.

'Yes? Great. Why are you ringing?'

'Just checking that everything is all right down there,' I said casually. There was a brief silence on the line, as if the sound waves needed time to get to their destination. Then, with a conspiratorial snort, he laughed.

'You're drunk!'

'No, I'm not drunk,' I said and hung up. I rang Fred and Arno, and both of them, having been woken from their sleep, asked immediately what the matter was. Each time, I said I had rung to see how they were. I told them I was having a good time, had met new friends and was developing muscle cutting down all those trees. I made them tell me in turn what they were up to. If they tried to hang up, I asked a new question which kept them talking. In that way I managed to hear Fred and Arno talking about ordinary things for forty and twenty-eight minutes respectively.

Next morning, quite early—I didn't know where I was and had trouble remembering what had happened—I was woken by the doorbell. The rest of the night had been restless and full of dreams, so I turned over with difficulty and tried to go back to sleep. During the few seconds I was asleep, I had a strange dream: I dreamed that I got up, pushed my grandfather's desk under the skylight and, like every morning, looked to see if Caitlin was awake yet. I experienced every movement as perfectly normal. I didn't have to pretend, nothing seemed to have changed.

It was only when my mother knocked on the door that I fell back into reality, literally with a thud, for I dreamed that I fell off the desk onto the bed, hurting my hands terribly. From the emphatic way she called my name, I knew there was someone to see me.

It was Ruth, Caitlin's mother. I pulled on my jeans, taking longer than normal because I had terrible trouble with the buttons—my only pair of jeans with a zip was in the laundry basket, covered in blood and mud—and went down the stairs. She stood in the hallway, slightly bent, carrying a bunch of flowers, blinking constantly as if the light in the stairwell bothered her. I was fairly sure she had never been here before, and from the way my mother fussed over her, taking her flowers, helping her out of her raincoat, showing her in, it was clear she also felt ill at ease. Ruth sat down on a straight chair, rather than in the armchair. She wore grey slacks and flat shoes and constantly rubbed her fingers along the seam of her trouser leg.

Seeing her made me gasp for breath. Ruth? I thought. Here? What's the time? I wanted to ask questions, but I didn't have enough breath, so the words imploded in my chest and made me cough. She must have realised how shattered I was, for she bent over to me and said: 'She's going to pull through.' After which she thanked me. Somehow, it sounded like a reproach. Thank you for what, I asked myself. That she'll never dance again? I wanted to know all sorts of things: what the doctors had done yesterday, if she had asked for me, if she was in pain, but Ruth was just as impatient and began, almost imploringly, to ask me about what had happened. I described the sequence of events, the way I had done for the police two or three times.

'I couldn't get it loose,' I heard myself saying far more often than necessary. 'I tried everything. I pulled as hard as

I could, until I nearly collapsed, but I couldn't get it loose.' My mother was listening, standing in the kitchen doorway. I stumbled over my words as I spoke. There were gaps in my memory and I had to close my eyes to concentrate. The couch I was sitting on was the only thing that held me upright.

I probably didn't tell Ruth anything she didn't already know, and her reaction was unsatisfied and unfriendly.

'It's all so terrible,' she said. 'She's alive, and yet it's terrible. Can you understand that? All the bruises and cuts. And the pain.' I nodded. I understood completely. I had the feeling I had never understood anyone so well. I turned my head to the window and saw a string of cars on the road. They slowed in the bend. Most of them stopped; people got out, stood on the shoulder of the road, pointing down. The trees on the slope were black with moisture.

'Do you know what the worst thing is for me?' she asked. She looked quickly at my mother. 'That I wasn't there. I wasn't where I should have been: with my child in her need. And I know she must have called out for me. Everyone calls for their mother when it comes to it.' My mother clasped her hand over her mouth and turned her head away.

'But it could have been worse,' Ruth continued. She made a small movement with her arm towards me. Everything she did seemed slow. She seemed to think deeply about every word she spoke.

'How are your hands?'

'They're healing,' I said, instantly blushing with shame. She seemed unaware of it.

'I know you're impatient to see her,' she said. 'But I must ask you to wait till tomorrow. I really think that it's too soon.' I was unsure how I wanted to react to that.

'No, no, I don't need to see her today,' I said, intending to reassure her, but as the words came out, I felt they were ill chosen. I confused her, as she did me, and perhaps that was why she left very soon after. The conversation had totally exhausted me, almost like an exam that goes on for hours and takes everything out of you. My mother brought the TV into the room and selected a channel which I watched for the rest of the day.

Early in the evening I got a phone call from the chief of the fire brigade. He said he had been on the spot that morning with the police. I looked out through the hall window and saw it was still raining.

'We've studied the wreck thoroughly. We couldn't see much yesterday with that weather. We now know where the fire started and how that rod could have been pushed through the floor of the car.' Rainwater poured down along the window. The garden was so wet it looked like a varnished painting.

'We've been able to ascertain that it could have been a lot worse. If the petrol tank had burst, for instance, you would both have died.'

'Yes,' I said. I couldn't think of anything else.

'The fire brigade is going to propose that you be given an award for bravery. I can't promise anything, of course, but we'll do our best.' I thought about the wreck on the slope. They had been there, that morning. They had found Caitlin's foot. What had happened to it? Had they taken it to the police, or to the hospital, with the black espadrille still on it?

'How did you get it out?' I asked, my tongue instantly drying out.

'What?'

'Her foot.' It sounded like a swearword. It took so long before he answered that I thought he had gone away.

'Hello?' he said suddenly, shifting the blame for the silence onto me. 'I didn't understand your question?' He must have hoped I wouldn't have the courage to repeat it, but I did.

'I asked how you got the foot out.' Another silence, shorter this time.

'We removed the amputated limb,' he said. 'Yesterday evening, as soon as the danger of an explosion had receded.'

'It *couldn't* be removed,' I said. At least, I thought I said it. In reality I *shouted* it. For a moment, it was as if I was still on the spot where it had happened, and as if I had to convince someone in a matter of seconds.

'Yes, you're right,' he said, drawing out the 'yes'. Maybe he did that to calm me down, but it had the opposite effect. I felt he was holding something back.

'Well then?'

'The rod had been pushed through the floor. Her foot was caught fast between the shaft and the floor. It wasn't humanly possible to pull it free.'

'So?'

'So what?'

'So what did you do?'

At the beginning of the conversation, the man's voice had sounded warm, like an older man's. Now he started stammering. His voice sounded higher than before and I guessed he was only thirty or so.

'The shaft had snapped at the other end. We could simply slide it back.'

'Snapped?'

'Yes, probably as the car fell down the slope. It was just a loose piece of metal.' I repeated the sentence in my head. And again. The chill of the floor was creeping up my legs. I would have liked to put my glowing hot hands around them. Before I hung up, it occurred to me that from now on I would probably always be either too hot or too cold.

I didn't read the papers that day. If I had, I would have been able to read about the girl Caitlin who had wanted to be a dancer. I would have found an interview with a surgeon explaining that re-attaching a foot can only be done in the most favourable circumstances, that the damage to the nerves and muscles was such that restoration of functionality was impossible, and that an amputation takes a future prosthesis into account. The scar tissue has to be positioned in such a way that pressure from the artificial limb won't cause pain. I would have been able to see journalists having their say about the fact that Caitlin had a licence, but, by our laws, was too young to drive a car. I would have been able to admire photos: of the wreck, of the road, of myself, my hair dripping wet. And of course there was a diagram of what the wreck looked like, where the rod had come through the floor and how Caitlin's foot was caught under it. The drawing was wrong. The diagram showed the rod pressing on the instep, but it had been higher up, near the ankle. I only discovered the mistake days later, at a time when I no longer had the courage to put things right.

And I didn't leave the house, not even to have a look at the wreck. It was removed by a tow truck the following day, making it even less worth the bother of putting on shoes and going outside. People came to the door, wanting to see me, journalists as well as others, and they also wanted to know

235

where Caitlin lived. My mother refused them all entry to the house.

&

ALTHOUGH I HAD HARDLY spoken to anyone, there was another detailed report in the paper the next day—the second day after the accident—longer and more elaborate than the previous day. My whole biography was in it—I had no idea where they got it all from. They went on about 'the hero of Sainte-Antoine' and about how courageous I had been and how fortunate a coincidence it was that I had been in exactly that spot at the right time. I read the articles with a kind of detachment, as if it were an exciting story and I didn't know the outcome. The facts were so changed and distorted that it actually seemed like the story of another, parallel event somewhere else in the country.

I tore the articles out of the various papers and arranged them roughly in a folder the way I had seen my grandfather do. If I got bored, I reread them, trying every time to approach them as if I hadn't heard the story before, and would only discover what it was about in the course of reading it. It was a strange, silly game I used to kill the time and exercise my imagination. I didn't break down. Heroes don't break down. That was a heavy responsibility. With hindsight, it was probably that responsibility that brought me close to a nervous breakdown.

'There's been a fire in the smithy, too,' said my mother, coming in from the garden, finding me at the breakfast table. She pretended she had only discovered it right then, but I knew she had known all along and had deliberately waited a day before mentioning it.

'I filled up the chainsaw just before the crash,' I said. I made a concentrated effort to raise my cup to my mouth. She stood still and looked at me fixedly.

'I must have spilled some,' I said, irritated by her incomprehension. 'And just after that I dropped a match.'

'Lucas!' she said warningly, but already turning away from me, busy with the coffee filter. 'How could that be possible?'

'It's obviously possible,' I said resignedly. She didn't pursue the topic. She pretended she was busy and had no time to discuss things like this, but I knew she didn't feel like hearing the details. It seemed as if she was hoping that, by not talking about it, the smithy would return to its former state. I realised more and more that she believed that things you didn't talk about were more readily forgotten.

Neither of us had any inkling of the sorts of questions doing the rounds in Montourin, until, a little later, a journalist from the *Régio-Gazette* came up the hill and walked into the kitchen before my mother could stop her. I dived into the living room, from where I followed the conversation.

'Is it possible your son reacted too quickly?' she asked in a deep voice. My mother didn't offer her a seat and I could hear her shoes clacking on the floor. 'They say that that rod was actually loose, and could have been slid back.'

'The petrol tank was about to explode,' said my mother. She just carried on tidying. It made more noise than usual.

'How could your son know that? A fire in the engine doesn't automatically mean the tank will explode.'

'He was prepared for the worst,' my mother replied.

'Why does your son avoid the press? Does he have things to hide?' I could feel her moving my way, but my mother, more resolute than I have ever heard her, asked the woman urgently to leave me alone and to go away. The wet footsteps moved away.

'I still think it's strange,' the hoarse voice said in parting.

'Yes, I'm sure you think it strange,' my mother echoed in a way that nearly made me laugh. When the journalist was out of the door, she came to me and said she didn't think she had ever been so rude to anybody.

I don't really know what I did the rest of that day. Did I sit and stare out of the window? Did I follow my mother about the house? The hours went on endlessly. Evening came. I didn't go to the hospital, and my mother didn't ask me why. I slept badly that night. It was near morning when I finally dropped off, and because my mother didn't wake me, I slept till after noon. The rest of the day I spent watching television. Towards evening someone rang the bell. Before I even opened the door, I knew it was Ruth.

'You haven't been to see her,' she said immediately. 'I know why: the fire brigade rang us, too.' She wore flat shoes with white socks and looked tired. Her eyes looked feverish, as if she was fighting some illness.

'I came to tell you that we understand. I mean, you mustn't feel guilty because you didn't push the rod aside. You couldn't know.' She broke off her sentence and looked away. Her eyes misted over, but before tears could flow she blinked. Her voice recovered and she went on.

'Caitlin remembers almost nothing. She has so many questions.'

'I'll come with you if you can't face it by yourself,' said my mother once Ruth had gone. I told her that was unnecessary. She wrapped a box of chocolates in polka dot paper and tied a ribbon around it. Next morning, straight after breakfast, I walked down the shepherds' path, the box of chocolates under my arm. Of course I had to pass the spot where the accident had happened, and that was what I was most worried about at first. I didn't want to be reminded of what had happened. I didn't want to breathe the smell of petrol, scorched earth and melting rubber. But walking past it was easier than I had expected, because all the time I was concentrating on what exactly I was going to say. The more I thought, the more I got myself into a mess. I thought of the way she was going to look at me and say, 'Did you say something?'

At Challon's Bluff, I sat down. I unwrapped the box and examined the contents. I let the box slide down the rock and returned home.

'So?' asked my mother when she found me at the kitchen table. I looked at her, and my expression must have shown her how desperate I was. She asked no further questions, not even about the chocolates.

For my part, I fell into a protracted silence which I kept up for several days. She did ask me questions, but I only answered with a yes or no. For the rest, I sat staring out the window, anxiously waiting for Ruth to come. My hands made it impossible to play patience. My mother gave me the books my grandfather had borrowed from the library long ago, but I have little patience with literature. Mostly, I sat with the phone balanced on my knee. I dialled random numbers, usually resulting in a female voice announcing that the number was not connected. Occasionally someone actually said 'hello', and then I would hang up. What did keep me occupied was channel surfing on television. I tried to watch everything at once and managed quite well. I could follow three films at once without feeling I missed anything. At first it gave me a headache, but I got used to it. They were thought-free hours when I got so absorbed by the rapid progress of different storylines that I forgot my own existence. But it wasn't good for my burns, which I unbandaged from time to time. Because of the contact with the air, the wounds formed dry crusts which I thoughtlessly picked at until they started bleeding, and after a while they became infected.

To make me feel even more peculiar, I was persistently constipated. The contents of my stomach seemed to have changed into a solid lump and I'd sit on the toilet for minutes on end without anything happening. It was extremely uncomfortable, made my mood even worse and made me, if possible, even more afraid of mixing with people. I decided to not eat anything; it seemed the only solution.

Ruth stayed away. It was as if she, like me, had given up. I slept far too much, except at night, because then I lay thinking about the accident, my eyes wide open. If I tried to look into the future, I saw nothing, and that was because I wouldn't allow myself to think of the approaching confrontation. The more time passed, the more acute became my indecision. In my mind, I talked constantly with Caitlin. If I shut my eyes, I saw her falling.

Early in the evening, around the time visiting hours at the hospital were over, I stood on the desk in my room, waiting for Ruth to come home, usually by herself, but occasionally accompanied by Soeur, who stepped out of the taxi cautiously, as if her legs were made of baked clay. Each time, I saw her look in my direction. Each time, I ducked and had to fight a feeling of constriction in my chest which made it impossible for me to breathe regularly for seconds at a time.

One evening we were startled by Copernicus screaming by the screen door. My mother poured him some milk in a saucer which he licked up ravenously.

'Soeur won't let him in any more,' she said when I came out onto the terrace to see what was the matter. A moment later we were having a row. I should be doing something, she said. I should get out. She thought I was making myself appear suspect, the way I was behaving like a dog that had been beaten. I should go and see Caitlin, no matter how much it worried me. The first few days I kept refusing on the pretext that my hands were still too sore. When the bandages had come off and the wounds had healed over, I just refused without looking for an excuse. All that time, it kept on gently raining.

Meanwhile, Benoît was relentlessly after me: he rang, wrote letters and eventually even sent a telegram which I found, accidentally, near the front door. It lay in a puddle of rainwater the sharp wind had blown under the door. I opened it and read that I should contact him. I didn't.

&

THE DAY AFTER the telegram, Soeur came. I had seen her coming; the taxi bringing her home from the hospital stopped in front of our door instead of moving on.

My mother was not home, and I didn't open the door. But from the moment she'd rung, I didn't dare move, switch on a light or get a drink for fear she was waiting somewhere by a door or a window expecting me to be coming home soon. It became a terrible evening. Cramped up, I sat where I was and the problem became so intense it began to feel as if I was being stalked by a dangerous animal. After a couple of hours had passed, I must have realised what was happening to me. I examined myself, and saw that I had locked myself inside a cage the size of this house, not just that evening, but for the whole past week, and that no one was going to get me out of it if I didn't free myself. A brilliant insight, but I had no idea what to do with it. My fear made logical thought impossible.

It was another hour before my intellect showed me the solution. My emotions resisted with all their strength, but I stood up instantly to deny them the chance to stop me. I walked outside, crossed the road and climbed over the low wall without using my hands. I detoured through the convent garden, at that moment not quite knowing what exactly I was planning to do. The geese floated on the water, graceful as moored sailing ships. The shrubs were full of scents and rustling sounds. The convent looked like a deserted factory building. By the time I got to the patio, my shoes were covered in mud. I knocked, and suddenly there were all sorts of sounds: a chair being moved, footsteps, the jingle of keys.

'Who's there?' asked Soeur from behind the door.

'Lucas,' I said. The silence which followed was predict-able and unavoidable. I waited for it to pass. I must have expected something else, for when she opened the door and motioned me to come inside, I stayed where I was. She looked me over briefly, and then peered with half-closed eyes over my shoulder, as if she expected me not to be alone. I entered and she shut the door. She sat down on the edge of a chair, both hands on the edge of the table for balance, her walking stick between her knees, as if to prevent her sliding down. She pointed out the other chair, diagonally opposite hers, its back to the window.

The kitchen smelled of insect spray. The furniture had been moved. The armchair had been pushed against the opposite wall, and a small daybed now stood where it used to be. They were preparing for Caitlin's return. She was going to come home and lie on a bed in this kitchen. The realisation struck me speechless.

'How are your hands?' asked Soeur, because I didn't say anything. I showed her. She looked at them, or at least I thought she looked at them until I noticed she had shut her eyes. She sighed.

'I was at your place earlier,' she said.

'I know.'

'Caitlin had a telephone call,' she said, emphasising each syllable. 'From Benoît.'

'Benoît,' I repeated. There was a teapot on the table, over a warmer. She lifted the mug she was holding up to her mouth and slurped the tea. The backs of her hands were covered in liver spots.

'That boy has been here a few times. I don't know if there was anything between Caitlin and him.' She looked at me questioningly to see if I knew any more. The kitchen was damp. The rain must have penetrated through the floor or the walls. I shrugged my shoulders.

'He didn't say much. Only that the . . . the business with the chainsaw wasn't an accident.' She paused, but I don't think she expected me to say anything. It was more to allow time for the words to get to me. She continued. 'He claimed it was a pay-off. He actually said: "I have something to settle with you, and because Lucas knows better where you hang out he promised to do it for me." Something like that. Caitlin couldn't remember precisely.'

'Yes . . . and?' I said, incredulously waiting for what would come next.

'That was all he said.'

I didn't answer. I remembered the morning I had seen the bathroom from under the surface of the water. That was how the world looked now: blurred, mottled, constantly in motion. Just like then, I had the feeling that the water was penetrating my head through my ears and filling it to bursting. Water just a little warmer than body temperature, making me glow and become drowsy. Soeur spilled a few drops of tea and I suspected it was my fault.

'It's not true,' I said vehemently. I knew I was speaking too loudly; there was no need for that. She turned her face towards me alertly, as if I had called her name. 'What do you think? That I pushed her into the gully? That I shifted that rod over her foot? How could something like that be a pay-off? How do you think you would set up something like that?'

'I know!' said Soeur, also speaking too loudly. 'But why does that boy say things like that? What's behind it?'

'He fell for her.'

'Why does he want to get you involved?'

'He asked me to do something to her. To avenge him,' he said.

'To avenge him?'

'Because she had turned him down.'

'But you told him you wouldn't do it.'

'I said nothing.'

'So you wanted to do it.'

'I didn't want to do anything. I wanted to go home.'

'He is your friend.'

'I thought he was my friend.'

'Didn't you feel just a bit that you had to do what he had asked you? If only to impress him?'

'That never crossed my mind.'

'Then why didn't you at least try to push that rod back?'

'Do you think I should have left her sitting there and taken the time to walk quietly around the car and have a tug at everything?'

'That is not what I am asking. I am asking why you could not have kept your cool.'

'I was in a panic. I had to make a decision.'

'And the fire extinguisher? It was underneath Caitlin's seat. According to the fire brigade, you didn't even *try* to get it out. You could have gained a lot of precious time if you had put the fire out first.'

'It didn't occur to me.'

'Perhaps you just decided it was the right moment? Two birds with one stone: you a hero and Benoît avenged?'

I wanted to get up, slam my hand down on the table, pull the chair out from under her, because I was furious and couldn't understand what business it was of hers. I felt how deeply she hated me, and how old that feeling was, perhaps as old as my grandfather. The aversion I had already felt for her as a child rose up massively inside me. She was old and had a sour smell. I shouldn't have come. I didn't want to talk to her, but she was forcing me.

Before I could get away, the sound of footsteps outside paralysed me. In a flash, I thought it would be Caitlin, but realised immediately that wasn't possible. Soeur went to the door with her bunch of keys, asked who was there and opened the door. It was Ruth. She seemed genuinely surprised to see me.

'Lucas?' she said. 'How are your hands?' While I replied, Soeur kept restlessly walking up and down, like a child caught at something.

'I've told him,' she said suddenly, her face turned to Ruth, but pointing at me. Ruth instantly looked at me. I had stood up. The situation seemed unfair. Two against one.

'But Soeur,' said Ruth, her arms limp by her side, 'I had asked you particularly not to . . .'

'It was necessary, Ruth. The question had to be asked. There is no need to go easy on him. Being silent about those things makes no sense; I should know.'

'What did you say?'

'I simply asked him why he panicked. You have asked me that question so often. Now I am asking him.'

I knew the moment had come to say what I wanted to say. They were forcing me. I turned the words over in my mind before saying them. But they tumbled all over themselves like spilled matches. I was so confused I started breathing faster to keep up with myself. I don't know if I did anything strange, but Ruth rushed to me and suggested we get some fresh air out in the garden. She held out her arm to help me walk. The candle under the teapot flickered.

246

She guided me towards the pavilion. Three cats followed us, apparently thinking we were carrying something edible.

'I can tell you why I panicked,' I said, knowing that the only way I would have the courage to give her an answer was to commit myself right away. She looked at me attentively, as if I was about to tell her a story.

'Caitlin taught me to think of the future,' I said. 'That was the first time I'd ever done that. She talked about *later*. Because of her, I'd started to wonder what I want to do later. What I want to be. The better I got to know her, the more I thought that my future was linked to hers.' This sounded well prepared. And so it was. Perhaps that's why it sounded insincere. I was embarrassed before I even finished speaking.

'When the accident happened,' I went on, talking in time to our steps, 'I saw not just her future disappearing, but mine as well.'

'In other words, you were in love with her,' she said. I felt just as ridiculous as I had expected. I think I nodded.

'When I saw the fire, I thought that everything was going to be destroyed, including me. When I was trying . . . just after the crash when I stood with the saw in my hands . . . I really didn't think I . . .' I began to stammer. The words wouldn't come. 'I mean . . . I thought. I thought very clearly. I thought I was being clever. Only later . . . the fireman said . . .' I don't often cry. It had been a few years since I had cried. I found it infuriating, not so much because of the tears, but because of the uncontrollable, ridiculous changes in my voice, making it go higher and higher and become more and more halting. I turned my face away from Ruth and decided not to say anything for a bit.

With a gentle push in my back she led me to the pavilion.

'I hear that all this wood has come from you?' she said carefully, as if afraid that what she said would make me cry even more. I shook my head, in a movement that could equally mean yes or no.

'We're grateful to you,' she said. I turned around, pretending to examine the quantity of firewood. Liquid dripped from my nose. I wiped it away with the back of my hand. Without the sunlight streaming in, the space seemed small and dank, perhaps not the best space to store firewood. We were silent for a while.

'My grandfather used to do this, too,' I said to show I was capable of speaking again. She nodded.

'Yes,' she said, 'he put himself out.'

'He had something to make up for,' I said. She stood behind me now, her face turned away, her head lifted up as if, through the window, she could see someone coming and was trying to see who it was.

'Yes,' she said thoughtfully.

'Why is Soeur doing this?' I asked suddenly. 'Why do those Jewish children persecute me after all those years?'

'They obviously haven't told you everything.'

'I know those nuns were put up against the wall. I understand that was terrible for her, but to still . . .'

'Have you ever wondered why Soeur wasn't killed too?'

'I don't know . . .'

'She wasn't there.'

'Oh.'

'The afternoon the Germans burst into the convent, Soeur had been called away. She had to go into Montourin to have her papers checked. Soeur maintains to this day that your grandfather had set it up. That he had organised it with the Germans.' She paused, as if to measure the effect of her words. I saw her looking at me sideways. Then she went on: 'Soeur and your grandfather knew each other from when they were small children. After years of doubt, she decided not to choose him. He never came to terms with her entering the convent. That's why Soeur is so bitter: she feels that she shares the guilt for the death of those five nuns, that she too should have been shot that afternoon.'

I felt as if I was waking from a life-long sleep, as if all the balls of my inner pinball machine were slipping into their slots. At the same time I felt as if I had been hit hard, somewhere between my eyes and my nose. I had a taste of blood in my mouth.

Ruth led me away from where we stood. She walked quietly ahead of me, looking around as if inspecting the garden. I realised that, although she didn't envy me my situation, she could feel no pity for me.

'I was there; I saw it all happen. This place is full of terrible memories. Yet I come back every year. Soeur is like a mother to me; I have no one else. I know she has her sharp edges, but you have to forgive her. We're all a bit in shock, I think. After all, Caitlin has lost her foot.' Horseflies came up from the pond, flying around our heads. Ruth hit out at them in vain.

'I keep thinking of Caitlin as a toddler,' she said. 'Even then she danced, her little arms lifted up high. She'd stretch her legs, and jump as high as she could.' The ground was soggy and dragged at our feet so that they made sucking noises as they came up. She was wearing light, flat shoes, and the small holes of the pattern in the leather were getting filled with mud. I could feel the cuffs of my trousers and my socks getting wetter and wetter from the grass.

'She was flawless when she was born,' she said. 'If you ever have children, Lucas, you'll find out: the first thing you do is touch. You can't believe your eyes, and so you touch: the hands, the nose. Caitlin was perfect. She had lovely, mobile feet, which curled up if you ran your finger along the sole. The doctor congratulated me.' The garden was still around us, the grass full of seeds. Suddenly, Ruth turned and looked me straight in the face.

'Do you know what I ask myself these days, Lucas?' I waited. 'Is anybody ever going to fall in love with her now?' I didn't know what to reply. Above all, I couldn't understand how she could say something like that. I thought it was a cheap shot, a blow below the belt. As if she too, through me, wanted to take revenge on my grandfather. She kept looking at me.

'Why don't you want to talk to Caitlin?'

'Because I'm not sure that I have saved her life,' I answered, distressed.

'It's still strange, Lucas. It's as if you are hiding something.'

She turned her back on me and strolled to the convent. Bewildered, I walked back through the garden. I was so upset I couldn't find the gap in the wall right away, and even once I was standing in front of my grandfather's house I suddenly wasn't sure which door I usually went in.

My mother still hadn't come home. I went to the phone and called Benoît. I had to call Directory first to get his number; he had always rung me, and I had never felt it necessary to ask him for his number. To my surprise, I heard his voice on an answering machine, saying I could leave my message or send a fax after the beep. I said I had to speak to him urgently. I didn't say who I was, but I only realised that once I had hung up.

I went into the living room to wait for my mother. It was gradually becoming clear to me that nothing was as it had been. As soon as she was inside, still in her raincoat and with her umbrella dripping on the floor, I told her the story of Soeur and Grandfather. She listened to me, her face expressionless. When I had finished, she said: 'I've had the feeling all my life that he lied to me.' Without interrupting the flow of her words, she removed a fleck of tobacco from her lower lip with her thumb and index finger. Then she simply went upstairs. I stayed in the armchair and read the half-wet newspaper I found in her bag. For the umpteenth time there was an article about me. The story of the rescue with the chainsaw seemed to stir the imagination of the town's inhabitants endlessly, perhaps because it was like a horror thriller. They couldn't read or talk enough about it. It was as if the national interest was at stake. There was a special feature about panic. The writer outlined how people react in a panic. Often, their reactions are exaggerated, because they no longer think logically, he said. People of an impulsive and quick-tempered nature will react wrongly in a panic situation. They actually assume they will make the wrong decision, with all its consequences. This attitude of self-doubt can lead in two directions: either they will watch without taking any action, precisely because they are afraid of making the wrong decision, or they get obsessed with the need to not just watch, and that obsession results in an over-reaction. A person like that will, for instance, apply heart massage to a person whose heart has not even stopped, killing a half-dead victim.

'Did the hero of Sainte-Antoine overreact?' the article asked in conclusion. I read the other reports on the page. I read things about me there which I knew nothing about and which I could not possibly have invented myself. The more I read, the more I was overcome by a feeling of hopeless resignation, as if I knew everything was going to slowly turn against me, and I didn't feel it worth bothering to try to do anything about it. Deep inside me, the conviction that I deserved no better kept growing.

I must have fallen asleep soon after, because I had a vivid dream in which I touched a newborn baby from top to toe, finding a heart-shaped birthmark on its lower back. When I woke up suddenly and decided I had better go to bed, I found my mother in the bathroom, bent over the basin. I thought she was cleaning her teeth. It was only when a strange odour reached me that I realised she was drunk.

᳒

NEXT MORNING, BENOÎT appeared in the living room. He wore a long, thin raincoat which swirled like a silken cape around him whenever he turned. He looked brilliant and colourful, like a plant after a shower. He had come in through the side door, so he must have walked through the garden, but there wasn't a speck of mud on his shoes. He carried a tall, fern-like pot plant, wrapped in cellophane, which crackled cheerfully when he put it down on the coffee table.

'So this is where you are,' he said. He took a few steps towards the window, turned and came back. His glance

252

rested briefly on the telephone which sat next to me on the cushion, but he didn't say a word about the many times he had tried to get through to me. The air in the room must have been stuffy for someone coming from outside, but I made no move to open a window.

'What's the matter?' he asked when I kept staring at him without saying anything. He smelled of ointment. He massaged his neck as he spoke.

'Of course you're wondering why I needed you so urgently,' he said before I could answer. 'They're looking for a new place for the refugees. Montourin is full of empty buildings; they won't need to look very far. We must be prepared. When the time comes, I want to be able to go into action without any delay.' I was amazed at his nerve. His words fell around me like stones. I could hardly believe that he was standing before me making this proposal after everything that had happened—particularly after his phone call to Caitlin.

'I'm going to denounce you,' I said, feigning calm. 'I'm going to go to the police and tell them everything.' He laughed, amused. He even winked. Fury exploded in me. I was glad of it: it was the first time since the accident that I had felt anything much at all.

'What are you going to tell them?' he almost giggled. 'That *I* pulled down the tree? That *I* threw the Molotovs? If it comes to it, I wasn't even there!'

I got up. I couldn't do anything else. 'You've gone too far, Benoît!' I said. My voice shook, and I wished it wouldn't because it made me sound so feeble. 'You've used me and I won't put up with it any longer.' His look showed only pity for me, and I realised I must look pathetic. I felt ashamed.

'Okay, go!' he jeered. 'Go on, go and see where you finish up. My dear friend, where do you think all the evidence points?'

'It'll be my word against yours,' I tried bravely.

'I don't think you quite see the consequences. They'll call you a communist faggot.' He removed the plant from the paper. The leaves opened out like spread fingers, and from the axil of each leaf little piss-yellow flowers protruded.

'You called Caitlin,' I said. I noticed that I was now so furious that hissing sounds interrupted my words. 'You told her the biggest lie anybody has ever thought up.'

His face was calm, as if we were having an ordinary conversation. He looked at me full of understanding. I could see the blackheads on his chin.

'It's fine,' he said, his voice infinitely mild. 'You don't have to work with us any longer. People who do it against their will are not much use to me. Practically no use at all, to be truthful. Although it does disappoint me. I had expected something quite different from you. But I won't try to change your mind. I couldn't; I'm not as persuasive as that. Anyway, I'd rather everybody made up their own minds. You just sit here quietly and recover. I'll just duck into the shed and fix a couple of cocktails, and then I'll leave you in peace. Although I must say I don't really like being treated this way.' I could see the muscles move in his cheek.

'Your gear isn't there any more,' I said, unable to mask the relief in my voice. 'I had an accident and the shed got half burned down.'

'Oh,' he said quietly. And again: 'Oh.' He looked around as if he had dropped something.

'Well, never mind. I'll find another solution.'

He left. I felt as though I was suffocating.

For the first time since the accident, I was angry enough to do something. I felt like a string someone has given an enormous tug, and which, minutes later, is still vibrating. I took a bath, changed my clothes and walked down the shepherds' path into Montourin. I was desperately anxious about going there, because I was sure I would be recognised everywhere. Fortunately, the police station was on our side of the town, so I didn't have far to go. Dead nervous I entered the building. The man at the desk was not the same man as last time, and for some reason that pleased me. I sat down on a bench, intending to wait until the guy who looked like a tap dancer would come by. I knew him best, and he inspired confidence. While I was waiting, several policemen asked me if they could help me. I told them I was waiting for someone, and they left me alone. When, after more than two hours, he came in, he took me into his office, which he obviously shared with other officers, but which, apart from three desks and six chairs, was empty. He invited me to sit down. Although it wasn't a sunny day, the blinds were down.

'Benoît?' he asked, when I had only just begun my story. 'Is that the Benoît I know?' I told him the family name, but as he didn't know it, we produced a description which made it clear we were talking about the same person.

'Does he live in the Rue Machiavelli?'

'That's right, in the Rue Machiavelli!' The man looked delighted. I wondered why.

'Great guy,' he said. 'Friend of your late grandfather, too.'

'He uses inflammatory language against foreigners,' I said. He spread his fingers on the tabletop. Behind him, a spiral staircase led to the next floor.

'He gets a bit too concerned,' he said, 'and he rather likes making his opinions known. But you can't blame him for that. He doesn't mean half of what he says.'

'It's possible that one day he won't stop at words,' I tried. He leaned back in his chair and rolled his pencil from one hand into the other. He shook his head, clicking his tongue as if trying to pacify me.

'With guys like that, a lot of what they say is just bragging. Anyway, what would you want me to do? We believe in free speech in this country.'

'He has dangerous ideas,' I said, sounding more resolute than I felt. He gave me a long, penetrating stare.

'What exactly do you mean?' he said emphatically. 'Doesn't his way of thinking please you? It is actually no different from that of your late grandfather.' He leaned forward across the metal desk and added: 'If your grandfather had stayed in local politics, we mightn't be in such a mess now.'

I felt cold sweat running down my back. I swallowed and said: 'Sooner or later he's going to use violence.'

'Then we'll have to wait for that violence,' he replied with a thin smile. 'And if I can give you some good advice: don't make yourself look suspicious by coming here making crazy statements. You've attracted enough attention as it is.'

And so I left to go home, feeling I'd been punched in the stomach, rather than given an encouraging pat on the back.

When I was back on the street, I realised I was barely ten minutes' walk from the hospital. I wanted to visit Caitlin, but walking towards the hospital I decided I couldn't turn up empty-handed. I would have to buy her something. Flowers would be stupid, considering her mother had no doubt told her about our conversation in the pavilion. Grapes cause cramps, and chocolate slows the digestion. I hesitated outside a delicatessen for a long time, counted my money, and finally, because I didn't have too much on me, retraced my steps, determined to try again next morning.

When I got home, the paper was on the table. There was an item about the Hero of Sainte-Antoine having been injured some five weeks earlier after a scuffle with a group of Arabs. He was thought to have turned up in the Cercle armed, and to have been beaten up by hostile Arabs. The report simply appeared among other items, and no connection was made with what had happened later. It wasn't at all clear why the report was there at all.

What surprised me most was the mention of the weapon. When the police had found me, the pistol was gone. So it had to be the Arabs who had sent in this report. It hadn't occurred to me that, of course, I had enemies in that camp, too. Desperately, I tried to imagine how I could explain this new fact in Caitlin's hospital room. It completely destroyed the balance I had so carefully achieved. It was hours later that a possible connection occurred to me, but I rejected this immediately because I couldn't accept that he had anything to do with this: Benoît and his fax.

&

FROM THEN ON, my story was caught in a vortex. I lost all control. Fiction and reality merged. The rumours being spread about me took on a life of their own. I didn't resist. I was in a daze.

It started with the second visit of that journalist. Without me having let her in, she was suddenly in the room, asking me why my hands were so badly burned. I thought the truth would be the best policy, and told her that hadn't happened during the rescue, but just before, during a fire in the smithy.

'Forgive me asking,' she said sweetly, 'but the editors are getting more and more questions and suggestions from people who have thought about the incident. I have to follow things up.'

Next day, there was another article in the paper:

Now that quite a few people from Montourin have inspected the site of dancer Caitlin R. Meadows' accident, we have found evidence that there were obviously two fires: in the car, but also in a shed some fifty metres further on. When we made enquiries from the police and the fire brigade, it appeared that, strangely enough, they had paid no attention to this. They knew nothing about the fire in the shed and could not supply answers to our questions. According to them, the weather that evening was terrible and it had been impossible in the confusion of the incident to pay attention to a small fire which seemed to have no significance.

Home handymen often cause small fires, and often no assistance from the fire brigade is required.

Your paper set about asking the person concerned, L. Beigne, for an explanation. The boy stated that he had indeed had a small problem while filling the tank of a chainsaw shortly before the accident. He put the fire out with his hands. Of course, the fact that his hands were burned is possibly part of the reason why he could not simply push aside the metal rod, which protruded unattached through the floor of the car, instead of taking such drastic measures.

The very same day, the police arrived. They found me stretched out in front of the television, and only when they insisted did I go to the smithy with them. They found the bucket which contained bits of glass and the left-over corner of a rag which had been used to make the fuses for Benoît's Molotovs. They searched around a bit longer and found Benoît's gun in the case of the chainsaw. They put everything in plastic bags and departed. Next morning this was in the paper:

The police have confirmed that stories circulating about the 'fairly radical ideas' of the 'Hero of Sainte-Antoine' are being checked. The curiosity of investigators was aroused by a detail in the case which at first sight seems, to say the least, remarkable: the fire in the shed fifty metres from the site of the accident.

'Of course, we don't want to slander the boy, but there is no getting round the fact that there are a few things which need investigation,' was the police comment. Otherwise, Lucas Beigne is known in the area as a quiet, sensible boy.

Although his hair is cropped short, he has never been seen in any uniform. It is generally assumed that he is not associated with any of the more radical political groups. Yet he seems to have been acting somewhat suspiciously lately: he recently bought a pistol from R. Dumaret's gun shop in

the Route sur Mérinne, which was subsequently stolen from
him by a group of Arabs.

The interrogation that followed went over me like a steam-roller. I was put in a separate room, with a police officer next to me who didn't let me out of his sight for a moment. A man in shirtsleeves asked questions, while in the corner a policewoman wrote down every word I said.

He asked me things about my grandfather, about the gun they had found in the smithy, which they claimed had been used to shoot out the windows of the presbytery on May 10, about my short hair, about the demonstration, about the overalls and goggles which had been found, wrapped in a grey plastic bag, in the bushes along the road to the convent, about the chainsaw and the linden tree in the square in the Cercle, about the purple jerrycan which I had filled with petrol at the Pluvier service station on Thursday afternoon, about the van in which my baseball cap had been found, covered in egg, and about the bottles and the fuses in my shed. I had only one defence: I kept mentioning Benoît's name. The man in shirtsleeves lost his patience and said he wasn't interested in Benoît, it was me he was questioning. I was not allowed to go home that evening. I was not allowed to see the papers. By chance, the television was on in the small room where I had to wait. My story had by now become such a hot item that the regional TV station had picked it up. To my amazement, I saw Benoît being interviewed. He looked clean and relaxed and looked into the camera with his long eyelashes.

'Lucas Beigne is a hothead,' he said. 'He probably reached for the chainsaw sooner than necessary because Caitlin is Jewish. He has said on more than one occasion that those

Jewish people shouldn't be staying in that convent, that his grandfather would not have countenanced it, and so on. Lucas went about with us occasionally, but we really thought he was too radical.'

'Didn't his ideas fit with yours?' asked the interviewer, who stayed off camera.

'Listen, we want foreigners out, but in a humane way. We would never go as far as Beigne. But this is a typical problem for our party: some of our hangers-on bring us into disrepute because they are hard to control.' The picture shifted away from him. I sat open-mouthed. I was so impressed by the ingenious way he had managed to twist the facts to his own purposes that I almost felt inclined to applaud. There were pictures of my grandfather's garden, the smithy and the site of the accident.

Off-screen, Benoît's voice continued.

'The police can search my property. I have an apartment and I rent a cellar with it to store some of my things. There I keep the guns I use for hunting—I have a permit for every one of them. Pistols and revolvers I don't use.'

The newsreader appeared on the screen. He added one more sentence before going on to the next item. He said it was expected that Caitlin Rose Meadows would lay charges against Lucas Beigne.

BECAUSE I DIDN'T have a record, and was a minor, I was allowed to go home to wait for the outcome of the investigations. I had to be available to the police at any time. Alex, who, according to the man who spoke to me, had also been questioned, had to stay. I read in the paper that he had said: 'I'm not a criminal. I campaign against crime.' He insisted from beginning to end that he had acted alone.

I ate even less than before. During the long days that followed, I did nothing except watch television and keep silent. But my mother wouldn't leave me in peace. She said I had to go and see Caitlin, or at least Ruth, to explain everything.

'If they lay charges, you'll have no end of trouble,' she said, 'and the whole business will cost us a fortune.' She asked me, begged me, to go to the convent. But I couldn't. I was totally constipated, and the discomfort prevented me from thinking straight. I did keep an eye on the convent courtyard. There was an amazing amount of activity going on, with trucks coming and going carrying old-fashioned hospital beds, nappies, blankets, tins of food. All the windows in the building were wide open. Furniture was hoisted from one floor to the next with ropes.

The bustle made me anxious. When my mother went out to Montourin, I locked the doors. For some reason I was expecting Benoît to suddenly appear and, smiling calmly, do something terrible to me. I couldn't tolerate any noise; I kept the volume on the television right down. If a siren sounded in Montourin, my toes curled in fright. I didn't leave the house. On no account did I dare go near the smithy. I knew the chainsaw was there, and I couldn't get rid of the feeling that I would be capable of starting it and pushing it into my leg, just above the ankle, like I did with Caitlin.

'I've been to visit Caitlin today,' I said to my mother

one evening. But she didn't believe me and called a doctor. He was a long-haired young man who said I was suffering reactive depression. My mother listened to the phrase with her hand clasped over her mouth, suppressing a sigh. The man stayed and talked to her for a whole hour, but I paid no attention to their conversation.

Finally, he came and sat in front of me. He sat down on the coffee table, so he came between me and the television screen, and said I should do something I liked doing.

'What are your hobbies?' he asked when I didn't answer.

'I don't have any,' I said. He clicked the biro he had in his hand. He shifted his weight, making the table creak dangerously.

'What did you do before the accident?' he asked.

'Cut wood.'

'Can't you go back to doing that?'

'With the chainsaw?' I said sarcastically, enjoying the surprised expression on his face. I could see he could have kicked himself, so, to finish him off, I said: 'Just imagine if there was another accident!' We came to an agreement. For the time being, I didn't have to do anything, except ring him up every day at the same time to tell him what I had done that day and how I was. I promised, but without any real intention of doing it. He left with a worried expression that didn't suit his casual style at all.

The same day, a few hours later, there was a knock on the living room window. To be honest, I got a terrible fright and my immediate reaction was to dive into the easy chair and wait for the visitor to go away. But it was too late. A girl's face appeared behind the window which is far too high up for someone of normal size, so I guessed she must have climbed onto the empty crates that stood there. She waved at me, said something and jumped down.

'You're the person I need,' she said as soon as I had opened the door. She didn't come in, but waited for me to come outside. I noticed how she quickly examined me and thought for a moment about what to say. She had brown hair with a reddish sheen, and her accent showed she was not a local girl.

'I'm here with a station wagon full of sacks of potatoes. I thought there would be someone to help me, but the removalists have just left and there's only an old nun.'

I was nonplussed.

'I wondered if you would have the time. There are only five of them.' I was so dumbfounded I just put my shoes on and went with her. The clouds hung low, but seemed too light to bring rain. The girl—young woman really—talked like a cheerful, carefree holiday-maker who had no idea of the drama that had occurred here this summer.

'What a wonderful view,' she said, pointing at the town. 'I've always wanted to live in a place like this, on the slope of a hill. Do you live here, or are you on holidays?'

'On holidays,' I said.

'Oh, your hands!' she said suddenly, slowing her steps. She pointed at the scabs on my fingers, but I said that the worst was over and that it didn't hurt any more.

'Burned?' she asked, concerned.

'An accident with petrol,' I said, shrugging my shoulders.

'Will you be able . . .'

'Sure,' I said quickly. 'No problem.' She was wearing open, flat sandals and dirty jeans cut off below the knee.

I imagined she was a farmer's daughter, delivering potatoes door-to-door, but I turned out to be mistaken: she was a volunteer worker for the SRR.

'You may be familiar with that organisation?' she said, and as I didn't reply, she added: the Society for the Reception of Refugees.

'I've worked for them for four years now,' she added quickly. 'But I've never had to cope with fifty-kilo sacks before.' We walked into the courtyard of the convent. In front of the cellar entrance stood her clapped-out, gold-coloured station wagon, covered in bumper stickers, its doors and hatch wide open.

'She told me to put them in the cellar,' she said. She pointed at the first of the sacks and took it by two corners.

'Okay?' she asked as soon as I brought my hands up. I smiled to reassure her. We went down the stone steps, and when we entered the cellar, I noticed that the setup was completely different. Instead of confessionals, dusty cartons and pallets with crushed doves under them, there were now grey metal shelves with huge quantities of preserved food—ten-litre tins of peas, among other things, and boxes full of unappetising-looking sweets.

'Lots of stuff here,' I said, just to say something. She showed me where the potatoes should go, let go of her heavy burden with a sigh and said: 'You should see it upstairs. Haven't you been there yet?' She led me up the inside stairs, the way I had gone with Caitlin, and took me to the first floor. There were bunk beds in the many small rooms now, instead of the heavy wooden beds the nuns used to have. She showed me the bathrooms, a television room with sagging couches, smelling of cigarette smoke, and a spacious, beautifully set up play room, which looked like a real kindergarten. In several places it was clear someone had been working on the stoves: chimney pipes had been disconnected and there was soot on the floor. The woman told me that the heating was the greatest drawback of this new location.

'I hope it will be a mild winter, because there is no money to install central heating,' she said. 'For the moment, we're repairing the old wood stoves that have been sitting here unused for so long.' She showed me the corridors where volunteers had painted over all the windows in the last few days and took me down to the ground floor, to the dining room with the ash floor where all the tables and chairs had been arranged and the big mirror removed. Buckets of water stood along the walls, like in the other rooms we had seen.

'The fire extinguishers haven't arrived yet,' she said when she noticed me looking at them. 'And we're expecting a return visit from those neo-Nazis.' I felt the blood drain from my face. It was as if she had emptied one of the buckets over me.

We brought the rest of the potatoes down to the cellar. I was hoping not to come across Soeur, but if I had to, it would be better now, with a big sack of potatoes in my hands.

'Do you know what that nun told me?' said the young woman as if she had read my thoughts. 'That the Germans shot five nuns here at the end of the war because there were Jews hiding in the cellar. Those geese . . .' She pointed at the pond. 'They were supposed to be a warning if anybody was coming. When the Germans had finished with the

266

nuns, they used up the rest of their bullets blowing the geese to pieces.'

When we had finished, she thanked me and I said goodbye. I crossed the road, but didn't go into the house. I went to the smithy and looked for my grandfather's axe. It was where I had put it away after the chainsaw had been fixed. I let the steel glide along my hands a few times. I went out and started hacking at the first piece of wood I came across. Because the pain wasn't too bad, I walked through the garden, some way down the hill to find a tree trunk. Just to be on the safe side, I took a pair of cotton work gloves with me.

For two hours I chopped without stopping. For a break I went over to the woodshed to fetch my grandfather's wheelbarrow. Returning to my tree trunk, I stacked the wood that was ready in the wheelbarrow, and because it only half filled it, I went on chopping for another hour. Although it didn't seem as hard as it had been the previous time when it had been so hot, I could feel myself getting impatient. The work hardly progressed. I felt like someone from the Middle Ages.

When my barrow was full, I walked to the convent with it. To my surprise, I saw that the gold-coloured station wagon was there again, this time with two second-hand children's bikes and a tricycle in the back.

'Fantastic!' the young woman called when she saw me coming. She had two friends with her who helped me unload like a pair of high-spirited girl guides.

And that is why I started working with the chainsaw again. I had been terrified of taking that step. I was convinced the blade would still be covered in blood, but I noticed someone had cleaned it and carefully wrapped it in an old woollen rag. It wasn't in its case, but under the damaged workbench. Getting used to the sound was the worst. But I carried on, dogged and determined. In no time, I had another barrowful of logs.

THAT WAS TWO days ago. Since then, I've cut down two trees and taken them into the convent. The pavilion is full. I've started a stack under the lean-to shelter for the geese. Benoît rang me. He said I needn't think I would get off so lightly and that he had no intention of allowing Alex alone to cop all the blame for what had happened. I'm on the alert every moment of the day. I listen in case he will come up the hill on Alex's motorbike.

This morning I went and stood by the side of the road because I had a feeling Caitlin would be brought home. After she had come past, had got out and gone into the convent on her crutches, I walked down to the hospital to talk to the nurses. On the way back, climbing the hill, I came to a decision: I'm going to visit her today. It's my last chance: my mother has got the police to agree that I can go home, to the city, and our train leaves just after seven tonight. I walk through my grandfather's garden up to the gate next to the house, open it, cross the road and clamber over the low wall into the convent garden. There are people in the courtyard, talking, faces I've never seen before, all turned towards the roof, obviously discussing the best way of dividing the space under the roof. At times, the geese make their words inaudible. I walk past them and stand at the kitchen door. As I lift my hand to knock, a cold, damp gust of air makes me shiver. I hear a 'yes' behind the door, but it sounds so muffled I can't tell who it is.

I open the door. Soeur and Ruth are not there, at least not in the part of the kitchen I can see. Someone could be in the back, but I can't hear any sound coming from there. I only see how Caitlin raises herself to see who is coming in. An expression of surprise comes over her face. She raises her hand briefly and then puts it down on the mattress to shift her weight. She keeps looking at me and I at her, as if we are both looking at apparitions.

'Lucas!' she says explosively. Her face looks yellow. She seems even bonier than before. She's wearing a lime green T-shirt with the sleeves cut out and with a print of three roses across the chest. 'You've come.' I take a few steps closer. I've come empty-handed, and I regret this. A gift gives you something to do. I don't know what I'm going to say. She's lying with one leg stretched out, the other pulled up. A sheet covers her up to the waist. At the end of her left leg there's a huge lump, as if there are a number of pillows under it. I stand next to the chair, on which there are books, a cake in its package and a small stack of paper serviettes.

'You're home,' I say unnecessarily.

'Just for a while. For a change of air. It will get too busy here later.' She indicates I should remove the things from the chair and sit down. I do so. My feet are prickly after the climb up the hill. My mouth is dry and my back damp.

'How are your hands?' she asks. I show her both palms. She reaches for them and very briefly touches the scabs with her fingertips. Her nails are shorter than I have ever seen them. Her hands are hot. Her eyes are large, but dull, like paint on glass. My head hurts.

'Have you got a glass of water?' I ask. I walk to the sink and open the cupboard she indicates. She watches me, every one of my movements.

'I was thirsty,' I say when the glass is empty. 'Are you in a lot of pain?' I point at her leg as I ask the question. She quickly looks at it and is silent, as if she has to think about it.

'Yes,' she says. The more I look at her, the more upset I become by her appearance. Her eyes are deep in their sockets and the skin below them is thin and grey. I can see the bones in her neck moving as she turns her head. Her skin seems faded—on her hands and arms, too. There are scars from burns on her elbows. She smells of starch and cough mixture.

'My muscles have become so slack,' she says. 'I've never sat still so long before.' Now she throws the sheet off her. It billows and falls in a heap at the end of the bed. She stretches her hand to the calf of her good leg.

'Just feel it,' she says. I reach for it, being very careful not to touch anything else, and find that the calf muscle feels as if it has become liquefied. The skin around it is warm and dry. Her left leg is stretched out. The knee is a bit shapeless and bluish and there are clear traces of bruises and burns on the shin. Under her calf there is a snow-white pillow. The stump is hidden by a protective cage.

'That has to be over it,' she says when I look at it. 'It's

unbearable otherwise. I can't take the weight of the sheet. I can feel it through the bandage. Stupid, isn't it?' She laughs apologetically. I help her arrange the sheet. Bending over her, I can smell the warmth of her body.

Through the lace curtains we see people moving. The sound of their voices occasionally penetrates dimly. Above the window we can hear the cooing of dozens of doves. They fly back and forth, throwing nervous shadows on the curtains. Someone calls out. A car starts. Caitlin has listened to me. I have told her everything, from beginning to end, the way I had planned. My words have upset her.

'Why? How can you do a thing like that?'

'I don't know, Caitlin. I was against the refugees moving into the presbytery. I thought it was unfair; that neighbourhood already has plenty of problems. I thought it was a way of making my voice heard.'

'A firebomb? A way to make your voice heard? You're out of your mind.' I have never seen her like this before. She is shaking. I have no defence.

'Benoît said it was our last chance to restore order.'

'Order? Is that what you aspire to? I had hoped you knew that at least: there is nothing as shabby and starved of imagination as order.'

'I let myself be carried away.'

She shakes her head incredulously. 'But the paper said that one man—Alex somebody—acted alone,' she says. 'He has stated you didn't know what he was using your petrol for.'

'That's part of the plan.'

She closes her eyes. Her eyelids are grey, finely veined.

'This is unforgivable, Lucas. I can't cope with this. I think you will have to go. I don't want to see you again.' She looks at me harshly. I don't get up.

'I'm terribly sorry, Caitlin. I can't tell you how sorry I am.'

'Go away, Lucas.'

'You're going to report me. You're going to ring the police.'

'Of course I will. Do you realise what you've done? Those families on the street, the damage, the fear, the hate campaign. You're a criminal. It's my duty to report you.'

'I'm telling you I am sorry. Why do you think I am here? Why do you think I'm telling you all this? I can't go on lying to you, Caitlin. You're too precious to me for that.' She says nothing more. Her mouth is open. Now I get up. I take the telephone from the table, unroll the extension cord which is coiled up by the wall. It reaches as far as her bed and I put the handset on the still-warm chair. Before leaving the kitchen, I look back. She does not look after me. She sits hunched forward, her face in her hands. I can't see if she is crying. I pull the door shut behind me. As I turn around, I nearly crash into the potato woman.

'Aha!' she exclaims. 'We need you again.'

The rest of the afternoon I help with the final preparations for the families' arrival. Of course there are a hundred things that need sorting out at the last moment, and while the women set the tables and go for extra bread, men are needed to lug mattresses up the stairs, carry crates of soft drinks to the fridge and make exposed powerpoints safe from little hands. There are wardrobes with loose doors and nails that need punching into floorboards. Regularly, I come

272

across Soeur. She is doing the rounds with a thermos flask and plastic mugs and pours coffee for me the same as for the others. In the kitchen, Ruth is washing the crockery that hasn't been used for years. She hands me the dripping plates without saying much.

At about five, the first refugee families arrive in army mini buses. The children drop their dolls the minute they see all the cats. Because my English is reasonable, they ask me to take one family upstairs, show them the rooms and tell them something about the area. I'm not supposed to answer their questions: I have to tell them there will be an information session that evening.

When I go home an hour and a half later, my mother is ready to leave.

'Hurry,' she says, 'the train won't wait.' I walk to the phone and call Caitlin. She answers immediately, from which I conclude the phone is still standing by her side.

'Caitlin speaking,' I hear her say.

'It's Lucas.'

'Oh.'

'Are you alone?'

'Yes.'

'Did you ring up?'

'No.'

'Why not?'

'I've been thinking.' She sighs and is silent for a time. I ask nothing.

'What I liked so much about you,' she said suddenly, 'was your vulnerability. Other boys I know behave as if they're certain about everything. You didn't. You had doubts about just about everything, and didn't try to hide it. I liked that about you.' Again she waits. I can't guess what is coming. My hands are clammy and my fingers leave damp traces on the receiver.

'Now I realise that your vulnerability has its downside.' I nod, but of course she can't see that. I have no idea what to say.

'I've lost my foot, Lucas. I'll never be able to dance again. I'm beginning to realise that more and more every day. When I think of my foot, I think of you.' After another pause she goes on: 'I want to do everything I can to remember you as my rescuer, not as the person who mutilated me. That's not easy. And just as I was beginning to manage, I heard about that firebomb. *My rescuer throws Molotovs.* You must admit . . .'

I make a sound to make her hear I am listening. I can't get anything else out of my throat.

'I'm going to wait for the police enquiry. They'll have to sort it out. I'm not looking for revenge. The last thing I want is to destroy your life. I owe you too much for that.' Another silence.

I try to break that silence, but can't get my thoughts in order. 'I'll . . . I want to help. If you like, I'll stay a few more days. I'm getting to know some of the families quite well now.'

'My mother was impressed with your English. You've done a lot of work. Even Soeur was delighted.'

'I've got four days of holidays left!'

'I'm going back to the hospital tomorrow. It's a pity, it's such fun here with all this activity.'

'I'll come to see you,' I say quickly and loudly, almost

shouting, as if I'm worried she'll hang up. But she does not say yes. All I hear is her soft breathing.

'Just leave things be for a while,' she says, and before I can say anything else, she hangs up.

From the kitchen door, my mother calls out that the taxi has arrived.

'I'm not ready yet,' I yell back. I run upstairs, into my grandfather's room, and shift the desk. I climb onto it. In the convent courtyard, everything is in motion. The geese cackle louder than ever. But you get used to their noise. Not a soul takes any notice of them.

Author's note

FALLING is about a boy who one day has his hair cut short, buys himself a gun and, soon after, causes irreversible damage. What interested me most when writing this novel were the pitfalls of sloppy thinking: a person who does not have his own point of view and does not question his own values becomes easy prey for smooth talkers with extreme views. Because of his lack of vision and courage, Lucas is swept along towards violent action. He makes a choice that is disastrous for Caitlin, the girl he loves. Like so many others, Lucas does not see the connection between right-wing extremism in his French village and the events that happened during the Second World War. Creating that anti-hero was mainly what made writing this book challenging for me.

The book has some of the characteristics of a classic *Romeo and Juliet* story. Past events have been kept hidden from Lucas. That makes him uncertain and indecisive and is the reason the gulf between him and Caitlin is so deep. Because Benoît and Alex have relatively simple answers to a series of complex questions, Lucas enjoys their company. Lucas is not strong, but neither is he bad. While writing this novel, I constantly kept the image of a wasp trap in my mind: you know how to get into it, but not how to get out. I wanted the story to work in the same way as the characters' reasoning: present arguments that sound plausible, but that turn out not to be valid when the readers and the characters collide with a reality that is complex and unpredictable.

What fascinated me about Benoît and Alex was their discourse: how they set up circular arguments with deceptive logic in order to blame social problems on immigrants. I wanted to examine why what they say sounds plausible and convincing. Another thing that interested me was the way Benoît pretends to be asking Lucas for advice. Many of his questions and requests are in fact orders. It is a way of discussing things that I have observed in everyday life, almost always between people in unequal relationships. Alex is Benoît's henchman. He is always ready with a snappy, simplistic observation. His one-liners mostly sound good, but they rarely make sense. With his clichés, he makes real conversation impossible.

I set the story in a French environment, but it is not clear if it is in French-speaking Belgium, France or some other francophone area. The only reason the novel is not set in my native Flanders is that the storyline needs a thickly wooded, mountainous landscape. Having made that decision, I then kept the setting vague, to indicate that the events could have happened anywhere.

I have been asked how I could have written something that is so cruel and gloomy. I think writing passages of this kind is less horrible than having to read them. The reader has to helplessly face what is happening in the story, but the writer is not helpless. The story, full of situations from which there is no way back, reflects life: there also, things happen without warning; without leaving you time to feel remorse, or to steer your destiny in a different direction. In life also, there may be feelings of regret and loss afterwards, but it is not possible to undo things. All that is then left is punishment and vengeance, but they do not offer redress.

Although the story development is at times horrifying, the novel is not despairing. Lucas makes mistakes, but he is still young. Because the reader gets inside the character's skin, a certain compassion remains, a hope for a way out. In that sense, literature can be a means of maintaining solidarity with the losers of our society. In real life, things often take a different course: public opinion washes its hands of the wrongdoer. Once the perpetrator has been condemned, people think the problem has been resolved. Consequently, new perpetrators keep coming forward.

I did not write this book from a belief that I could change things. People will always succeed as well as fail. They will sometimes make the right decision, sometimes the wrong one. What I do believe in is empathy, and teasing out ideas in stories. You cannot un-think thoughts and ideas. Like insights, they are memes. Once they have been told, they become contagious and spread. That goes for sloppy thinking, but also for more complex opinions. The latter just need more words and more time.

Had someone asked me twenty years ago what future I saw for this book, I probably would have said I expected that by about the middle of the twenty-first century's second decade it would be completely outdated. By that time, Europe would surely be a melting pot, and the world would be colourblind. But, in hindsight, I can see I was mistaken. Nationalism, fundamentalism and racial intolerance have grown. The question of how we can keep people out of our group has gained ground. We have stopped wondering how we can prevent people falling behind or being abandoned by the group. People obsessed with defining identity, for themselves and others, have come forward – despite the fact that identity is precisely that it is an experience; a lived reality, which is different for each person, and which cannot be precisely articulated. In that sense, I do feel sorry at times that this book is still in print. I hope that, in the future, *Falling* will become a novel one reads mostly to understand the mindset of the twentieth century: a tale from the past; a bizarre historical document.

Anne Provoost

ABOUT THE AUTHOR AND TRANSLATOR

Belgian writer ANNE PROVOOST is the author of a series of provocative novels that examine topics as varied as right-wing extremism, sexual abuse, and religion through the eyes of young protagonists. *Falling* was made into an English-language feature film. Anne is a member of the Royal Academy of Dutch Language and Literature and a member of PEN. Her works have been published in eighteen different languages.

JOHN NIEUWENHUIZEN is an Australian-based, award-winning translator of Dutch and Flemish literature. In 2007, John was awarded the NSW Premier's Translation Prize and PEN Medallion. In 2015 he was recognised with an IBBY Australia Honour Book award for Translation for his translation of *Nine Open Arms* by Benny Lindelauf.